CHARLESTON BUZZ KILL

TOM TURNER

AUTHOR OF THE CHARLIE CRAWFORD MYSTERIES

ACKNOWLEDGMENTS

Once again, to the best daughters in the universe—Serena and Georgie.

JOIN TOM'S AUTHOR NEWSLETTER

Get the latest news on Tom's upcoming novels when you sign up for his free author newsletter at tomturnerbooks.com/news.

ONE

Vermelle LeGare had one of the oldest, most prominent surnames in Charleston. Fact is, the nicest street in Charleston was LeGare Street—pronounced Le-gree, as in Simon. Close seconds being Tradd and Church Streets.

Vermelle, though, was black and poor, a fifth-generation cleaning lady. Her husband, Willie, had just dropped her off at the corner of Broad and Church—a ten-minute walk to the house on Stoll's Alley where Vermelle was working that day. Willie'd dropped her there because he had a big roofing job that day and didn't want to be late. Vermelle didn't point out to Willie that his being on time would make her late for Mr. David.

Mr. David was David Wayne Marion, a rich, handsome fifty-year-old man. Vermelle knew just how rich he was because his net worth had been published in an article in the *Post & Courier* when he took an ill-fated run at becoming governor. Seventy-five million, mostly in real estate, she recalled.

After he lost in his bid to become governor, Mr. David veered off in a whole different direction and—of all crazy things—ended up becoming the star of a TV reality show. He had money, looks, and success, so fame was all that was left. But Vermelle had seen the show and… well, she intended to keep her opinion to herself.

She walked down Church Street and marveled once again at the beautiful houses on the street shaded by live oak trees with their wide, majestic canopies. Her favorite was a four-story brick Georgian with a dark mahogany door and antique glass fanlight above it. The house had graceful pediments above the windows and a perfectly proportioned wall to its right. On the second floor was a classic piazza where she imagined the husband and wife sipped their sloe-gin fizzes as soon as the clock struck five. Maybe earlier.

1

On the next block, she passed the garage door of an elegant Federalist-style house and chuckled to herself at the angry red letters stenciled onto its garage: *Do not block driveway. Violators will be persecuted to the full extent of the law.*

Did that mean hanged, she wondered, or merely tarred-and-feathered? And wasn't it... *prosecuted*? White people didn't make mistakes like that... did they?

Her favorite wall in Charleston was on the next block. Its surface was dirty concrete with patches of green lichen making it look a thousand years old. The highlight of the wall was the most intricately detailed wrought iron gate she had ever seen. She wondered if it had been crafted by Philip Simmons, a blacksmith by trade and a black man by birth whose work, she had heard, had ended up in the Smithsonian Museum.

Then she passed the decrepit house with a severe lean to one side, that always caught her attention. It was a stately colonial with imposing columns but was run-down and neglected. Like the owner couldn't afford to keep it up. She had heard Mr. David on the phone once making fun of a woman who was, "house-rich and check book poor" and wondered if this was her place. Mr. David went on about how the woman was from an old Charleston family but had been spotted using food stamps on the down low at the local Harris Teeter food market.

Vermelle turned left on Stolls Alley and walked over the bumpy, broken-brick pavement. The roads were in far better shape up on Nunan Street—in the heart of the 'hood—where she lived in her two-bedroom freedman's cottage. She had observed how the well-to-do south of Broad Street folks leaned toward the old, worn, distressed look. She had heard the word 'quaint' used a lot but just couldn't see it.

At number 5 Stoll's Alley, she rang the bell and waited.

David Marion's Greek Revival featured grey stucco over brick—the brick peeking through in several places. Vermelle had heard how at one point in history brick had lost favor with the rich folk so they had simply stuccoed over it. As she fumbled for her key, she looked over at the bulky two-inch-thick shutters with cut-outs of palmetto trees and the flickering gas lanterns that David Marion kept on at all time.

After a minute or so, she knocked and waited.

Nothing.

She knocked again.

Nothing.

Out of options, she tried the doorknob. To her surprise, it opened.

That was odd. She pushed it open and stuck her head in.

"Mr. David, it's me, Vermelle."

She walked into the hallway, the rare herring-bone heart-of-pine floor at her feet.

"Mr. David," she said again a little louder, "it's Vermelle."

She walked into the living room recently decorated by Madeline Littleworth Mortimer herself.

"Mr. David?"

She figured he must have hurried off to shoot a scene for his dopey TV show and had forgotten to lock the house. It had happened before.

She went down the hallway to his bedroom to get the sheets, towels, and his dirty clothes; the first thing she always did.

The bedroom door was open, and she went in.

And there, sprawled atop the 1000-count Egyptian sheets of his king-size bed, lay David Wayne Marion buck naked and with a bullet hole in his forehead .

First, Vermelle screamed, scaring the hell out of Mr. David's Labrador retriever, napping at the side of the bed. Then she called the cops.

Finally, she fled the house and headed straight to the AME Church up on Calhoun. All she could do now was pray for the soul of poor Mr. David.

*****

First on scene at Marion's house, at 9:10 a.m. was a Charleston Police Department rookie who was mostly clueless about murder scene protocol. But at least he knew enough not to disturb the scene, which was better than most.

Next to arrive was homicide detective Delvin Rhett, a wiry, well-dressed, twenty-eight-year-old black man. His father was a philosophy professor at the Citadel, the military college just up the road, a strict disciplinarian who outlawed hip-hop in his house and forbid his kids to call their friends, 'dawg' or 'niggah'.

After Rhett did a cursory once-over of the crime scene, he called the uniform over. "Tape off the house, Bobby," he said, "Stay outside, and don't let anybody in except the ME, the techs, and my partner."

Bobby scratched the back of his head. "Your partner's the new guy, right?"

"Yeah, Nick Janzek."

Bobby nodded, then pointed down at Marion's body. "You know who this is, right?"

"'Course I do," Rhett said, "now go watch the door."

Rhett flicked his hand and Bobby headed toward the front door of the house.

The detective took out his iPhone and started snapping pictures of Marion. He clicked off a few shots of the four bloodstained pillow, a couple more of the blue needlepoint pillows with the monogramed initials, DWM, on it, and several more full-lengths of Marion's body, tanned to a dark brown and in sharp contrast to the pure white sheets. Marion, for an older guy, had a nice assortment of traps, lats, delts, and a quasi-six-pack. He clearly spent time in the gym, and judging by his lack of body fat, steered clear of the Golden Arches.

A few minutes later Rhett heard the front door creak open.

"Delvin," he heard a voice, "where y'at?"

It was his partner, Nick Janzek, a Boston transplant doing his best to talk southern.

"In here," Rhett shouted from the first-floor master.

A few seconds later, Janzek walked in. He was wearing khakis, a blue blazer, a striped tie, and looked more like a forty-year-old accidental preppie than a highly decorated homicide cop from the mean streets of Beantown.

Janzek, six-feet and a solid one hundred seventy-five pounds, had catlike emerald-green eyes and dark hair he wore on the long side. A two-inch scar ran down the left side of his face and stopped just above a sturdy chin that had taken a few shots over the years. He came in and looked down at David Marion's naked body.

"Guy make you feel a little inadequate?" Rhett asked.

Janzek didn't respond.

"Never seen a Johnson like that on a white boy before," Rhett said.

4

Janzek shook his head and sighed. "Okay, Delvin, knock it off."

Janzek pulled on his plastic gloves and took in the whole scene for a few moments.

Then he noticed something and went around and crouched down at the foot of the bed.

"Whatta we got here?" Janzek said pointing to a lump under the bedding.

"I didn't see that," Rhett said, walking closer.

Janzek untucked the sheet and covers and pulled them back.

It was a balled-up pair of women's underwear. Black and lacy. Janzek took out his phone and snapped a few shots.

"You know who this guy is, right?" Rhett asked.

Janzek shook his head and shrugged

"Seriously?" Rhett said. "You don't know?"

Janzek shook his head. "Why? Am I s'posed to?"

"Shit, man, you livin' under a rock. It's that guy, D-Wayne, from the reality show, *Charleston Buzz*."

Janzek scratched his head. "He a rapper... like Vanilla Ice or something?"

Rhett snarfed a laugh and shook his head. "Not hardly. Some white guys have nicknames like that, too."

"Is that the show that's got the whole town pissed off? S'posed to make us look bad or something?"

"Us? How you figure you're *us*," Rhett said, "You being a Yankee who got down here day before yesterday."

"Correction," Janzek said, "it's been four long months of your bullshit."

Rhett laughed. "Aight, so here's the lowdown on the guy. D-Wayne's the star of the show... was I guess that would be. Even though he lives down in New Orleans most of the time."

"How you know all this?"

"How do you think? I watch the show," Rhett said. "Enough to know the guy married a little cupcake half his age. Just had a kid, too."

"So, if he lives in New Orleans, what's he doing here?"

"Shootin' the second season of the show. Rents this place, I think."

"And the wife?"

"Article said she lives down there, raising their kid."

5

Janzek rubbed his chin for a moment, then picked up the panties.

"Okay, then, if she's down there," he said, holding up the underwear, "then who d'you suppose these bad boys belong to?"

"Could be anyone," Rhett said. "Dude's a notorious poon hound."

TWO

Janzek and Rhett had spent the last forty-five minutes searching the house, taking a close look outside, and in an unlocked BMW parked in the driveway. At the top of their list of things they wanted to find was either Marion's cell phone or computer. But so far, they had come up with neither.

The ME, Jack Martin, showed up next. Martin had a thing about Janzek. He had gotten the notion from a murder they worked a few months back that Janzek thought he was smarter than everyone in the room because of his big-time homicide rep up north. And maybe Janzek secretly did think that, but he sure as hell would never broadcast it.

Martin bent down to take a closer look at Marion's fatal wound.

The bullet hole was above the bridge of David Marion's nose, just below his hairline, and it exited just past the middle top part of his head.

"Trajectory indicates the shooter was probably down at the foot of the bed, I'd say," Janzek said.

Martin looked up at Janzek.

"Is that what you'd say, Nick?" He looked back down at the stiff. "Kind of depends which way his head was facing. Shooter could have been anywhere."

Rhett stepped in closer. "Yeah, but chances are, he lined up ol' D-Wayne right after he walked in," Rhett said, backing up his partner.

"Thanks for weighing in, Delvin," Martin said. "Seems you boys don't need me here at all. Got this thing all doped out."

Janzek and Rhett rolled their eyes but held their tongues.

Martin walked around the bed and started examining the wall behind the head of the bed.

Janzek had already located the slug in the wall but decided to let Martin find it himself. He turned to Rhett. "That TV show," he said. "How'd our guy here get along with the other people in it?"

"You mean, aside from pissin' off every guy and screwin' every chick?"

"Is that right?"

"Yeah," Rhett said. "Which is why people watch it. D-Wayne and this guy named Saxby were always goin' at it."

Jack Martin, whose back was to them, turned his head partway around. "Don't forget that doofus, Rip. The guy who was banging D-Wayne's wife."

Rhett nodded. "Yeah, but that was before D-Wayne married her."

"Jesus Christ," Janzek said, "Am I the only one in the world who never watched this trash?"

"Probably," Rhett said. "Poor culturally deprived bastard."

"And what's with these guys names anyway?" Janzek said. "D-Wayne, Saxby, Rip... Can't they have nice, normal names like Bill, Bob or," glancing over at Jack Martin, "Jack?"

"Yeah, Jack's a good Christian name which exudes masculinity," Martin said. He held up the slug he had just carved out of the wall. "Looks like a .22."

Janzek got closer and examined the slug Martin was holding in his blue latex glove. "Or possibly a .223."

"Like I said, a .22," Martin said.

Janzek let it go. Besides, hearing about the cast of the TV show was way more interesting. He turned back to Rhett.

"So, give me a rundown on all the players on the show."

Rhett cupped one elbow and put his hand to his chin. "Okay, but first, I gotta tell you about this one episode. May be relevant here... so, what happens is, the whole cast goes hunting—"

"Oh yeah, that was a good one," Martin said, looking up. "None of those turkeys could shoot for shit."

"Except D-Wayne's wife," Bobby the uniform piped in, from around the corner in the living room.

Janzek glanced over at Rhett and smiled. "Dude's got really good hearing."

"Yeah, he's right, too," Rhett said. "That girl bagged a shitload of quail, but the guys couldn't hit their dicks with a hammer."

Janzek heard the front door open. "Who is it?"

"Me," said a woman wearing a blue windbreaker with CSU printed on the back. Her name was Ruthie Mueller and she was a crime scene tech.

Janzek's first instinct was to cover up Marion.

"Hubba hubba," Ruthie said, glancing down at the body, then doing a double take, "ho-lee shit, D-Wayne."

Martin got up from his crouch, one of his knees popping. "Ruthie, I need you to dust the hell out of this place," Martin said. "I'm looking for prints of either the perp or the broad who lover boy here was bangin'."

"How you know he was bangin' someone?" Ruthie asked.

Martin looked over at Janzek. "'Cause Janzek found a pair of Hanky Pankys in the bed. Guy's wife is down in New Orleans s'posedly."

"Victoria's Secret, actually," Janzek said, eyeing the label.

"Whatever," said Martin.

Ruthie laughed and glanced over at Martin. "I'm impressed you've even heard of Hanky Pankys."

"My old lady's brand," Martin said. "But hers are chartreuse."

"TMI, Jack." Ruthie said, kneeling next to Janzek, who was on all fours, looking under the bed. "What you looking for, Nick?"

"Anything," Janzek said. "But I'd really like to find the guy's cell phone. I looked all over. No cell, no computer so far. The two things that would probably help the most."

"He got a home office maybe?" Ruthie asked.

"We already tried there," Janzek said. "Nothing."

"Tried his car, too," Rhett said. "Nada."

Janzek got to his feet.

"Come on, Delvin," he said, "why don't you and me go look around outside again. Talk to the neighbors."

Rhett followed Janzek out of the bedroom, through the living room and out into the driveway.

"This oughta be good," Rhett said glancing at his watch. "White folks down here really dig it when a black dude drops in at breakfast and starts firing questions at 'em."

*****

9

It turned out that nobody on Stolls Alley had seen or heard a thing. Same for Water Street, Church Street and Atlantic Street. They did get one useful piece of information, though, while going door-to-door. One of the neighbors, who said she was a friend of Marion's wife—widow, that would be—gave them her phone number.

Janzek thanked the woman, then went to his car to rehearse what he was going to ask when he made the death-notification call. He'd done them a hundred times before, and it never got any easier. You had to just get right to it and keep the words and euphemisms to a minimum. Then, sneak your questions in as subtly as possible.

He dialed.

A woman's voice answered on the third ring. "Hello?"

"Mrs. Marion?"

"Yes, this is Jessie."

"My name is Detective Janzek from the Charleston Police Department. Mrs. Marion, I am very sorry to have to tell you," there was just no way to soften it, "but your husband was shot and killed in Charleston last night."

"What?" she said. "Oh, my God, what happened?"

Most first reactions were more delayed and more hysterical.

"He was shot at his house on Stoll's Alley. I am very sorry for your loss, ma'am."

"Oh, my God," she said again.

"Are you in New Orleans, Mrs. Marion?"

"Yes, yes, I am… oh my God," a third time, "I-I just can't believe it."

She started to sob. It sounded slightly forced. Like she'd just remembered that was what newly minted widows were supposed to do.

"I assume you'll be coming up to Charleston, Mrs. Marion?"

"Yes, yes, of course," she said. "I go by my maiden name, Jessie Lawson."

"Oh, okay, thanks for telling me that," Janzek said. "Well, I will make myself available to you when you get here, and, of course, keep you informed about any developments in the case."

"Thank you, Detective," she said, sniffling. "I appreciate that."

Then Janzek heard a baby bawling in the background. Maybe it saw its mother crying and got upset.

"Ms. Lawson, if I may, I have a few questions."

10

"Sure, go ahead."

"When did you last see your husband? And when were you planning to see him next?"

"About three days ago actually. He was planning on coming down here this weekend, but something came up on the show and he had to stay up there."

"'Something came up?' Do you know what?"

"I think they had to re-shoot a few scenes unexpectedly. He had to stick around."

Her sobbing had stopped, but the baby was still going at it with a vengeance.

"And when you last saw your husband, did he happen to mention anything out of the ordinary? Any problem he might have been having with another person maybe? Or had he ever mentioned anyone who may have threatened him in the past?"

Jessie Lawson didn't speak right away. "No, sorry," she said, after a few moments, "nobody I can think of."

"And you didn't overhear anything? A phone call maybe? I know this may sound repetitive, but did you observe anything that maybe seemed a little... off?"

"No, I'm sorry. Wish I could be more helpful."

"That's okay. My last question, do you have any idea at all who might have done this? Someone who may have had a motive. Anyone you can think of. Even if it may seem far-fetched?"

She didn't hesitate. "I just can't possibly imagine. Deep down, David was the sweetest man in the world. Yes, there was that role he played on the show... but in real life, everyone loved him. I just can't possibly imagine someone... murdering him."

Not exactly Delvin Rhett's take on D-Wayne, but maybe D-Wayne was a better actor than people gave him credit for.

"Well, thank you, Ms. Lawson. Again, I am very sorry for your loss. I'll be in touch with you when you get to Charleston. In the meantime, if there's any way I can be of service, please don't hesitate to call."

He always said that even though no one ever did.

"Thank you, Detective."

Then he gave her his number and hung up.

Only good thing he could say about a death notification was that it was easier done on the phone than in person.

11

THREE

Janzek and Rhett had gone back to the police station on Lockwood after interviewing the rest of Marion's neighbors. Janzek wanted to take a look at Marion's reality show for himself.

It was three in the afternoon and he and Rhett had just binged on four episodes of *Charleston Buzz*. Janzek flicked off the clicker, shook his head, and said four was all he could take. Even though he had pretty much hit the wall after the pilot.

"I think I'd rather watch that Jersey smut mouth than those airheads," Janzek said.

"Snooki, you mean," Rhett said. "Love that girl."

"Jesus, Delvin, is there anything beneath you? Anything you won't watch?"

"Yeah, *Duck Dynasty*," Rhett said, shaking his head. "Bunch of gay bashin', red neck, ZZ Top cracker boys."

Janzek held up his hands. "I'll take your word for it."

Rhett shook his head and smirked. "Okay, Mr. Masterpiece Theater."

As far as *Charleston Buzz* went, it seemed like the lives of the recurrent characters in the reality show consisted almost exclusively of sex, drinking and selfies, with most of them having no discernible means of support. Not that Janzek had anything against sex, drinking, or selfies, but give it a rest once in a while.

"I don't get how that one, Naomi, can live in that big house on Beaufain when she's a goddamn dog-walker," Janzek said.

"Yeah, I wondered about that, too. I got a theory that the show subsidizes 'em. I mean, none of 'em, with the exception of Samantha, and Greg the banker, really do anything. And it wouldn't surprise me if Greg's a teller."

Janzek nodded and tapped his desk a few times. "So as far as

Marion goes," he said, "you've seen all twelve episodes, what exactly's the skinny on the guy?"

"Well, actually, he's one they don't need to subsidize. Best way to sum him up is, he's rich as shit and has a thing for girls half his age. No, make that a third his age. Supposedly made a ton of money in real estate before the crash. Built a bunch of office buildings, then retired."

"Retired to a life of hittin' on every chick in Charleston between the ages of training-bra and twenty-five," Janzek said.

"Exactly."

Janzek flashed back to something Jessie Lawson had said. "His wife told me he was going to go down to New Orleans this weekend but cancelled at the last minute. What's your take on that?"

Rhett shook his head and smirked. "Same as yours. Guy met a chick who gave him reason to believe he might get lucky."

Janzek nodded and leaned back in his chair. "So first he got lucky, then he got really... *unlucky*."

*****

Rhett talked Janzek into watching episode five of *Charleston Buzz*, tempting him with the fact that the second half of the episode was when the cast goes hunting at a plantation.

"I tell you, man," Rhett said, at a commercial, "I realize even more the second time around how much of a snake that Saxby is. Always talking about D-Wayne behind his back. Bunch of scenes where the camera catches him rolling his eyes after D-Wayne just said something ridiculous."

Janzek nodded as the show came back on. "Which is pretty much all the time. What about that guy Rip?" He pointed to him on-screen.

"What about him?"

"He strikes me as just kind of a big goof."

"Yeah, that's about right," Rhett said. "Lotta yap, most of it pretty lame."

Janzek was about to hit the wall as he watched more junior high-school flirtations between Rip and one of the girls. "Is the hunting scene coming up pretty soon? I can't take much more of this."

"Yeah, they're about to head down to Rip's family's plantation,"

Rhett said. "That's what he calls it anyway, but it's really more like a trailer park in the middle of a thousand-acre swamp."

"Not exactly '*Gone with the Wind*'?"

Rhett shook his head. "Not even close. A bunch of broken-down huts... makes the 'hood' look good."

"Rip's on my interview list for tomorrow," Janzek said, looking down at his notes. "So why don't we split 'em up? I'll take Rip, Saxby, Samantha, Lisa, and Ashley. You take Greg the banker, Ted, Naomi, and Darcie."

Rhett laughed.

"What?" Janzek said.

"What?" Rhett said, "It kills me. You pretend you can't stand the show, but I can see you're all fired up to go Q&A the smokin' hot blonde and the pink haired one with the humongous Winnebagoes."

FOUR

The four-story brick house at 69 Bull Street was impressive.

Weighing in at more than eleven thousand square feet, it featured three wide piazzas, the Charleston word for a balcony. It had enough parking for twelve cars which was unusual since most lots in Charleston allowed for only a few spots and many houses had no parking at all. It was a deep lot, and the house was set back about seventy feet from the street behind an ample front yard. Many of the houses in the area were rented out to students at the College of Charleston, the twelve-thousand-student, liberal arts college that dominated the city located just north of Beaufain Street and south of Calhoun.

The first thing you noticed about the house at 69 Bull, nicknamed the Boy's Club, was the putting green. Yes, putting green. In fact, it was a perfectly manicured inch-for-inch replica of the green on the sixth hole at Augusta National, the golf course where The Masters is played every year.

A man on the second-floor piazza had his left arm around a tall, willowy brunette and his right hand around a highball of Makers Mark. The man, close to sixty and the girl, twenty years old max, were looking down at the two men putting on the green below.

It was 11:30 p.m. and it was a good bet that the two putters were drunk. On the edge of the putting green stood a jumbo red plastic cup of brown liquid that belonged to a man lining up his putt. The man next to him had a Heineken in hand, which he would put down when it was his turn. On the sides of the putting green were lights, a scaled-down version of the kind you'd see at a professional baseball field for a night game. It was the job of an older black man in a white dinner jacket to bring the lights out of the cellar every night and set them up. It was also his job to make sure the men's needs were attended to,

15

which meant fresh drinks and cigars which he fetched from the bar and humidor inside.

The men were playing a simple game in which the fewest putts won the hole. After they'd finish a hole, the one who'd just lost got to choose where they'd place their balls before putting toward the next hole.

They were betting a thousand dollars a hole.

"What's the score?" the man from the second story shouted down to the two putters.

A man with wavy white hair looked up.

"He's up three," he said, taking a long pull on his Heineken. "But not for long."

"Time for double-or-nothing maybe?" the man on the balcony said.

"Good idea," the man with wavy white hair said, looking over at his shaven-headed opponent. "Double or nothing?"

The man with the shaved head smiled and walked over to his drink on the edge of the green.

He picked it up, took a sip, then drained it. "You're on, brotha."

*****

The man with the shaved head won the double-or-nothing bet. They had tied the first two holes, but after a belt of bourbon, the man with the shaved head sunk a thirty-five-foot putt. The spectators on the balconies above gave him a spirited ovation as he collected an $8,000 check from the wavy-haired man. Then they went inside to refresh their drinks.

"Oughta call you Tiger Woods," one of the girls said to the shaven-headed man, whose name was Thad Whaley.

He chuckled as she handed him a glass of Woodford Reserve bourbon that she had just gotten from the bartender. It was the way he liked it—neat, no water, no ice.

"Thanks, darlin'," Whaley said, waving the check in the air. "This oughta help pay for your education."

She laughed and clinked her wine glass with his.

Stanton Conger, the wavy-haired man, came up to them with a fresh Heineken in hand.

"Hey, Jolene, you seen my girlfriend?" he asked the girl.

Jolene blushed, and glanced at Thad Whaley, who laughed knowingly.

"I'm just guessin'," Whaley said, "that, judging by Jolene's reaction, *your girlfriend* might just be someone else's girlfriend at the moment."

Conger wasn't amused. "Who's she with?" he demanded.

Jolene's eyes flitted from side to side, then locked on to Conger's.

"Mr. Williams," she said under her breath.

Mr. Williams was the alias of William Kidd.

All the men had aliases.

Whaley laughed and said to Conger. "Hey, man, looks like sloppy seconds?"

Conger shook his head, smiled, and looked around the large room. "Two-timin' bitch," he said and chuckled. "Which one of the girls here needs a boyfriend, Jolene?"

Jolene scratched her head.

"Well, there's Leah, girl whose room is next to mine. I'd say she might."

Conger tried to remember what Leah looked like.

"Where is she?" he asked, reaching into his breast pocket, and taking a cigar out of a silver case.

"Up in her room," Jolene said, "doing homework."

Conger shook his head. "Christ, back when my daughter was in school, I could never get her to do homework," he said. "What's she look like... Leah?"

"What are you worried about?" said Whaley, putting his arm around Jolene's shoulder and working it down toward her braless breasts. "We got nothing but perfect tens here."

Jolene pretended to like getting pawed by Whaley. "She's really cute," she said.

"How 'bout bein' a good girl and goin' and fetchin' her?" Conger said.

"Sure," said Jolene, putting down her wine glass. "I'll be right back."

She started walking, then she turned back. "Anything special you want her to wear?"

Conger looked at Whaley and smiled. "As little as possible."

Jolene went over to the elevator, as Whaley and Conger watched the wiggle of her perfect ass.

"Ah, my little sociology major," Whaley said.

"That'll get her far in life," Conger said, his attention suddenly focused on a man who had just walked in from one of the piazzas.

"What does it matter?" Whaley said. "With looks like that she's got nothing to worry about."

With his beady eyes, Conger eyed the man who came off the piazza as he walked up to the bar.

"Fuckin' Murray," Conger said under his breath, flicking his head at the guy at the bar. "Guy's really tryin' to rub it in my face. But I got my guy payin' him a visit pretty soon."

Whaley turned toward the bar and glanced at Lex Murray. Murray was a tall, stoop-shouldered man who looked to be in his late fifties.

"What can you do?" Whaley said with a shrug. "He was a founding father here, just like you."

Conger shrugged. "Yeah, but you'd think twenty years in the slammer would disqualify him from comin' back."

Whaley shrugged again and shook his head. "Nothing like that in the bylaws."

Murray shot a look over at the two men and locked eyes with Conger. Then he smirked and looked away.

"Supposedly, he's got ten million stashed away," Whaley said

"More like twelve," Conger said.

"You would know," Whaley said. "Where do you figure he's got it? Swiss bank account? Grand Caymans?"

"Guy never trusted banks," Conger said.

"So, what then? Coffee cans in his backyard?"

Conger squinted in thought as he emptied his beer bottle. "Have to be one hell of a lot of coffee cans."

FIVE

Lex Murray took his first sip of the $200 bottle of scotch. Man, had he missed booze in jail. Almost as much as women.

His cell phone rang. He looked down, punched the green button, and went back out onto the piazza.

"Hello."

"Mr. Murray?"

"That's me."

"I have a very important message to deliver to you."

"I'm listening."

"I need to do it in person."

"Who the hell are you?"

"Doesn't matter. I'm walking into the Boy's Club right this minute."

"Okay. I'm up on the third-story piazza."

Murray clicked off and took a long pull on his drink.

A few minutes later, a barrel-chested man, mid-forties maybe, with deep-set eyes, stepped off the elevator on the third floor and walked out to the piazza.

Murray, who was sitting in a rattan chair, eyeballed the man but didn't say anything.

"My name's Jim," the man said.

"Jim who?"

"Just Jim."

"Okay, mystery man, Jim," Murray said. "What do you want?"

"I'll take a Budweiser."

"I meant—"

"I know what you meant."

"Sorry, we don't stock swill like that," Murray said.

The man laughed. "Okay, gimme a… Beck's then."

Murray flagged down the waiter, asked for a Beck's and another McCallam for himself.

Jim sat down in the matching rattan chair across from Murray.

"This is a pretty nice place," Jim said, looking back inside. "Looks like a hangout for Charleston's blue bloods. How come they let you in? A guy who just got out of the jug."

Murray wasn't amused. "'Don't kid yourself. I started out life as a blue blood. Me and a couple guys I went to Chapel Hill with started this place."

"What's Chapel Hill?" Jim asked.

Murray shook his head. "A college," he said, "I'm guessing you never made it through junior high. No offense, 'course."

"None taken," Jim said, looking around. "So, that's enough small talk. Time for business."

The waiter showed up with their drinks.

"So, go ahead," Murray said, waving his hand, "let's talk business."

Jim took a long pull on his Beck's and burped.

"'Scuse me," he said. "They probably don't allow that here either."

Murray didn't look amused.

"All right, cutting to the chase. You owe my client a lot of money."

"Your client? Who would that be?"

"You know exactly who I mean," Jim said. "You owe the man two million dollars."

Murray just shook his head and sighed. "Two million, huh?"

"Yeah," Jim said, "Cash or a check will be just fine."

Murray leaned in close to the man.

"Let me give you a little history lesson, Jim."

"Spare me," Jim said. "Just give me the money."

Murray chuckled, shaking his head. "Lesson goes something like this. Thirty-five years ago, 'your client' and I were in college together. The aforementioned, Chapel Hill. He came from a rich family, I came from a family, well, let's just say... rich in tradition. Anyway, one day we were sittin' around having a couple beers, as college boys will do, and we came up with this business plan—"

Jim waved him off. "I know all about it. Mighty good business plan it was too."

"I'm flattered to hear you say that," Murray went on. "Anyway, I was the guy who implemented the business plan," he said. "Your client was the guy who—thanks to his family money—financed it."

"Built it up to quite the little multi-national operation, I understand?"

"I prefer 'conglomerate,'" Murray said. "And just for the record, I paid your client back every nickel."

"Funny," Jim said, "that's not how he remembers it."

"That's 'cause I paid him back in product," Murray said. "Which was the way he wanted it. Ain't my fault he put it all up his nose."

"They teach you to say ain't at that Chapel Hill place?"

Murray killed the last of his scotch. "I got a question for you."

"What's that?"

"Let's just say I wanted to pay him back what he says I owe him, which, by the way, I don't. How the hell's he figure it's two million when it was only a hundred grand he staked me with? I'm not gettin' the math here."

Jim set the beer down on the table.

"That's easy," Jim said. "Interest over thirty-five years adds up."

"One million nine-hundred-thousand in interest?"

"Yeah, well, I assume my client is looking for a little more vig than your local savings bank."

*****

The girl, Leah, whose room was next to Jolene's, came downstairs in a low-cut top and a black micro skirt.

Jolene introduced her to Whaley and Conger.

"What were you up there studying, darlin'?" Conger asked.

Jessie took a dainty sip of her scotch and Mountain Dew.

"Microphysics," she said.

Conger looked at Whaley and laughed. "I don't even know what that is."

"You don't have to," Whaley said.

Leah, who in heels stood five inches taller than Conger, looked down at him. "What about you, Mr. Smith," she said, using Conger's alias. "What do you do?"

Jolene shot her a look. The girls weren't supposed to ask

21

questions like that. Absolutely nothing personal. But Leah was new that semester and didn't know any better. Stern lecture to follow.

"Let's just say I own a few buildings," Conger said.

"Yeah, like half of downtown," Whaley said.

"Only a third."

"And what about you, Mr. Jones?" Leah asked. "What do you do?"

Jolene shot Leah another look, but Leah didn't catch that one either.

"Plastics," Whaley said.

Conger laughed.

"What?"

"Little joke. Before your time," Whaley said. "Actually, I'm a surgeon."

"For real?" Leah said. "What kind?"

"Cardiac," Whaley said.

"Wow," Leah said.

"But enough about me," Whaley said. "Maybe you and Mr. Smith want to go up to your room and study up for your next microphysics test."

Stanton Conger gave Whaley a grateful nod of approval.

"I'd like that very much," Leah said, putting on the seductive voice she'd practiced in front of her mirror.

SIX

Janzek was outside Saxby's house.

Saxby Wentworth-Kuhn lived with his mother. The house took up practically half a block and at first glance looked like the White House. That is, if the White House was chocolate brown.

It had taken Janzek a while to track down Saxby. Finally, he had just Googled him, which led him to Saxby's mother's house that turned out to be a big Greek revival monster they lived in together at the corner of Rutledge and Montagu. Janzek had first called the New York office of the *Charleston Buzz* production company, SLAM!, but the woman there said she had no authority to give out his address. Telling her he was a cop didn't swing it either. All it did was elicit a, 'did he do anything wrong?' response. Janzek was tempted to respond with a cheeky, 'you mean besides being on that tacky show of yours?' but bit his tongue.

Finally, he had just gone to the house hoping to catch Saxby—maybe buffing up his Ferrari or pinching his American Beauty roses. The house was surrounded by a fifteen-foot wall and inside it stood statuesque live oak trees. There were signs everywhere, "No Trespassing," "Beware of the Dogs" and "Surveillance Cameras in Use." One even said, "These Premises Protected by a .357 Magnum." In addition to the threats of snarling dogs and trigger-happy guards, Janzek imagined a moat filled with alligators and piranhas.

But despite all the security measures—implied and otherwise—and the threats to bodily harm, Janzek found a side gate open and walked back around to the massive front door. It looked like something you'd find at a Bavarian castle.

He rang the doorbell.

A few moments later a black man dressed in a black suit, white shirt and black tie came to the door.

Janzek had figured butlers went out with Mr. Carson.

"Yes, sir, may I help you?" the man asked, which was when Janzek noticed his shoes. Grey, lizard-skin and pointy-toed—they looked as if they'd be good at climbing chain-link fences running from a cop.

Janzek flashed his badge, "My name is Detective Janzek, Charleston Police Department, I'd like to have a few words with Mr. Wentworth-Kuhn."

The butler's eyebrows arched.

"Yes, sir, I will announce you," he said, turning around, and walking into the house.

Janzek heard his cell phone chirp and took it out of his pocket.

It was a text from Rhett.

"D-Wayne funeral tomorrow. U wanna take it? Or me?"

He heard footsteps and the man from the five episodes of *Charleston Buzz* he'd seen suddenly appeared. He looked thinner, his face more gaunt, which was surprising because he heard TV foreshortened the human body and made you look fatter.

"A real live detective," Saxby Wentworth-Kuhn said.

Janzek put out his hand. "Hi, Mr. Wentworth-Kuhn, I'm Detective Janzek."

"Lose my last name, it's too big a mouthful. Call me Saxby."

He said it in a theatrical way, so it came out amped up with drama, like 'Call me Ishmael.'

"If you've got a few minutes, I just need to ask you some questions about the death of David Marion."

"Poor old D-Wayne," Saxby said. "I figured someone would show up, sooner or later."

Janzek saw a man and a woman come up behind Saxby. One was an exotic, muscular-looking, Hispanic man in black tights and a lime-colored T-shirt with a swoosh on it. The other was a young woman with a short, military haircut.

Saxby turned to face them.

"This is my personal trainer, El Tigre," the Hispanic man bowed, "and Carla June. She does—"

"—hair and nails," the girl said, stepping forward and shaking Janzek's hand,

"Okay, guys," Saxby said. "I'm not going to need you for a while."

The two smiled, turned, and walked away.

"Sorry, I think they just wanted to see a detective up close."

Janzek nodded. "Can we go sit down somewhere?"

"Sure, come on in, let's go sit in the salon du thé," Saxby said, pronouncing the last word, *tay.*

"The what?" Janzek asked.

"Salon du thé," Saxby said again. "That's what *ma mere* calls it. It's French for tea room. Where she has her morning cup, but since she's never up in the morning..."

Janzek snuck a look at his watch as he followed Saxby. It was just past noon.

"So damn sad about my bro, D-Wayne," Saxby said, leading Janzek into a small room that had walls covered with portraits of unsmiling, stodgy-looking people dressed in dark clothes. It also had an elaborate, metal, water fountain that was gurgling fitfully in one corner of the room.

Saxby put out his hand as they approached a seating arrangement. Janzek sat down in a love seat and Saxby in a worn, leather chair opposite him.

"I'm sorry," Saxby said, looking around. "I'm not being much of a host. What would you like to drink, Detective?"

Janzek thought the right thing to do was ask for tea, but then, he didn't drink tea. "Just water would be fine, thanks."

Saxby nodded and picked up an antique-looking silver bell from the table beside him and rang it.

The butler appeared almost immediately as if lying in wait around the corner.

"Yes, Moses," Saxby said. "We'll have iced water for the detective and a Beefeater 24 gin martini for me, please," then turning to Janzek. "The martini's in honor of D-Wayne. That's what he always imbibed." Then he winked. "Copious amounts of them."

Janzek figured that was a good segue. "Speaking of David Marion, I'm sure you must have given thought to who killed him? You knew the man pretty well. Tell me what you can about any enemies he might have had, or any theories you have about his murder."

Saxby tapped his finger on the table next to him.

"Yes, I have given it a fair amount of thought, but I have no clue. Honestly, I think he pissed off a lot of people. But that's a long way from going to his house and putting a bullet in his head."

Moses appeared with their drinks. Janzek's water had a spring of mint in it. A nice touch.

"Thank you, Moses," Saxby said.

"Thanks," Janzek said.

They both took sips. Saxby's was actually more like a gulp. He set his glass down, one-third full now.

"But that's exactly what someone did," Janzek said picking up the thread. "Went to his house and put a bullet in his head. So, my question is, in your opinion, could it possibly have been someone from the show?"

"I don't know," Saxby said, working the thought around in his head for a moment. "Rip's kind of a loose cannon. Plus, D-Wayne stole his girlfriend, then went and married her. But I really don't have a clue."

"Wait," Janzek said, raising his hand. "I didn't get that Jessie was actually Rip's girlfriend... just that he slept with her a couple of times."

"Three times, to be exact," Saxby said. "But it was getting to the point where Rip might have considered her his girlfriend."

"You think?" Janzek said, "And, if I've got my facts straight, you were sleeping with her, too."

"Yeah, but she definitely *was not* my girlfriend," Saxby said. "She just came over to my stabbin' cabin a few times."

"Your what?"

"My stabbin' cabin."

"Oh, gotcha," Janzek said. "You don't mean here, do you?"

Saxby couldn't contain his laughter. "No, man, are you fuckin' crazy? Not with my mother around." He appeared shocked at the utter uncoolness of the whole concept. "Nah, I got this awesome loft over on Upper King."

"So that would be... your stabbin' cabin?"

"Yeah," Saxby beamed with pride. "One of the producers came up with that name."

"It's catchy," Janzek said, taking another sip of water. "So, what about you. How did you get along with Marion?"

Saxby held up his hands and shook his head. "Whoa, whoa, don't be goin' down that road. Don't make me out to be a guy with a motive. That shit between me and him, that was just another thing the producers dreamed up. You know, dramatic tension, stuff like that." He put up finger quotes for that last bit.

"But it seemed you guys went at it a lot." Janzek said. "Seemed more than just dramatic tension."

"Well, yeah, 'cause it was in the script."

"Wait a minute, I thought it was a reality show," Janzek said. "Cameras rolling, all of you just being yourselves?"

Saxby laughed and took a pull on his empty drink. It made a slurping sound.

"Put it this way," he said. "The producers always felt it necessary to—let's just say—enhance reality. Give it a good jolt of steroids. Like those reaction shots of me, every time D-Wayne said something stupid... which, I gotta tell ya, was pretty much all the time."

"I know what you mean," Janzek said. "So, they actually coach you how to react?"

"Shit, yeah. They'd say something like, 'Okay, Sax, now give me your best I-hate-your-guts look' or, as the head producer called it, my Snidely Whiplash look."

Janzek looked at his watch. He had been there half an hour and had very little to show for it.

But Saxby seemed to be just revving up. Suddenly he started waving his arms excitedly like he was trying to fly. "Or like that episode where we all went out for dinner," he charged on, "and D-Wayne gets really drunk and lectures all of us like we're a bunch of children. The producers came up with that whole bit, too."

Janzek looked over at the slow-dripping fountain. It was like Chinese water torture. "I guess I haven't seen that one yet."

Saxby's head snapped back. "What? You haven't seen episode nine. I thought you were a fan."

Janzek had no clue how he had reached that conclusion. "Yeah, well, but I still haven't seen 'em all. Something to look forward to."

Yeah, right.

Saxby smiled like he forgave him.

"Fact of the matter is, D-Wayne and I actually got to be pretty good friends. You'd never know that from watching the show, I know. We went out one night—no cameras or anything—and talked about how we were gonna go on Oprah and Jimmy Kimmel together. You know, hype the show and stuff."

"Yeah, and did you?"

Saxby looked down at his shoes. "Turns out we were a little overly ambitious there. But our agent got us on Channel 9 and the Joey Milchman show."

"Can't say I'm familiar with Joey."

"He's real popular down in Savannah."

Janzek nodded. "I'll try to catch it one of these days."

Saxby rang the bell for another drink.

Janzek looked at his watch again.

"So, you hung out with Marion a fair amount. Did he ever get any calls, or anybody sketchy-looking ever come see him? That you noticed? Or did he ever talk about someone who may have been hassling him, threatening him, anything at all like that?"

Saxby started nodding, then he thrummed his fingers on the table again. Finally. "No, not that I can think of, but do dirty looks count?"

SEVEN

The cast member who Janzek was most looking forward to interviewing was Samantha. Not that he'd ever admit it to Rhett. She seemed like the most normal of them all. Pretty, too. He planned to call her up after he went to Marion's funeral.

He walked into the police station on Lockwood Avenue and went into Rhett's cubicle. Rhett was hunched over his computer.

"Hey," Rhett said, looking up. "You got my text, right?"

"Yeah, sorry about that. I was in the middle of interviewing that guy Saxby. Forgot to get back to you."

"Don't worry about it. How was the Saxman?"

"Not much help."

"Kinda like tits on a pickle?"

Janzek shook his head slowly. "Jesus, who writes your shit?"

"Southern color, man."

"Is that what you call it?" Janzek said. "So, I'll handle the funeral."

Even though victims' funerals never really got you anywhere, you still did them anyway. If you put stock in movies, perps would often show up for a funeral and the hero would—through some combination of wiliness and intuition—figure out who the killer was, track him down and slap the cuffs on him. Case closed in a couple of hours.

Janzek had been to literally hundreds of funerals and, so far anyway... nada.

Sometimes there was a benefit or two, though. Like good booze at Irish funerals. Or good food at Jewish ones. At the last one he went to—his first in Charleston—he had observed one Sheila Lessing, a prominent woman in Charleston, as she arrived—tardily. A half-hour later, she had left—impressively—in a football-field-length black limo. The next month they met and became kind of an item.

But that's another story.

*****

Janzek found out later that freak-show funerals, which David Marion's turned out to be, were quite common in New Orleans. Which was probably where Jessie Lawson got the idea. But Marion's funeral was definitely a first in Charleston.

Janzek got out of his car on Calhoun Street and walked into the staid funeral home, expecting an expensive oak casket. Worst case, an open one. Not that he'd have minded all that much. He'd seen plenty of waxy dead bodies in boxes before in Boston.

A man standing just inside the front door, in a brown suit and cauliflower ears, directed him to a room. Janzek nodded and walked inside.

And there—in all his glory—was D-Wayne Marion.

He sat on a green sofa, larger than life, on the far side of the room in one of the most bizarre tableaus Janzek had ever witnessed. It looked like a frozen scene from a play. Displayed on a dais, Marion looked like a well-dressed, professionally stuffed animal. Taxidermed to near perfection.

Janzek remembered the green sofa from the living room of his house on Stolls Alley. In one of Marion's hands was a half-filled martini glass—Beefeater 24 gin, no doubt—and in the other, a lit cigarette. He was wearing white ducks, a blue shirt with a Polo logo and an oh-so-hip straw pork pie hat. There was the faint trace of a smile on his face and his Labrador retriever—very much alive but dozing—lay at his feet.

Janzek tried hard not to react to the outlandish scene. But he had never seen anything quite so weird in his entire life. He wondered if he was looking at a wave of the future.

A reality funeral.

He looked Marion over again. Then he realized the purpose of the jaunty pork-pie hat on his head. It was pulled down to cover the gaping bullet hole in his upper forehead that even the best embalmer in the world couldn't completely cover up.

Janzek walked into the room and sat down in third row center. Then he glanced to his right where he heard a whirring, mechanical sound. It was a man behind a camera with a SLAM! logo on it and it was pointed right at him. Janzek quickly looked away.

Just as Marion's over-the-top wedding had been filmed a month before on the show, and later televised, so, too, it seemed, would be his way, way over-the-top funeral.

Janzek looked to his left and saw Saxby, sitting next to an older woman who looked as though she had recently gone under the knife of a team of New York's finest plastic surgeons. No question about it, it had to be his mother, the woman notorious for knocking back cocktails with her Cheerio's. She hadn't been in any of the first five episodes, so this was Janzek's first sighting of the woman.

Janzek looked back at Marion, who, of course, hadn't moved a muscle, even though he looked very much alive. Behind him hung a framed diploma from Episcopal High School and, beside it, another from the University of Virginia. Also framed was a certificate for a fraternity called St. Anthony's Hall.

Janzek realized he was looking at a carefully arranged grouping of the most meaningful things in Marion's life.

To the other side of Marion hung a framed picture of him astride a horse, holding a raised polo mallet. On a table in front of him stood an architect's model of a sleek, twenty-story office building. And, just below the building—a poignant touch—was a photo of what Janzek guessed was his ten-week-old son.

A bald man in a black suit with a cigarette in his hand, who Janzek guessed was the funeral director, walked down the center aisle and went up to Marion on the elevated stage. He carefully removed the cigarette that had burned out from between Marion's rigid digits, and replaced it with the fresh, lit one. Then he pulled Marion's fingers together, tight on the cigarette. Janzek thought he heard a faint crackling sound.

An older couple, the woman's eyes red-rimmed, the man's blank, sat in the front row. Marion's parents, Janzek guessed. D-Wayne's father's eyes had an unfocused look like he might possibly have traveled a few miles down the Alzheimer's highway. Next to them sat a woman in her forties with two teenage girls. Marion's sister and nieces, Janzek guessed. A white-haired, straight-backed, black man sat next to one of the girls. Aristocratic Charleston families seemed to have one or two loyal retainers like him. Usually with names like Ezekiel or Jasper, Delvin Rhett had once explained to Janzek, rolling his eyes.

Finally, Janzek's glance strayed to the grieving widow and child whom he had yet to meet.

Jessie turned and looked over at him as if she felt his stare. Slowly, a Mona Lisa smile crept across her face. She raised her head majestically and he half-expected her to wink.

It was not the look of a woman deep in mourning.

EIGHT

Janzek was leaving the funeral home on Calhoun when his cell phone rang.

"Yeah, Delvin, what's up?"

"Where y'at?"

"Calhoun and Ashley."

"Do a U-ie and meet me at 69 Bull, just south of Calhoun," Rhett said. "Go on up to the top floor."

"Whatcha got?"

"Something pretty bizarre."

"It must be National Bizarre Day," Janzek said, doing a U-turn.

"You, too?"

"Yeah, Marion's funeral."

"How bizarre could a funeral be?"

"Trust me."

"Bet you never been to one with rattlesnakes."

"One of these days," said Janzek, pulling up to 69, Bull Street.

He flashed his badge to the man at the front door, who clearly wasn't thrilled to see him. He told the man where he was going, then took the elevator up to the top floor of the four-story home.

An open corridor led to eight identical doors in a long hallway. One was open, with a Charleston Police Department uniformed cop standing outside of it like a sentry. Janzek had seen him before but didn't remember his name.

He walked up to him.

"Nick Janzek, Violent Crimes."

"I know."

"Delvin Rhett in there?"

The uniform nodded.

"Thanks," Janzek said, walking in through the open door.

33

Rhett was talking to a woman who looked to be in her early twenties. He was sitting on the corner of a wooden desk and she on a well-worn couch with a woman next to her. The woman looked to be in her forties and had a deep-creased frown on her face.

Rhett looked up. "This is my partner, Detective Janzek," he said, then to Janzek. "This is Leah Reynolds and Doctor Marshalk from Roper Hospital. Miss Reynolds was, ah, assaulted by a man a little while ago."

Janzek nodded to Leah Reynolds. "I'm sorry to hear that," he said. "And I apologize for making you repeat what you told Detective Rhett, but if you would, please?"

The girl looked down and the doctor looked uneasy.

"Well," Dr. Marshalk said, "as Detective Rhett said, Ms. Reynolds was accosted by a man here in her room." She looked at Leah Reynolds, who had covered her eyes. Marshalk put her arm around her. "Don't worry, I'll stay right here with you. I'll stay as long as you need me."

Leah Reynolds' shoulders raised up then slowly seemed to deflate as she sobbed quietly.

"I know it's painful and raw," Dr. Marshalk said, "but these men are here to help."

Janzek nodded. "Thank you, Doctor."

The girl looked up at Janzek, tears in her eyes, then shook her head and looked back down.

Dr. Marshalk waded back in. "Let me try to help. Leah was... well, having sex with a man. In the middle of it, he took his tie and tied it around her neck, cutting off her supply of oxygen."

Janzek saw where it was headed. Sexual asphyxia.

Leah put her hands up to her face again.

The doctor went on. "What happened was, he kept tightening it... until finally, Leah lost consciousness."

"I thought he was going to kill me," Leah blurted out. "He kept pulling it tighter and tighter until I passed out."

Janzek wanted to offer solace, but there wasn't much he could say. "Then, after a while, you came to?"

Leah nodded. "Yes, and he was..." She started to sob even louder.

Janzek looked over at Rhett, who was shaking his head.

Nobody said anything for a few moments.

"I know this is really hard for you, Leah," Janzek said finally, as softly as he could, "but, please, tell me what happened next."

"I started screaming. After a minute or so my friend, Jolene, came running in. She had her cell phone in her hand and told the man she had called the police when she heard me screaming. The man hit her with the back of his hand, then walked out."

"Describe this man, please, Leah," Janzek said.

Rhett held up his notebook. "Got it right here, Nick," he said. "White man, late fifties or early sixties. Tall, weighs around two-twenty-five to two-fifty, grey, wavy hair. That about right, Leah?"

She nodded. "With a big mole right here," she said, indicating her right cheek.

Rhett wrote that down.

Then, Leah lost it completely and broke down. Her whole body started shuddering, and she was sobbing in long, spasmodic jolts. Dr. Marshalk put both arms around her and pulled her close.

Rhett turned to Janzek. "A couple of uniforms showed up and one knew Dr. Marshalk. He called her, and she came right over."

Janzek glanced over at Rhett. "Got the name of the guy who did this?"

"Yeah, Mr. Jones. He was here with his friend, Mr. Smith."

Janzek started to roll his eyes but caught himself.

"And this Mr. Smith," Janzek asked Rhett, "you got a description of him, too."

Rhett held up his pad. "White male, five-eight to five-ten, around a hundred-eighty pounds. Bald, scar on his forehead cutting into his eyebrow--"

"How old?"

"Like his friend, late fifties, early sixties."

There was nothing more Janzek needed to know and nothing he could do for Leah Reynolds. Fortunately, she seemed to be in the best hands she could be.

"Leah, again, we are very sorry about what happened and will do everything we can to catch this man, I promise you that," Janzek said, standing up. "We're going to go now, but one of us will be in touch. I hope you feel better soon."

Leah didn't look up. "Thank you."

Janzek glanced at Dr. Marshalk. "And thank you, Doctor. Thanks for all your help."

Dr. Marshalk nodded and smiled at him.

Janzek and Rhett walked out, nodding at the uniform cop as they went past him. Janzek pushed the button for the elevator. "What is this place, anyway?"

"I asked the girl," Rhett said. "She said a sorority."

"So where are the Greek letters on the front?" Janzek said as the elevator door opened. "All the other ones around here have 'em."

"I know, and did you check out the cars in the parking lot? They're all like Beemers, Jags, and Lexuses."

"I noticed that." Janzek pushed the button for the first floor. "And that putting green in front, what's up with that?"

Rhett shrugged. "I got no idea. Not like most college girls spend a lot of time practicing their putting."

"Let's go scope out this place a little." Janzek said as they stopped at the first floor.

He pressed the button for the second floor and the elevator doors closed.

On the second floor, the elevator door opened onto a huge oak-paneled room. It had a black and white checkerboard marble floor, a long bar at one end and very expensive looking furniture.

"Sure doesn't look like a sorority house to me," Janzek said. "Unless it's for billionaires' daughters."

"Yeah, I agree. I mean, looks like they hired some New York decorator and said, 'Go crazy, spend as much as you want.'"

They were looking around the room when a man carrying a case of liquor walked in a side door. He looked surprised to see them and in no hurry to roll out the welcome mat.

"Sorry, but not open 'til two. Are you new members?" He eyed Rhett like there was a snowballs chance in hell of him being one.

"No," Janzek said, holding up his ID. "Charleston Police. Mind if we have a look around?"

The man set the case down on the bar then walked around behind it. "Why? What are you looking for?"

"Nothing in particular," Janzek said. "You got something to hide?"

"Nothin' at all. But you guys just show up out of the blue... I just wonder why."

Janzek pointed to the case of forty-year old Glenfiddich scotch on the bar and said to Rhett. "Not exactly the brand of sorority girls and frat boys."

"No kiddin'," said Rhett.

Janzek looked back up at the bartender.

"This place sure ain't catering to the Pabst Blue Ribbon crowd. My name's Nick Janzek, my partner, Delvin Rhett."

The man nodded as he opened the box of Glenfiddich. "Billy Reece."

"Let me ask you—" Janzek wasn't quite sure how to phrase the question "—what exactly is this place?"

"What do you mean? It's Delta Phi Omega."

"Okay, but you get my drift, what goes on here?" Janzek said. "Doesn't strike me as a place where the sisters get into pillow fights on a Saturday night."

Reece put two bottles of Glenfiddich on a shelf behind the bar. "I'm not sure what you're asking?"

"Okay, let's start with, how many girls live here?"

"I think about fifteen or sixteen."

"That's it? In this whole big house?" Janzek asked.

"Yeah, they live on the third and fourth floors."

"And who exactly are the guys who come here?" Rhett asked.

Reece pulled out a sponge from a sink behind the bar. "What do you mean?"

"He means exactly what he asked, who are the guys who come here?" Janzek said, "Last night there were two guys here in their late fifties, early sixties. A little old for frat boys, I'd say. They paid a visit to two of the girls upstairs."

"Sorry," Reece said, squeezing out the sponge, "I'm *still* not sure what you're asking."

Janzek shot Rhett a glance like, *is this guy stupid or just uncooperative.* "Let me put it to you in the form of a question a moron could understand," he said, his patience exhausted. "Are the guys who come here paying for sex?"

"Hey, man, I'm just the bartender. I make drinks and that's it."

Rhett decided to play good cop. "Look, Billy, we're big fans of bartenders," he said, with a wide grin. "We partake of your services on a regular basis and know that, among other things, you're damn good observers."

"Yeah," Janzek cut in, "so, the question is, what have you observed? What the hell goes on here? And while we're testing your powers of observation, what's the name of a big guy around sixty years old, weighs somewhere between two-twenty-five to two-fifty, wavy, grey hair, and a big mole on his cheek? Name's Mr. Jones."

"I don't know anyone by that name. Or who fits that description. Guys just come here, have a few drinks and socialize."

Janzek shot another glance at Rhett.

"And on a typical night, describe the guys who come here?" Rhett asked.

Reece's eyes went up and down the bar, like he was looking for another customer who was friendlier.

"All different kinds," he said finally.

"How old?" Janzek asked.

"Oh, you know, all ages--"

"Cut the shit, Billy," Janzek said. "You mean all ages between fifty and your grandfather?"

Reece started re-wiping the already immaculate bar and didn't answer the question.

"You ever see guys give the girls money?" Janzek asked. "You know, in exchange for their scintillating conversation?"

"How would I know? I'm just--"

Janzek leaned closer to Billy and tried to find his eyes.

"I know, I know," he said. "Just swabbin' the bar, mindin' your own business, mixin' up Glenfiddich and Red Bull for the lollipop crowd, right?"

NINE

Lex Murray's bulldog, Moonie, was in a really bad way. Throwing up, weaving all around the living room of Murray's rented house, howling and scratching itself so hard that one leg had started to bleed.

Murray had no idea what was wrong with her and took her to the vet immediately. The vet didn't come up with anything either except to guess that it might be something Moonie ate, though he pointed out how much her pupils were dilated. Murray took her back home, put her in the fenced-in backyard of the house on Lamboll Street and watched her from the kitchen. She was running around in circles, like an invisible Wile E. Coyote was on her tail.

Murray's cell phone rang. He looked down at it and didn't recognize the number.

"Hey, Lex," the voice said. "How ya doin'? It's Jim."

He knew a few Jims.

"The guy from the sorority house last night," Jim said, "Workin' for your old buddy, you-know-who."

"Yeah," Murray said, "what do you want?"

"I thought I made that clear," Jim said. "Two million dollars."

"Yeah, yeah, I'm workin' on it," Murray said.

"I'm not sure I believe you, Lex," Jim said. "Hey, by the way, how's your dog doin'?"

Murray glanced out the kitchen window at Moonie. The dog was lying down now. In a ball, shaking.

"You fucking psycho!" Murray said. "What did you do to her?"

Jim laughed. "Nothing you and your boys didn't do to thousands of people."

"What the hell are you talking about?"

"A little heroin in her Purina Dog Chow. She'll live."

Murray slammed his fist into the wall next to his refrigerator.

"Where are you, you son of a bitch? I'm gonna come there and beat the shit out of you."

Jim laughed loud and hard. "Are you now? Well, come on over, tough guy. 17 Ludwell Avenue in West Ashley. Like I said, all I did was give your hound a little of your own medicine."

"That's bullshit, I just peddled pot and coke."

"Yeah, well, you know what they say, those are just gateway drugs to the heavy shit," Jim said. "Hey, when you come over here—to beat the shit out of me and all—make sure you bring the two million. Okay, tough guy?"

*****

Murray decided against following through on his threat to Jim. Guy looked like he probably had a few unlicensed automatic weapons lying around the house. Instead Murray packed two suitcases, put Moonie in the front seat of his car and headed down to Hilton Head. Something he'd been planning to do anyway. But, on his own schedule.

Hilton Head was where he had buried the money—twenty years before—before he did the hitch at MacDougall Correctional. A big four-bedroom condo down there had been his base of operation: on the water and an easy drop point.

Moonie had her head out the window now, her long pink tongue flapping around, seemingly recovered from her overdose earlier in the day.

Murray had a vague idea where he'd go after he dug up the money but figured twelve million dollars could buy him a pretty nice lifestyle just about anywhere. Leading contenders at the moment were Bermuda and several places on the west coast of Mexico. It would not be a permanent move, but long enough so that Jim whatever-his-name-was would move on and take his whole intimidation act with him.

He had spent five years filling the large Tupperware containers with hundred dollars bills back then. There were about fifty of them, all stacked neatly in a Mosler safe. Once he'd filled up the safe back in 1999, he'd dollied it over to his old El Camino and humped it up into the back of the truck bed. Then he'd driven it into the back yard of an old freedman's cottage in the middle of nowhere that he'd paid cash for the day before. What he liked about the house most was that it had no neighbors anywhere near it. He had dug a big hole in back, rolled the safe up to the edge of it, then eased it down into the hole. There had been a full moon that night, he remembered, and all he'd heard was the lapping of the water from a nearby tidal swamp.

Nobody but a few snakes and maybe a hoot owl or two knew about his buried treasure.

As Moonie slept in the seat next to him, Murray wondered if the True Value hardware store was still in business on Lagoon Road in Hilton Head. He needed to get a shovel and a flashlight.

He ejected the third CD of the Carl Hiaasen book out of the CD player of his Mercedes as he got off of Highway 17 and onto 95 South. Between thinking about Bermuda and Mexico, trying to follow the book's plot, and driving, Murray had taken no notice of the man in the black Yukon a hundred yards behind him.

TEN

Janzek was on the computer in his office when he got a call. It was Sheila Lessing. Sheila was a Charleston woman who had made it big in finance. Specifically, she had become a partner at Blackstone, a New York private equity firm and old boy's network if there ever was one, at twenty-nine. Twenty years later she had cashed out and now ran her own money and was a major South Carolina philanthropist. And, as of four months ago, an FON. Friend of Nick, make that special friend of Nick. He had met her shortly after he broke up with a woman named Geneva Maybank. They'd had had a good thing while it lasted, but, ultimately, she had wanted more and more of his time. Time that he didn't have to give her. It was a familiar cop story.

"Hey, Sheila," Janzek asked, "how's life up in the mountains?"

"Nice," she said, "really nice. Looking forward to seeing you up here next week."

Oh, God, he had forgotten all about that.

"You forgot," she said, "didn't you?"

"Sorry," he said. "I've just been really slammed."

"David Marion's murder?"

"Yeah, that and this other thing at the college."

"What happened there?"

"It's a long story."

"You can tell me all about it over a couple drinks up here."

"Sheila, I—"

"Don't even think about it, Nick. You're not backing out. You need a break, I can tell."

"Sheila, I just—"

"Tell you what, just come for a long weekend. I could send the helicopter for you, so you don't need to spend all that time driving."

Janzek laughed. "Are you kidding? Just to remind you, I'm a cop who makes a shade more than the counter girl at Krispy Kreme. What do you think the papers would say if they saw me get on a private chopper in the middle of a high-profile murder investigation?"

"Come on, Nick, I've been looking forward to this for a really long time."

"Me, too. The good news is there's still a lot of summer left."

Sheila Lessing was a very powerful woman who, for all her life, had been turning 'no's' into 'yes's.' She sighed dramatically. "The helicopter could pick you up in the backyard of my house on Sullivan's." Sullivan's Island was a fancy beach town just over the bridge from Charleston. "Nobody'd ever see you get on it."

"I just can't go now. I'm really sorry."

Sheila didn't say anything for a few moments. Then: "God, will you please just get a new profession?"

"'Fraid it's a little late to be an investment banker."

"I'm sorry," Sheila said, exhaling, "I know I'm acting like a spoiled child, but are you sure you can't—"

"I'm sure. It would be as if you—in the middle of one of your high-powered negotiations—said, 'sorry, gotta buzz off to St. Barth's now.'"

Sheila laughed.

"What?"

"How do you even know about St. Barth's?"

"How do you think? Read about it in my dentist's office."

*****

Rhett walked in just after Janzek hung up with Sheila. Janzek was shaking his head.

"What's wrong?"

"Nothing, man. Whatcha got?"

"I agree with you about parking a guy across from the sorority house," Rhett said.

Janzek stood. "Let's go talk to Ernie about it. We're going to need him to authorize some extra manpower for all we got going on anyway."

Rhett followed Janzek down to Ernie Brindle's office. Brindle, a short, intense, fifty-year old man, with hair going every which way, had been chief of police for over ten years. Unlike Janzek's chief up in Boston he wasn't a ballbuster who demanded that every case be solved yesterday.

Janzek stuck his head in Brindle's office. Brindle, at his computer, looked up and saw them.

"Got a second?" Janzek asked.

"For you, Nick, I got a minute," Brindle said, looking over his half-moon reading glasses. "For your partner… two seconds."

Brindle liked to bust Rhett's chops.

"Funny man," Rhett said with a chuckle.

Janzek and Rhett sat down opposite Brindle. "We got a manpower problem, Ernie," Janzek said.

"I'm listening," Brindle said.

"Way I see it is, our homicide is obviously top priority, but the girl's assault is not far behind."

"Yeah, I agree. Are you telling me you can't handle both?"

"No, we can," Janzek said, "but, for starters, we need you to authorize posting a guy across the street from the sorority house, where the assault took place."

"What for?"

"'Cause we want him to take a camera and monitor who comes and goes."

Rhett leaned forward in his chair. "We're thinking sooner or later the guy who did it is gonna come back."

"Probably he'll stay away for a while," Janzek said, "but eventually he'll show up."

"The bar there is open from two in the afternoon 'til two in the morning," Rhett said. "Can you give us a guy for that time?"

Brindle tapped his fingers on his desk. "Yeah, I can do that. But are you sure you're not biting off more than you can chew? Taking on both."

"What do you think?" Janzek asked.

"I think you can handle 'em," Brindle said, "or I wouldn't have assigned 'em to you. But you can forget about having any spare time for a while. You okay with that?"

Janzek and Rhett both nodded.

"Then get goin'," Brindle said, making a shooing motion with his hands. "Go get these sombitches."

Janzek and Rhett stood and walked toward the door. They went back to Janzek's office and sat down.

"Back to the sorority," Janzek said, picking up a pen and tapping it on his desk. "My guess is that not only is the guy who did it gonna stay away for a while, but most of the regulars, too."

"You figure Billy the bartender got the word out?"

Janzek nodded. "Yeah, no question. Oh, hey, I forgot to show you. I took a few pictures when I was at Marion's funeral. Maybe you can identify some of the people there."

Janzek handed Rhett his phone.

Rhett started clicking through the pictures of the funeral.

"Are you fucking kidding me?" Rhett said. "What a show! Look at 'ol D-Wayne—" He pointed—"Dude's havin' the time of his life."

"Yeah, except he's dead."

"A mere technicality," Rhett said clicking to the next picture, "I mean, look at the guy…smokin', drinkin', carryin' on."

Rhett clicked to the next picture. "Rip and his latest squeeze."

"Which reminds me," Janzek said, "he's next on my list."

Janzek pointed to the older couple Rhett had clicked to.

"My guess is that's Marion's father and mother."

"Yeah, I think you're right," Rhett said as he clicked to the next. It was the woman in her forties, the two girls next to her.

"That's probably his sister," Janzek said, pointing again.

Rhett nodded. "The whole cast of the show wasn't there?"

"Click the next one."

Rhett clicked it. "There we go," he said, looking at the cast standing behind the smiling corpse of David Marion posing for a picture. Several of them had big smiles and were flashing gangsta hand signals.

"Jesus." Rhett shook his head. "What's wrong with these people? Don't they know you're supposed to wear black at a funeral? I mean what's with all the lime green and puce and shit?"

Janzek looked down at the shot. "What the hell's puce?"

Rhett pointed at a dress. "Kind of a purple. One of the favorite colors of the brothers who ply the pimp trade."

Janzek laughed.

Rhett clicked the camera again and pointed. "How hot is she? The girl on top of your list."

It was the blonde, Samantha Byrd.

Rhett clicked to the next one.

"Who's that?" Janzek asked, pointing at a middle-aged woman who actually was dressed in black. "She's not on the show, is she?"

"Nah, but I saw her on the website," Rhett said. "I think she's like the producer or something."

"I didn't notice her when I was there," Janzek said, pointing, "but look at her eyes, almost looks like she's crying."

"Yeah. I see what you mean. Rest of 'em, though, look like they're in a mosh pit."

Rhett clicked the phone again. "These guys in the background with the movie camera's, are they who I think they are?"

"Yup," Janzek said. "Can you imagine this episode? Oughta do wonders for their ratings."

"Un-fucking-believable," Rhett said, "And if you play your cards right, maybe you'll make it onto Season Three. I can just see the episode description now: *Charleston Detective Attends Rager at D-Wayne Marion's Funeral.*"

ELEVEN

Rip Engle was a friendly guy with big teeth and bushy, dirty blond hair. Goofy was a word that came to mind. Janzek guessed he was about twenty-five but when he went and read his bio on the SLAM! website found out he was actually thirty-six. He sized him up as a guy who, when he was a kid, was always trying to keep up with his older brothers. Whose ambition was no more than to do his damndest to be one of the boys.

Rip had a modest one-bedroom apartment on Wentworth Street, which featured a big stack of dirty dishes in his kitchen sink befitting his bachelor status. His living room was dusty and had the smell of mold and cheap, old perfume. The place was in desperate need of a cleaning lady.

Janzek and Rip were sitting in bamboo chairs, which should have had cushions on them, but didn't. Rip, no doubt, had bought them at a tag sale. The two were facing each other, with a table between them that looked like a three-dollar special from Habitat for Humanity.

"Dude was a good guy," Rip said. "Sometimes took himself a little too seriously, but hey, who doesn't from time to time. Right, bro?"

Janzek nodded and took out his notebook and pen. "You got a theory how it might have gone down, Rip?"

"Not really, I mean D-Wayne could piss you off, 'cause he got drunk and obnoxious sometimes, but killin' the dude...? I can't see it, man. Gotta say, though, he and Saxby sure went at it a lot."

"Tell me about that."

"Well, they just, I don't know... *went at it a lot.*"

"About what?"

"Damned if I know. I remember last Thursday, them having the mother of all pit bull rumbles."

"Thursday, you mean the day Marion was killed?"

47

Rip did the math. "Yeah, guess it was."

Janzek wrote that down in his notebook.

"What else can you tell me about their fights?"

"Just that they were really loud."

"But not… physical."

Rip shook his head. "Almost, though."

"Where were you the night he got killed?"

It took a few moments, then it dawned on Rip.

"Wait, you're not thinking—"

"Gotta ask. It's all part of my investigation. I ask everybody the same questions," Janzek said, though it was not always true.

Rip nodded. "Okay, so, way I remember it, I went to a RiverDogs game that night, had a buncha beers, then went home."

The RiverDogs was Charleston's minor-league baseball team.

"By yourself?"

Rip gave him a look like Janzek must be smoking something.

"Dude, I never go home by myself," he said, "Well, actually one time back in 2016."

He laughed and beat his thigh with his hand, like he had just cracked a real doozie.

"I saw one episode of your show where Marion stole your girlfriend... Lizzie was her name, I think?"

Rip shook his head. "Guess you don't know how it works, dude. Holly and the TV guys make that shit up to spice up the show. You don't really think that ol' D-Wayne could actually snake a chick from me… do you?"

"I don't know, I—"

"Not on my worst day. Besides, I heard that the panties found in his bed were from Victoria's Secret." Rip said. "I mean, trust me, man, I'd never go out with a chick who wore undies from that place. I mean, how uncool is that? Chantelle... the only way to go. Rive Gauche Tangas to be more specific. Slid a few of those off in my day. Know what I'm sayin'?"

Janzek had absolutely no idea what he was saying. Last thing he knew, Victoria's Secret was a perfectly fine maker of women's underwear. He decided he didn't need to probe the subject further. Instead, he shifted forward in his bamboo chair and locked onto Rip's eyes.

"Marion was married, but the story I got was that didn't keep him from chasing woman on the show."

"On the show, off the show, anywhere he could find 'em. Dude was incorrigible, man."

Janzek gave Rip extra points for the word 'incorrigible' but wondered if the guy was capable of constructing a sentence without 'dude' in it.

"So, tell me about specific women Marion was... seeing."

Rip tapped his foot on the floor like he was counting.

"Well, he was doin' one of the producer's assistants, then the make-up girl for a while. He hit on Naomi, in the show, a few times. Then the same day he had the fight with Saxby, the day he was killed, he got dropped off at the set by this stone-cold fox in this sweet green convertible. Aston Martin or something."

Janzek leaned forward. "Can you describe her?"

"Blonde. Big hair. D-Wayne had a thing for blondes with big hair. Liked 'em flashy and sassy. Sorry, that was all I saw of her, she was driving."

"Did you remember anything else about the car?"

"Like what?"

"Well, like the plate? What state? South Carolina? Out-of-state? And, how old would you say she was?"

"Maybe late thirties or so, something like that? But hot, really hot." Rip winked at Janzek. "You know what they say about older women, right, Nick?"

"No, what do they say?"

Rip thought for a second, scratched his head, and thought some more. "Hell, I forgot."

TWELVE

Ernie Brindle had emailed Janzek and Rhett that he wanted to see them.

He was on a call when Janzek and Rhett walked into his office. He motioned to the chairs facing his desk and cut the call short.

"So, I want to tell you about something I just got," Brindle said. "But first, catch me up on what you got on David Marion and the girl who got assaulted."

Janzek exhaled and leaned back in his chair. "Got something hot off the press," he said. "One of the guys on *Charleston Buzz* told me he saw a blonde in a green Aston Martin drop off Marion at the set day before he was killed."

"So, what's your theory?" Brindle asked. "That she was the one in bed with him?"

"Could be. I checked DMV for green Aston Martins. Only two in the area. One in Mount Pleasant, another one downtown, both registered to guys."

"Did you speak to the owners?"

"Yeah. One was like, 'are you kidding? No one drives it but me.' Other guy said his wife drives it sometimes, but she's a fifty-five-year-old brunette."

Brindle tapped his desk. "Guess the car could be from anywhere, right?"

Rhett nodded. "Yeah, I'm gonna put out a BOLO in an email to the whole department."

"Good idea," said Brindle.

"Besides that," Janzek said, "of all the people we've interviewed, I'd say we got two suspects and a possible."

"So, tell me about 'em."

"Saxby Wentworth-Kuhn, for one. Guy on the show with Marion."

50

"Yeah, I know who he is."

"You a fan, Chief?" Rhett asked.

"Everybody's a fan... of fucking train wrecks. Most people won't admit it, though."

"It's pretty amazing," Rhett said.

"What is?" Brindle turned to Rhett.

"How our fair city, the size of Mesquite, Texas and El Monte, California, has not one, but two TV shows."

Brindle cocked his head and studied Rhett. "Where do you come up with shit like that, Delvin? Mesquite, Texas and El Monte, California?"

"One time when I had nothin' better to do I looked up all the cities the size of Charleston," Rhett said, "Those are just two. A few others are Sioux Falls, South Dakota, Cedar Rapids, Io—"

"Okay, okay. But why would you want to know that shit?"

Rhett shrugged. "I don't know, just intellectual curiosity, I guess."

Brindle shook his head. "You're fucked up in the head, you know that, Delvin."

"Maybe a little," Rhett allowed.

"Hey, how 'bout we get back to our suspects?" Janzek asked.

Brindle turned to Janzek. "Yeah, why're you thinkin' Saxby. I mean, he's an obvious one, but I'm not seeing the profile of a killer."

"Yeah, I don't disagree, but here's a little backstory. He's the guy who came up with the whole concept of the show in the first place, then he went and sold it to SLAM! But the plan was—the way he envisioned it anyway—he'd be the star. Instead he ends up playing second fiddle to Marion. Not only that, but Marion implies—on national TV—that Saxby's gay."

"I see where you're going, but is that enough to kill a guy?" Brindle asked. "Or is it all just a bunch of showbiz shit to get ratings?"

Janzek tapped his finger on Brindle's desk. "You got a point. Everyone we've talked to so far claims that most of the quote-unquote *reality* is actually scripted. But we got a little more on Saxby."

"Oh, yeah, what?"

"Guy's got a sheet."

"No shit," Brindle said. "For what?"

"Nothing all that big," Janzek said, looking over at Rhett. "You got it, right?"

Rhett pulled a piece of paper out of the breast pocket of his jacket and handed it to Brindle.

"An assault up in New York back in 2008," Rhett said. "He got convicted but got off with community service 'cause it was his first offense."

"What exactly happened?" Brindle asked, scanning the sheet Rhett had handed him.

"I called up NYPD and tracked down the arresting officer," Rhett said. "It was a bar fight. Saxby hit some guy with a wine bottle."

"Then six years later," Janzek said, "he gets into a fight with a guy at a traffic light in California. Road rage or something."

"So, Saxby's got a temper on him," Brindle said. "Okay, so give me a theory how it went down."

"Alright," Janzek said. "Like everyone else on the show Saxby drinks like a fish. So, he has a few and goes to Marion's house. Girl's maybe just left, and Saxby gets into it with Marion. About how Marion's hi-jacked Saxby's show, or maybe he gets in his face about something he said about Saxby on the show. Whatever. Saxby's got a piece on him, the thing escalates—and with that temper of his—he loses it. Puts one between Marion's eyes."

"Actually, a little higher than that," Rhett said, pointing to his forehead.

"Close enough," Janzek said.

"Another one is," Rhett cut in, "Saxby maybe finds out D-Wayne is puttin' the wood to a girlfriend of his, goes to his house and *blam, blam*."

"But, like you said, Marion's been hinting that Saxby's gay?" Brindle said.

"Doesn't mean he is," Janzek said. "From what I've seen, Marion never seemed to let the facts get in the way of his bullshit stories."

"Matter-of-fact," Brindle said. "I did notice that."

Janzek shrugged. "Like I said, Ernie, we're still early in the game. Just throwing shit around at this point. Seeing what sticks."

"So, okay, Saxby's a possible. Who's number two?" Brindle asked. "Based on what you got there, I'm still seeing Saxby as more like an... *improbable*."

"I admit it, what we got so far is a little thin," Janzek said. "Doesn't mean something more solid won't come along."

"Yeah, okay," Brindle said. "So, who's number two?"

"Jessie Lawson," Janzek said, "Mrs. D-Wayne."

"Because?" Brindle asked.

"Because she's sick of him fucking around all the time," Janzek said. "Or wants all their money to herself? Hell, I don't know, maybe she's got a guy on the side. Another reason it could be her is 'cause she's supposed to be such a good shot."

Brindle looked doubtful.

Janzek shrugged. "Or if that's not enough, maybe 'cause husbands and wives kill each other on a regular basis. I can tell you this for a fact, at the funeral she didn't play the grieving widow role too convincingly."

"Okay," Brindle said. "That one needs fleshing out. Gotta put some meat on its bones."

Janzek nodded. "I agree, they all need work. But since this isn't a case where we wrap it up in a neat bow in the first forty-eight, we're scrambling here."

"Okay, who's next? The possible."

"What I was talking about before. Either the blonde in the Aston Martin. Or maybe her boyfriend or husband if he found out. Or if it was some woman other than the blonde in bed with Marion, then maybe her or her husband or boyfriend."

"That's a lot of *possibles*." Brindle said.

"Yeah, I know."

"Anyone else?"

"Not really." Janzek said. "I interviewed Ashley and Lisa from the show and didn't get anything. They got pretty small roles. I'm waiting for Samantha who gets back from some job thing tomorrow."

"How 'bout you, Delvin?"

"I talked to Ted, Naomi and Darcie," Rhett said. "Didn't really get anything useful out of them. Got Greg the banker later today."

Brindle nodded. "All right, well, keep me in the loop. Anything new on the girl who got assaulted by the gasper? And what's with that place on Bull Street anyhow?"

"Good question," Janzek said. "Best we can tell is it's a fancy cat-house for fat cats. The working girls, in this case, being college girls who like to dress well."

"Sounds like a place we should be shutting down," Brindle said.

"Yeah, easier said than done," Janzek said.

"We looked into it a little more," said Rhett. "Turned out all the girls who live there all have scholarships—"

"—from some charity called Charleston Philanthropies, LLC," Janzek finished. "We're trying to find out who's behind it."

Brindle was shaking his head. "So nowadays, philanthropy is another word for whoremongery? I mean, Je-sus Christ! Okay, now I gotta tell you what I got. There's a real bad actor in town. Know the name Lex Murray?"

"Who?" Rhett asked.

"Lex Murray."

"No, who's he?"

"Before your time probably," Brindle said. "A big-time drug dealer from Hilton Head. Lived here on and off. He did like a twenty-year bit at MacDougall. Just got out and showed up here. Rents a place down on Lamboll."

"I remember hearing about him," Rhett said. "Dude used to live high on the hog. Boats, jets, women, the whole nine, right?"

"Yeah, that's him," Brindle said, "I thought it might be good to keep an eye on him, so I had Gates watching his place."

"Good idea," Janzek said.

"Yeah, you woulda thought."

"Why, what happened?"

"Gates took a little snooze on the job," Brindle said, reaching into his desk drawer. "Woke up and found this on his windshield."

Brindle handed Janzek a note on a lined, yellow, sheet of paper.

"'Dear Mr. Undercover Policeman,

Had to go on an unexpected business trip to Schenectady, New York. Please water the plants, save newspapers, and keep an eye on the place for me.

Your pal,
Lex M.

THIRTEEN

Lex Murray decided he was going to dig up the money and take it to Savannah, Georgia, which wasn't too far from Hilton Head. Then, he'd open up a few bank accounts and park the cash in safe deposit boxes. He'd probably need a whole wall of them. His next move would be to move all the money down to Grand Cayman, where he had a friendly relationship with a local bank—at least he had twenty years ago, before his stint at MacDougall.

After all the money moving, he intended to go to Bermuda. Check it out, see how he liked it.

He had taken the exit off of 95 and was now on 278 in Hilton Head. He saw a sign for a Home Depot and knew they'd stock plenty of shovels and flashlights. He pulled in, bought one of each, plus a couple of candy bars and two large bottles of water, then headed for the house on Bolton Road.

He got there a little after eight at night. The small one-story house was abandoned, just as it had been twenty years before, but now it looked as though it was in danger of collapsing at any moment. The main culprit was a round hole in the roof, which looked like a cannonball had crashed through it. He peered through a window and saw cobwebs, mold, and rotted floors. A crusty, old sleeping bag lay in one corner, in what once had been the kitchen. A door to what he guessed was a bathroom was closed and a few liquor bottles were strewn around the floor.

That was kind of strange. The sleeping bag and the liquor bottles. Though they could have been there for a long time. He certainly didn't remember them being there twenty years ago.

He was happy to see that the house still had no neighbors and figured that was probably because the land around it was so swampy.

As he turned away from the house toward the road, he saw a

black utility vehicle, which seemed to have pulled over. It slowly accelerated and drove away. He didn't think anything of it.

He decided to go back to his Mercedes, which was parked in the house's driveway, and listen to more of the Carl Hiaasen novel until it got completely dark. He intended to do his digging under the cover of darkness.

*****

He looked at his watch when the CD came to an end. It was 9:03 and dark outside.

He opened the package that the flashlight had come in and put the two AAA batteries in it. Then he opened the car door, got out, opened the back door of the Mercedes, reached in, and grabbed the shiny new shovel.

He walked around the house and clicked on the flashlight, looking for the marker he had left there twenty years before.

He found the large, oval-shaped rock right away, even though knee-high wild grass had grown up all around it. He had gotten it from the side of the driveway in front, way back when, then carried it back and set it down over the buried safe.

He almost felt like kissing the stone. It had served as a loyal sentry for all these years, guarding his buried treasure. Instead he grabbed both ends of it—it seemed heavier now, probably because he was twenty years older—and tossed it unceremoniously to one side.

Then he started digging. It took him no more than ten minutes to hit metal with his shovel. Man, what a sweet sound! Twenty years ago, he had lowered the safe down, so it rested on its back, and now all he had to do was dial the combination, open the door, reach in, and pull out the Tupperware containers.

Five minutes later, he had all the dirt cleared from above the safe and was ready to plug in the numbers of the combination. The combination was a number he couldn't possibly forget, because it was on a tattoo on the inside of his right wrist. When guys at MacDougall asked him what the numbers stood for, he explained that it was an old girlfriend's birthday. A chick who had ended up marrying a cop in Jacksonville, he said. Sounded plausible and everyone bought it.

The front of the safe was about a foot and a half below the level of the ground around it. He stepped down on top of it, his feet straddling the door. He crouched down and dialed the combination. Just as he'd practiced it every day. He heard the final click and felt his heart beat faster.

He stepped off the safe, knelt back down, pulled open the door and saw the cash-filled Tupperware boxes neatly arranged eight across and seven deep.

He licked his lips and punched the air with his fist.

"Thanks, Lex," the deep voice behind him said, "I can take it from here. You're a really good digger, man."

He jumped when he first heard the voice, like someone said 'boo' watching a scary movie when he was a kid. He didn't even want to turn around. But he did.

The man named Jim was standing above him, cradling a Tec Nine in both hands.

"Pretty handy with that shovel. Toss it over there," Jim said, pointing.

Murray thought about trying to knock the gun out of Jim's hands, but knew he'd be a dead man if he tried.

With a resigned sigh, he turned and tossed the shovel to his side.

FOURTEEN

The article wasn't in the *Post & Courier*, the newspaper of record in Charleston, but the *City Paper*, which was more of an alternative. It was free and frothy and occasionally you'd run across the word 'fuck' in articles. The headline read, *SLAM! Hidden Camera Records Bedroom Frolics*. Janzek was sitting down to a breakfast of coffee and a blueberry muffin at the Bake Shop on East Bay Street when he saw the article. Right after he read it, he called Rhett, who was at the office already.

"Listen to this," Janzek said. "*'The producers of "Charleston Buzz," the reality show portraying Charleston as Peyton Place—for you Millennials substitute "The Affair"—are camera-happy. Their ubiquitous cameras are reportedly set up just about everywhere to record every deliciously sordid detail in the soap-opera lives of their eight oversexed and over-served cast members. Now it seems one of these stationary, wall-mounted cameras may have been installed in several cast members' bedrooms to record their lovemaking. We have been told by one of the show's producers—who we would deem quasi-reliable (when it suits his purpose, that is)—that cameras have long been rolling in certain cast members' boudoirs. Among them are said to be Rip, Naomi and Saxby...'* Are you thinkin' what I'm thinkin', Delvin?"

"Loud and clear," Rhett said. "That maybe one was rolling in D-Wayne's bedroom."

"Exactly," Janzek said, lowering his voice as a couple walked in to the Bake Shop. "But I sure as hell don't remember seeing any camera there. Do you?"

"No. Definitely not," Rhett said. "Unless they had it really well hidden. I mean, the new ones are real small."

Janzek thought for a few moments. "I don't think there was one. One of us would have spotted it, or it would have dawned on one of the producers, or someone connected with the show, to call and tell us about it."

"Yeah, maybe. Unless they decided *not* to tell us about it."

"In any case, we gotta go talk to them. I'll swing by and pick you up. We can take a run over to the SLAM! office."

*****

Janzek made some calls—specifically, one to Rip Engle—and found out where the SLAM! office was located. SLAM! was based in Hollywood but had leased out an office on Upper King Street. It was in a loft building you entered from Liberty Street, Rip said, which ran between St. Philip and King Streets.

On the way there, Janzek called the SLAM! office but just got a recording that said, "*This is* SLAM!... *keepin' it real. Leave a message.*"

When they arrived, Rhett hit the buzzer for the SLAM! office.

"Yes, who is it, please?" a professional-sounding woman's voice said a few moments later.

"Charleston Police," Janzek said. "Could you let us in, please?"

"Of course," said the voice, "we're up on the third floor."

SLAM's space didn't look particularly office-like. It was an enormous, high-ceilinged room with exposed pipes and industrial lighting. Straight ahead stood a bar with eight bar stools. Off to the right, a ping-pong table. Beside that, a pool table.

To the left stood a man and a woman, smiling and welcoming.

"Gentlemen," said a tall, horsey-looking woman in jeans and a Rolling Stones, big-lip T-shirt. "Welcome to SLAM! South."

Janzek recognized her as the middle-aged woman dressed in black he'd photographed at David Marion's funeral.

"Thanks," Janzek said, showing his ID. "I'm Detective Janzek, this is Detective Rhett."

"And I'm Holly Barrow," then turning to the man next to her. "And this is Hudson Rock."

Cute. Janzek nodded at the man.

"We've been expecting to hear from you," Holly said.

"What do you mean?"

"That article in *City Paper*," she said. "We figured that might arouse your curiosity."

Janzek nodded again. "Yeah, it sure did."

Barrow motioned with her hand. "Come on over to the bar. We're buying."

"We generally don't start drinking at ten in the morning," Janzek said.

She laughed. "We got all kinds of non-alcoholic stuff." She slipped behind the bar as Hudson Rock followed.

Janzek and Rhett sat down in two bar stools.

"What's your pleasure?" Holly asked.

"Water, please," Janzek said.

"Got a Coke?" Rhett asked.

Barrow nodded. Hudson Rock did the honors.

"Okay," Janzek said, "we have a critical question. There were no hidden cameras in David Marion's bedroom, correct?"

"Correct," Barrow said.

"Is that because he was a married man? And—in the unlikely event—he ever had a, ah, dalliance, he wouldn't want there to be any evidence?"

"I like the way your mind works, detective," Holly said. "I actually asked David if we could install one in his bedroom and he gave me a very succinct two-word answer."

"And that was?"

"'Fuck no.'"

Janzek nodded. "I'm just curious. This article in the *City Paper*, was it initiated by you or a reporter of theirs?"

"Well, we like to maintain good relations with the press," Holly said. "Actually, Hudson was interviewed by the reporter."

Janzek put down his water and looked over at Rock. "Okay, Hudson, take us through that interview, if you would."

Hudson nodded. "Sure. It was just another routine interview, the guy saying how he noticed we had cameras everywhere. He made some lame joke about them being in the girl's showers or something. I said something like, 'No, but in their bedrooms—'"

"Putting them there was kind of an experiment," Holly cut in. "But here's the reality. Obviously, we can't show people actually having sex on the show, so the cameras weren't that useful. The first one we put in a smoke alarm in Naomi's bedroom."

"No," Rock said. "Actually, it was in Saxby's stabbin' cabin."

"Oh, right," said Holly, then turning to Janzek. "Stabbin' cabin meaning—"

"I know," Janzek said. "So, what was the upshot?"

Holly sniffed dismissively. "You ever watch someone sleep for nine hours straight?"

"Can't say I have."

"Well, trust me," Holly said, "it doesn't make for scintillating TV."

"The fact of the matter is," Hudson chimed in, "most of the time they're in bed, they're sleeping. It's like a ratio of ninety-nine to one"

"What is?" Janzek asked.

"Sleeping to fucking," Hudson explained with a straight face.

"Good to know," said Janzek.

"And like I said, since—unfortunately—we can't show people having sex on the show," said Holly, "the whole thing was kinda pointless. We eventually took the cameras out."

Janzek glanced at Holly, then Hudson.

"But you didn't tell the reporter that, I'm guessing? That you took them out."

"Oh, God, no," Holly said. "Might as well let him and his small-town imagination conjure up a whole library of torrid sex tapes."

"I hear you," Janzek said. "Hey, look what it did for Paris Hilton."

"I'm impressed, Detective," Barrow said. "Wouldn't have figured you'd know about stuff like that."

"I'm hurt, Ms. Barrow."

FIFTEEN

"Saxby, it's Nick Janzek, I got a few more questions for you. When can I come talk to you?"

"I just walked in the front door," Saxby said. "And in our household anyway, it is now officially cocktail hour. So, come on over and knock one back with me."

Janzek looked at his watch. It was one minute past noon. One of the first things Janzek noticed when he moved to Charleston, was how much people in the so-called Holy City liked their cocktails.

Early and often.

"Give me half an hour. Is the gate gonna be open?"

"Just hit 1861 on the security pad," Saxby said, then added, "a terrible year in American history."

*****

Mr. Carson, or his latter-day successor, let Janzek in.

"Welcome back, Detective," said the middle-aged black butler.

"Thank you," Janzek said. "Sorry, but I never got your name?"

"Moses Gronowski," the man said with a grin.

"No shit," Janzek said. "Polish-African-American?"

"That I am," Gronowski answered proudly.

"Now there's a combination you don't run across every day."

"Best of both worlds."

"Amen, and I'm half of it."

Gronowski nodded. "I figured."

Janzek slapped him on the back. "Can you take me to Mr. Wentworth-Kuhn, please? Salon du thé, I'm guessing."

"Follow me. Actually, he's in the library with his mother. It's long past tea time for the missus."

62

Gronowski led Janzek down a long hallway to the library. The room contained a lot of imposing furniture that managed to appear both impressive and dreary at the same time.

Saxby's mother was indeed the person Janzek had seen with Saxby at David Marion's funeral—a pretty woman who looked fifty at first glance but grew older the closer you got. She sat in a brown leather chair across from Saxby.

A smile fluttered across her face as she saw Janzek approach.

Saxby turned and stood. "Detective Janzek, I was just telling my mother all about you."

"Yes, but you didn't tell me how fabulously handsome he was," Saxby's mother said. "I'm Penelope Kuhn, Detective. So nice to meet you."

"Nick Janzek, ma'am, nice to meet you, too." Janzek gave her hand a delicate shake.

"Moses," Kuhn said, "get the man a drink, please... I'm having champagne if you'd care to join me."

"Thank you," Janzek said, turning to Gronowski. "Just water, please."

"You're no fun," Penelope said. It came out as 'fud.'

Janzek had noticed a slur and wondered how much was left in the champagne bottle.

"Have a seat," Saxby said, gesturing.

Penelope Kuhn slapped the spot next to her. "Right here."

What could he do? He sat down next to her and dialed up his all-business look.

"I need to ask you some questions, Saxby," thinking that Penelope would take the hint.

"You can ask them in front of me," Penelope said. "I'm a big girl." Janzek eyed Saxby. Saxby nodded. "Ask away, partner."

Gronowski handed Janzek a glass of water and reloaded Penelope's champagne flute.

"Thank you," Janzek said, eyeing Saxby. "So, look, I'm not going to beat around the bush here. I did some checking and found out you were arrested twice for assault. I need to know about those incidents?"

Saxby glared at him. His mother reacted differently. "Oh, my God, those were both *toooo* ridiculous," she said, waving her hand

63

dismissively. "And *soooo* long ago. My son was practically a child at the time."

Saxby maintained the glare but shifted it to his mother. "Mother, I can handle this, thank you very much."

"I know, I just—"

"You gotta be kidding," Saxby said defiantly, turning back to Janzek. "So, you seriously think I had something to do with what happened to Marion?"

"The day he was killed it was reported that you and he had a loud argument off-camera during one of your shoots. What was that all about?"

Saxby laughed and shook his head. "About nothing. Christ, I can barely remember, just D-Wayne calling me out on something I said about Jessie."

"Which was?"

"The truth. How her first husband died in the saddle."

"Really, Saxby," Penelope said, wiping her cosmetically enhanced chin with a linen napkin, "why must you use that horribly tacky expression?"

"Well, it's true, the old fart's ticker shut down in medias coitus... is that better?" Saxby said.

"No, it's disgusting and disrespectful."

"Wait, so you're saying Jessie was married before?" Janzek was thinking she was only about twenty or twenty-one now.

Saxby and his mother both nodded.

"How old is she?"

"Twenty," Saxby said. "She married Penn Pomeroy back when she was eighteen. It was one of those January-December marriages you see a lot in—" he did the little quote thing with his fingers "—so-called 'polite society'."

Janzek wasn't sure how relevant to his case this was, but he sure was curious. "So, what exactly happened?"

"Jesus, I just gave you two explanations," Saxby said. "Neither of which my mother approved of."

"No, I understand how he died," Janzek said, "but she was eighteen and he—"

"—was seventy-nine," Penelope said.

"Like that Playboy Playmate, Anna Nicole Smith," Saxby said.

"And that old groaner from Texas. Except Jessie thought Penn was rich and he wasn't."

"We all thought he was," Penelope said. "He had that beautiful house on LeGare Street."

"Mortgaged to the hilt," Saxby said. "I remember going to the funeral. She was, like, licking her chops. Couldn't even hide it. Then, I guess, she found out the truth when she met with the lawyer."

Two husbands in the ground and she couldn't even drink legally. Jessie Lawson was definitely Janzek's next stop.

SIXTEEN

Janzek called Jessie and asked if he could meet with her at three o'clock that afternoon. She said yes and suggested the Starbucks across from the Charleston Place hotel where she was staying. That gave him time to go see Rip Engle before Jessie. He wanted to double-check a few things.

Janzek punched in Rip Engle's cell number as he slid into the seat of his car.

Rip answered on the first ring.

"I was hoping we'd talk again," Rip said. "I like the idea of helping solve a murder."

"Well, I like you helping me," Janzek said, thinking that Rip sometimes seemed more like a fourteen-year-old than a guy in his mid-thirties. "I have a question for you. When you had the cast down to your plantation to shoot quail, what happened?"

"What do you mean, what happened?"

"I mean, how many quail did you actually shoot?" Janzek said, "I heard you didn't have that much luck?"

Rip laughed. "Put it this way, we had plenty of luck finding birds. We just couldn't hit the goddamn things."

"Nobody could?" Janzek asked. He knew the answer.

"Well, no one except Jessie. She was Annie fucking Oakley out there. I mean, Jesus, bro, that girl's a hell of a shot."

"Yeah, that's what I heard."

"I guess her old man taught her—" Rip stopped, getting where Janzek was going. "Wait, dude, you're not thinking... I guess that's exactly what you were thinking. That thing about the pre-nup, huh?"

Pre-nup?

This was the first he had heard about a pre-nup. It could be a game-changer. Something he wanted to hear about face-to-face.

"Where are you right now?"

"I'm at the Bull Street market. A late lunch."

"Where on Bull Street is it?"

"Well, it's actually on King," Rip said, then raised his voice and asked, "Hey, what's the number here?"

Janzek heard somebody say, "Fifty-two."

"It's Fifty-two King."

"Okay, got it," Janzek said. "Be there in five minutes."

*****

Janzek didn't waste any time as he sat down at the table opposite Rip. Rip was wearing shorts, a tight yellow T-shirt, and his trademark dopey grin.

"So, David Marion and Jessie had a pre-nuptial agreement?"

"No," said Rip.

"But you said—"

"That D-Wayne wanted her to sign one after they got married," Rip said.

"I guess he figured better late than never. A *post-nup*, I guess you'd call it."

"Do you know when he brought up this 'post-nup' idea to Jessie?"

Rip thought for a moment. "A week ago? Little more maybe? I heard she went ballistic. Tell ya this, she showed up at the show loaded for bear."

"Exactly what day was that?"

Rip thought for a second. "Tuesday."

"And did she sign it?"

"No way. And the next day, I heard, she got on a plane to New Orleans."

"So maybe... she got out of town before he could get her to sign it?"

Rip shrugged. "I think so. All I know is she was as pissed off as I've ever seen her. And the two of them were pretty good at airing their dirty laundry in public."

"What did you hear them say?"

"She was yelling at him, 'Are you fucking kidding me... fifty thousand a year?'

Even Janzek would have trouble getting by on that. "Anything else you recall them saying?"

"I remember D-Wayne saying something snarky like, 'What are you so worried about? I see a lifetime of marital bliss ahead for us.' She just looked at him like maybe... maybe she wasn't so sure about that."

"So, that was it?"   "Yeah. After a while, she kinda cooled down," Rip said. "But you just knew that wasn't the end of it."

"Do you have a sense for what else was in the post-nup?"

Rip gave him a blank look. "Nah, not really, bro."

Janzek stood up. "Thanks," he said, looking down at Rip's salad. "I appreciate your help. I got a date with Annie Oakley now."

"Well, give her my best. She was my old girlfriend after all," Rip said. "One of the many."

"Yeah, I know," Janzek said, "tough to keep 'em all straight, huh?"

SEVENTEEN

Janzek wanted to be totally prepared for Jessie Lawson. So, he called her and asked if he could push back their meeting at Starbucks to six. He had some more digging around he wanted to do. She said fine, but she had to be somewhere at seven.

He went back to the station and spent the next two and a half hours doing some checking. He found out several eye-opening things.

*****

Jessie was staying at the Charleston Place hotel because—as she told Janzek—there was no way she was going stay at the house where her husband had just been brutally murdered. She had been having meetings with various lawyers and accountants for the past few days. She had found out—among other things—that as of yesterdays close of the stock market her net worth was seventy-eight million dollars and change. It was less than she expected—because D-Wayne had a way of exaggerating things—but she could get by on it. She had already contacted a real-estate broker in New York City about buying a part-time place there. She had always thought New York was more her speed, Charleston was a little too provincial for her.

*****

She wore too much make-up for Janzek's liking. And her lips looked cosmetically enhanced—definitely bigger than the ones she'd been born with.

They hadn't gotten off to a great start. Because, as usual, Janzek dived right in. Clearly, a little too abruptly for her. But Janzek couldn't help himself. He knew he was probably guilty of what he had been accused of many times before: something southerners called 'that pushy Yankee syndrome.'

His offense with Jessie had been that he said again how sorry he was, about the death of her husband but, in almost the same breath, asked her about the state of their marriage at the time he was killed. "It was fine," Jessie said, then sighed theatrically. "Okay, he cheated on me, and that didn't make me happy, but that's just the way it was."

Janzek wasn't expecting such a direct answer.

"I heard that D-Wayne approached you about signing a marital agreement last week."

Jessie had been looking down. Her eyes shot up to Janzek's. "Where'd you hear that?"

"One of the cast members. Is it true?"

"D-Wayne brought it up, but he brought up a lot of things that never went anywhere."

"Are you saying this never went anywhere?"

"I'm saying we had no marital agreement."

"But was he still asking you to sign one at the time of his death?"

"What difference does it make? There wasn't one," Jessie said. "I get why you're asking. I'm not stupid, you know. So, are you looking to charge me with something?"

"No, Ms. Lawson, I'm not accusing you of anything, but it's my job to figure out who had a motive to kill your husband."

"I know, I get that. So, are you saying my motive would be to kill him before he made me sign that thing?"

If the shoe fits... "Some might construe that as a motive. Fifty thousand dollars a year if you got divorced... I'm pretty sure that wouldn't have made you too happy."

Jessie's jaw hardened. "Was it Rip who told you this?"

She looked furious now.

"I can't say."

"D-Wayne was never going to go through with it."

Janzek wasn't convinced, but he felt he had exhausted the subject. He wasn't sure how to introduce the next one, so he just barreled ahead. "You were the only woman who went to shoot quail at Rip's family plantation. Is that correct?"

"That was no plantation. More like a glorified pig farm with a fancy name."

"Which was?"

"Balmoral Plantation."

"But you were the only woman who went, right?"

"You know, Nick, you're really starting to piss me off," she sighed theatrically. "And I was so prepared to like you. Okay, yes, I was the only woman, and the fact is I shot way better than any of the guys down there. They couldn't hit a barn door from ten feet away. So, does that mean I shot my husband? Well, for one thing, I was in New Orleans, six hundred miles away. For another, believe it or not, I loved my husband."

Janzek nodded. She would hardly be the first woman to profess undying love after killing her husband.

It was time for the 'gotcha' he had been saving up.

"I did some checking—" long, dramatic pause "—and you were scheduled to fly up here the morning after your husband was killed, is that correct?"

Jessie nodded. "Very good. You get a gold star. He had to stick around for the show, so I decided to join him."

"But instead of flying you drove. Why?"

"Because I had some pieces of furniture that I wanted to bring up here," Jessie explained. "I got off first thing in the morning—twelve-thirty a.m. it was—then drove straight through with a couple of quick pit stops."

Janzek leaned forward like a hungry predator.

"So, you're saying, you got in to Charleston the morning after your husband was shot?"

She glared at him and raised one eye. "Yes, that's exactly what I'm saying."

"Ms. Lawson, I checked the records at the Charleston Place garage, and you got there at nine in the morning."

"Yeah, so?"

"So, it's an eleven- to twelve-hour drive and you just said you took off first thing in the morning?"

"Yes, exactly. Like I said, just after midnight—last time I checked that counts as first thing in the morning. Second of all, I drive like a bat out of hell, particularly in the middle of the night when no one's on the road. It took me nine hours."

She shot Janzek a triumphant look.

71

"Mrs. Lawson," Janzek said, amping up his best matter-of-fact tone. "I checked your credit card charges a little while ago. They indicate that you bought gas with a Mastercard at a Hess station just west of Atlanta at six o'clock at night the day before you say you got here. In other words, five hours before your husband was shot to death. Atlanta is four and a half hours to Charleston. I guess the way you say you drive, more like three and a half or four."

Jessie sighed deeply. "You're a regular Sherlock Holmes, aren't you, Nick?" She seemed not the least bit chastened.

"Ms. Lawson, you lied to me. You were actually here in Charleston when your husband was shot."

"Okay, busted. I lied. So sue me. I drove up early to catch my husband in the act and, you know what?"

"What?

"I did."

"What time was this?"

"When I caught him?"

"Yes."

"Around ten o'clock at night."

"What happened?"

"It was simple. I walked into the house on Stolls Alley—it was unlocked—and there he was in bed, with his latest bimbo."

"Who was she?"

"Never saw her before in my life. Blonde, trampy-looking, you know, been around the block a few times."

Janzek immediately thought of the woman in the Aston Martin.

"So, what did you do?"

"I just laughed and called him an asshole."

"That's it?"

"Well, no, then I spat at her."

"You spat at her?"

A grin spread across her face. "Yeah... seemed like the right thing to do at the time."

"I need you to describe this woman to me, please. I don't exactly know what trampy-looking means."

"Sure, you do: cheap, fake tits, Dolly Parton hair. I just got a quick look at her. Bitch buried her head under the covers."

"Any identifying marks, moles, birth marks, anything like that?"

Jessie sniffed her disdain. "Yeah, come to think of it, this little nipple ring on her left tit. No, actually, it would be her right one."

"Would you be able to describe her face? To a sketch artist of ours."

Jessie scratched her head. "Um, not really. Her face was kind of a blur. Wasn't like she sat there and chewed the fat with me."

"I understand. So, what happened next?"

"I went to Oak. Had a bottle of red wine and a nice, juicy steak. I guess you missed that credit-card charge."

"No, I saw it. You used an American Express card for that one. At 11:04, to be exact."

"Whatev," Jessie said. "Fact is, when I left my husband, he was very much alive. Probably started humping that bimbo right after I left."

"Something else, I also found out you have a carry permit for a concealed weapon?"

"Yeah, so. Lots of people do. This *is* South Carolina, land of the gun."

Janzek nodded. "Did you have a gun on you that night?"

"No, it was under the seat in my car."

Janzek looked her in the eyes. She didn't blink or look away.

There wasn't much more he could ask her. He thanked her, said he'd no doubt be back in touch and left.

It was an okay interview. He'd caught her in a lie but that was a long way from catching her with a smoking gun.

EIGHTEEN

Later that day, Ernie Brindle walked into Janzek's office. It was 6:45 p.m. Janzek looked up from his computer.

"Hey, boss, what's up?"

"It's almost seven o'clock and I'm buying. Normally I don't conduct business at Moe's, but tonight I feel like making an exception."

Moe's was a bar on Rutledge Avenue that had about as many TV screens tuned in to sports as it had different brands of beer.

Janzek smiled and stood up. "You're the boss and I do what you tell me to do. I'm assuming I can bring along my African-American colleague?"

"He'd get his nose seriously out of joint if you didn't."

Janzek walked down to Delvin Rhett's office.

"The boss is buying," Janzek said.

Rhett looked up from behind his desk with a grin.

"Moe's?"

Janzek nodded. "Yeah, I hear he's got his very own table there."

*****

"Okay, boys," Brindle said, sitting at a corner table at Moe's. "Catch me up on D-Wayne. Then I want to tell you about what happened down in Hilton Head. That guy I was telling you about, Lex Murray…? He bought it."

"No shit," Janzek said, taking a sip of beer.

"Yeah," Brindle said. "Just like D-Wayne. Single shot in the forehead."

"Keep going," Janzek said. "You have our undivided attention."

"Okay, so they found his body jammed in a safe buried behind a house he owned down there."

74

"You're kiddin'," Janzek said. "What do you mean in a safe? How'd they find it?"

"What happened was this homeless guy had been crashing in this abandoned house out in the middle of nowhere. Guess he'd been drinking and passed out on the shitter. Said he heard a noise, looked out a window and saw someone digging a hole outside. Then he heard a voice and saw a guy standing in a hole and another guy holding a gun on him. A few minutes later the guy with the gun shot the guy in the hole. Guy in the hole was Lex Murray. Homeless guy said the shooter took a whole bunch of plastic boxes out of this buried safe, put 'em in his car, then stuffed Murray's body into the safe in the hole and filled it up with dirt."

"Wow," Janzek said, "Lucky the homeless guy was there, or we'd never know about it."

"I know," Brindle said, killing the rest of his beer.

'I'm assuming that those plastic boxes were full of cash?" Janzek asked.

"I'd say you're correct in your assumption."

"Got a guess about how much it might have been?" Janzek asked.

"Well, I remember reading about his trial back then," Brindle said. "A guy who worked for him flipped and testified that he had stashed around ten mill or so. But they had no idea where. Never found a nickel."

"You thinkin' maybe this is all somehow related to D-Wayne?"

"I don't know," Brindle said. "Maybe, maybe not. Only thing the two murders have in common is both vics got shot in the head. Different caliber weapon from what the Hilton Head chief told me, but the ballistics aren't final yet." Brindle raised his hand to the waitress. "I know the chief down there a little. I'm gonna ask him to put you guys in the loop."

"Yeah, do that," Janzek said. "So, now we'll catch you up on what we got."

"Still lookin' at D-Wayne's wife and that wing nut, Saxby, from the show?" Brindle asked.

"Yeah," Janzek said. "Why is it everyone calls it *that show*? Like what they're really saying is, that piece of shit."

"'Cause we got manners here in the South," Brindle said. "Pretty good with our euphemisms, too."

Janzek raised his beer mug to Brindle, then told him about his meeting with Jessie Lawson and her story about her walking in on her husband.

"Like you said before, we gotta find that girl who was in bed with him," Brindle said. "She's the key."

"Trust me, ain't for lack of trying. I got two sketchy descriptions is all. One from Jessie Lawson, which was more body than face, the other from Rip which I told you about."

"We went around to all the other cast members and asked if they saw the blonde," Rhett said. "But no one else had seen her close up. One or two from a distance, but that was it."

"I also went and talked to a bunch of D-Wayne's friends not on the show," Janzek said. "But no luck to speak of."

The waitress showed up with three mugs of beer.

"But going back to Jessie," Rhett said. "I just don't buy that she's our girl. She's just too... obvious."

"Yeah, well, maybe," Janzek said, "but I got news for you, Del. That's usually whodunit. The most obvious."

"But is that what your gut's tellin' you? You really think it's her?" Brindle asked.

"I don't know," Janzek said, putting his mug down. "I got a bunch of reasons to think it was her. And one big one to think it wasn't."

"So, let's hear 'em," Brindle said.

"Okay, reasons why," Janzek said. "First of all, as we all know, Jessie can shoot. Easy for her to put one between her husband's eyes. But, hell, from that close, maybe Steve Wonder could, too. Number two—" he told Brindle about the post-nuptial agreement that D-Wayne tried to get Jessie to sign.

"I mean, here's my thinking," Janzek said, "When D-Wayne first brought up the post-nup, she skipped town, hightailed it to New Orleans. But eventually, it seemed to me anyway, he was going to force her to sign it. Sooner or later. Sounded like, from what Rip said, he was dead set on getting her to."

"I hear ya," Brindle said, nodding.

Janzek turned to Rhett. "So, obvious suspect, yeah. Motive, absolutely," he said. "I mean the difference between fifty thou a year and inheriting close to eighty million."

"That's what she's getting?" Brindle said, his eyes huge.

"So, I heard."

"Hell, I'd kill for that," Brindle said.

"Me, too," Janzek smiled and turned to Rhett. "Also, I didn't get a chance to tell you this yet, but when I met with Jessie a little while ago, she told me she wasn't in town when D-Wayne was killed. Well, turns out she was. Girl was flat out lying to me."

"Wow, she's beginning to sound more and more like our girl," Brindle said.

"I know," Janzek said. "And with a carry permit to boot. By the way, I picked up a warrant to search the hotel room where she's staying. Going there tomorrow morning."

"Good idea. Think any way she might see that coming?" Brindle asked.

"I don't know," Janzek said. "I'm just not sure how worthwhile it's gonna be."

"What do you mean?"

"Well, if she did it, she probably woulda taken a ride over the Ravenel Bridge by now and tossed the gun. Still... worth checking."

Brindle nodded. "Okay, so give me the reason she didn't do it."

Janzek picked up his beer mug. "'Cause when she paid D-Wayne the surprise visit, the mystery woman was there. Least Jessie said she was anyway."

Brindle nodded. "Gotcha," he said. "So, you're saying that if she killed him, she'd have had to kill her, too."

"Yeah, exactly," Janzek said. "Not like she's gonna leave an eyewitness behind."

Janzek's cell phone rang. He pulled it out and looked at the number.

"Hang on a second," he said to Brindle and Rhett. "Hello."

He listened for a few moments, said thanks, and hung up.

"That was Donny Fulton on the stake-out at 69 Bull. A couple of well-dressed men in their late fifties just went in," Janzek said, turning to Rhett. "You and I should go check these guys out, Del."

"Always happens," Rhett said, sliding out of the booth. "Just when I was starting to get comfortable."

"Make you a deal," Brindle said, "I'll be buyin' again when you got all this shit wrapped up. We'll turn off our cell phones, line up the drinks, and hunker down."

"Deal." Janzek said, standing up. "And you won't be getting off so lightly then. I'll be hittin' you up for a lot more than a beer and a half."

NINETEEN

The man at the door of the four-story brick building on Bull St. looked like he'd rather let in serial killers than Janzek and Rhett. The man's attitude seemed to be quite different from that of the man who had let them in last time they were there. The first man wasn't exactly welcoming, but he didn't make them feel like they were Hannibal Lecter and Buffalo Bill trying to bust in. Which led them to the obvious conclusion that the word had come down to keep the cops out, or at least slow them down a little.

Janzek had been doing everything he could to find out who was behind Charleston Philanthropies LLC but was having a tough time. He thought the key might be to find out who owned the house at 69 Bull. In the past, finding out the owner of a property had been simple. He just went to the official Charleston County site, which listed the owners of every property in the county and their mailing addresses. Once he got that he could go to the address and track down the owner. The stumbling block was the address for Charleston Philanthropies was a PO box. Specifically, PO Box 311, Summerville, S.C.

Janzek had dispatched a uniform to go to Summerville and see if the post office there would release the name of the person who rented the box, but the uniform had come back empty-handed. The woman at the post office said that he needed to get a judge's order for her to reveal the identity of the owner. So, that had to be his next step.

Technically, they also needed a warrant to go into 69 Bull Street, but they were trying to finesse it, hoping the guy at the door wouldn't know any better.

"We just need to ask one of the students here a few questions," Janzek said to the man at the door. "Her name is Leah Reynolds."

"She moved," the man said.

Smart move, Janzek thought. "Where to?"

"A dorm somewhere," the man said, keeping the info to a minimum. "I don't know the address."

"We still need to go inside," Janzek said.

"Can't it wait 'til tomorrow morning?" the man said.

"No, it can't," Janzek said, taking a step toward the door.

Reluctantly, the man opened it and let them in. "Make it quick, okay?"

Rhett turned to him. "You mean, having cops in your club is kind of a buzzkill?"

The man's silence answered the question.

In the elevator, Janzek pressed the button for the second floor and turned to Rhett.

"Do you remember the name of that girl who called the cops?"

"Yeah, Jolene," Rhett said. "Lived next door to Leah."

They got out on the second floor and walked into the big room where the bar was located.

Across the room, they saw the two older men who Officer Fulton had spotted going in. One of them looked pretty close to Leah's description of the man who had assaulted her. The two men were sitting at a table near the bar with four young women. One of them looked barely eighteen.

Janzek and Rhett walked over to the bar. "Hey, Billy," Janzek said, "we're back."

Billy scowled. "So, I see."

"How 'bout a couple of Coca Cola's?" Janzek said.

Billy got out two glasses, filled them and handed them to Janzek and Rhett.

"Thanks," Janzek said, pulling out his wallet, "what do I owe you?"

"For you, detective," the bartender said, "on the house."

"Thanks, that's very kind of you. Hey, would you mind taking a picture of me and my partner here. We never get to go to fancy places like this." Janzek asked handing Billy his iPhone.

"Sure," Billy said, aiming the iPhone, "get closer together... that's it... say cheese now."

"Cheese," Janzek and Rhett said together.

"Aww, that's cute," Billy said, snapping off a few shots.

Then he handed the iPhone back to Janzek.

"Thanks," Janzek said, turning to Rhett and ushering him into position. "Now let me get a few of you alone, Del, relaxing and enjoying your Coca Cola."

"Ah, okay," Rhett said, smiling uncertainly into the iPhone.

Janzek snapped off about ten shots then put the iPhone back in his pocket.

He took a long sip of his Coke, then set it down on the bar.

"Well," he said to Billy, "thanks for your hospitality, it's time for us to go back to work now. City doesn't pay us to sit around drinking Coca-Cola's in fancy places."

"You're welcome, Detective," Billy said, "always a pleasure seeing you."

Janzek chuckled. "Once more with genuine sincerity, Billy," he said. "I'm not sure I heard the love."

Billy smiled wanly.

They walked over to the elevator, got in, and pressed the button for the fourth floor. It was one of those slow elevators that go about two and a half miles an hour.

"What the hell was that all about," Rhett asked, "the pictures?"

Janzek already had his cell phone out. He scrolled down the pictures he had taken and stopped at one. In the foreground was the top of Rhett's blurry shoulder. In the background was the two men at the table, surrounded by the four girls.

The men's faces were in sharp focus.

"Wanted to see if either of these guys were the ones who attacked Leah Reynolds," Janzek said, pointing. "I thought it would be pretty traumatic for her to have to come here and ID the guy in person."

"Pretty slick move," Rhett said, with a smile.

"But first, we gotta find out where Leah's living. Show her these shots."

They got out of the elevator and went and knocked on the door next to Leah Reynold's old room.

The girl named Jolene came to the door and told them Leah had moved to a dorm room at 20 Warren Street. They asked for her cell phone number and Jolene gave it to them.

Then they called Leah, who had just gotten back to her dorm from a class and told her they'd be there in ten minutes.

On the elevator down, Janzek spotted something. It was a tiny surveillance camera mounted above the wood crown molding.

Janzek pointed to it. "Might have some interesting stuff on it."

Rhett took a step to get a closer look. "I saw a DVR in the security guy's office," Rhett said. "I'd assume the video from this thing gets stored on the DVR's hard drive."

"Wouldn't hurt to have a look."

"Yeah, definitely," Rhett said. "All we gotta do is get the guy to lend it to us."

"That might be easier said than done," Janzek said, pulling out his wallet to count how much he had. "How much you got on you, Del?"

"Mmm, maybe about eighty bucks."

The elevator door opened.

"I got a little over a hundred. Hundred and twenty-three, to be exact," Janzek said. "Think that guy would loan us his machine for two hundred bucks?"

"I don't know, Nick, you can be pretty persuasive."

TWENTY

The drove up to Warren Street with the DVR in the back seat.

"Think Ernie'll reimburse us?" Rhett asked.

"Yeah, I do," Janzek said. "That was money well spent."

They parked and went to the front door of 20 Warren. Leah buzzed them in, and they took the elevator up to her room. She was hanging pictures on her walls. They showed her the photos of the men in the bar on Bull Street, but she said they were definitely not the ones who had accosted her.

"How are you doing anyway?" Janzek asked, noticing she looked pale and sickly.

"I'm okay."

"You did the right thing, you know," he said, "moving from Bull Street."

She nodded and tried hard to smile.

"Well, you take it easy, okay," Janzek said, patting her on the shoulder.

This time she managed a smile.

They walked out of her dorm room and went back to the station.

*****

The DVR did, in fact, make for extremely interesting viewing.

They got Ernie Brindle to look at the entire tape with them. They figured that Brindle knew more of the movers and shakers in Charleston than they probably ever would.

"That's Jack Pinckney," Brindle said, pointing at a man picking his nose in the elevator. "He's a trust and estates lawyer to the blue bloods. Gets 'em off on DUI's, too."

The film kept rolling.

"Oh, yeah," Brindle said, pointing to the next photo. "None other than Eustis P. James, owner of TV stations, thoroughbred horses and fast sports cars. I pulled him over a coupla times for speeding back when I was a uniform. But a couple hundred bucks in fines wasn't gonna slow that guy down."

A balding man in a polka-dot bow tie was next. "I don't know who he is," Brindle said.

Then another two faces came into focus. "That's Thad Whaley, a big cardiac surgeon, and Stanton Conger. Conger owns half the damn city. Major-league prick, too."

Two other men walked into the elevator.

"Ho—ly shit," Brindle's eyes got as big as a soccer goalie on a penalty kick. "That's Lex Murray, guy I was telling you about. The dealer who bought it down in Hilton Head. No idea who that is next to him. Doesn't exactly look like a member of the country-club set, though."

"They don't look all *buddy-buddy* either," Janzek said, observing the body language. "What do you suppose Murray's doing there?"

"I have no clue," Brindle said. "But I need you boys to get on it and find out."

Janzek looked over at Rhett. "We been talkin' to the bartender there," he said. "He knows a lot more than he lets on."

"Good," Brindle said, "see what you can get out of him."

"We'll do that when we take back this machine," Janzek said.

Rhett smiled and patted the DVR. "Little sucker's worth its weight in gold."

*****

First thing Janzek did back at his office was to call a homicide cop named Dwayne Embrey in Hilton Head. Brindle's contact, the Hilton Head chief, had given him Embry's name as the point man for Lex Murray's murder. Janzek's first impression of Embry was that he was pretty territorial. As in, he didn't want any Charleston guys horning in on his action.

Janzek volunteered that they'd email Embry a photo of Lex Murray and the man with him in the elevator.

Embry thanked him, said he'd be in touch if he had anything, and hung up.

Then Janzek called Leah Reynolds at the dorm.

"Leah, it's Detective Janzek again. I'd like to come see you and show you some pictures of other men. See if any of them may have been the one who assaulted you."

Leah did not jump at the opportunity. "Ah, sure, but I'm pretty busy today."

"How about tonight?"

"Can you make it around eight?"

Sure, Janzek thought, he didn't have much of a life. Might as well be at the beck and call of a college kid and her study habits. "That's fine, see you then."

He planned to kill three birds with one stone: find out whether Leah could point the finger at one of the men in the photos, see if the doorman of the building on Bull Street could ID the man with Lex Murray, and ask Billy the bartender the same question while at the same time trying to find out what Lex Murray was doing there.

TWENTY-ONE

It turned out Samantha Byrd, the blonde hottie from *Charleston Buzz,* actually had a real job. Unlike just about everyone else on the show, except Greg the banker. She was a real estate agent at Palmetto Properties and Janzek guessed she was probably very good at it. He wondered how being a cast member affected her work. Pro and con, he concluded. 'Pro' because she probably got prospective buyers as customers who were curious about her and the show and wanted to rub shoulders with a star, albeit one who was a dozen rungs lower on the spectrum than Meryl Streep. But that could quickly turn into a con, he reasoned, them asking her a million questions about the show when all she really wanted to do was sell them a damn house. No doubt she needed the commission to buy groceries and pay the rent since the cable gig, he figured anyway, wasn't exactly making her rich. There were probably other pros and cons, too, but Janzek wasn't going to overthink it.

He was in her office on Broad Street, a large open room with eight desks including hers. Fortunately, only two other people were at their desks. They were pretending to be working but were, in fact, listening intently to the Q & A between Janzek and Samantha.

Janzek had broken the ice already, having commented on how nice the office was and how he had seen Palmetto Properties signs all over town. She said, yes, they had a lot of listings and the market was pretty hot right now, so that got the small talk out of the way.

She was tall and had blonde hair, with a striking, light-up-the-room smile. She looked very fit, like she might be a runner. In fact, Janzek thought maybe he had checked her out once running along the Ashley River on East Bay Street. He guessed she was around thirty, and she didn't display any ring of commitment on her long, slender fingers.

He had just asked her his standard question about who she thought might have had a motive to kill D-Wayne Marion. She looked a little taken back by the question and blinked a few times.

"I really have no idea," she said, finally, "I mean, it never occurred to me that it might be someone on the show."

"Probably wasn't," Janzek said, "but I have to ask."

"I understand," she said. "Have any of the other people on the show come up with any possible... I guess you call them, perps?"

"I've heard a theory or two."

"Who?" Samantha asked, lowering her voice, and leaning closer.

"Well, I really can't say," Janzek said. "It's—you know—confidential information. Just like anything you say to me will be confidential."

"Well, as you can see, I don't really have anything to say... on that subject anyway," Samantha said.

Janzek turned, looked over and caught the eye of a middle-aged woman a few desks away. She quickly looked back down at her computer.

Janzek lowered his voice. "How would you characterize the relationship between Jessie Lawson and D-Wayne Marion, Samantha?"

She didn't hesitate. "Rocky," she said. "Stormy comes to mind, too."

He liked direct women. "Did you hear any talk about the state of their marriage?"

"Like I said, somewhere between rocky and stormy." Samantha said. "See, I kinda think Jessie put heavy pressure on him to marry her. Well, God bless her, I guess. I mean, she got what she wanted, right? D-Wayne went fifty years without ever taking a stroll down the aisle. My sense is there probably were a lot of women over the years who would have said 'yes' to him."

"But your sense was he never popped the question until Jessie came along?"

A smile appeared on Samantha's face.

"I'm not so sure he was the one who *popped* the question."

"Meaning, she did?"

"Meaning she asked the question and answered it, too."

Janzek nodded and glanced back at the woman a few desks

away. He'd caught her red-handed again, clearly struggling to hear their lowered voices.

"You mind taking a little walk outside with me?"

She looked at her watch. "I have a showing in forty-five minutes."

"Won't take more than twenty."

"Yeah, sure." She got up and started walking toward the front door. He followed.

There was an Italian ice cart on the sidewalk just down from the Palmetto Properties office.

"Buy you one?" Janzek asked, pointing at the cart.

"Thanks," she said, shaking her head, then patting her hard belly. "Diet."

"Like you need to," he said, immediately regretting that he'd slipped into the personal.

"You're sweet," she said. "I'm glad we came out here. That woman, Doris... talk about no life. She's always eavesdropping on me."

Janzek stopped walking and turned to Samantha.

"So, Jessie and D-Wayne fought a lot?"

"Oh, yeah," Samantha said, "like cats and dogs. She got out of control sometimes, like she had no clue how to reign it in."

"Did she ever threaten him?" Janzek asked. "Maybe you overheard something?"

Samantha laughed. "Yeah, one time she said—" She paused, like she wasn't sure whether she dared say it or not.

"What?"

"That she was going to cut his balls off."

"I take it that was after—"

"Yes, one of his numerous indiscretions."

A green sports car drove past them, catching Janzek's eye. Not an Aston Martin, but it reminded him. "Speaking of which," he said, "did you ever see D-Wayne get dropped off by a blonde woman in a green Aston Martin?"

Samantha shrugged. "I wouldn't know an Aston Martin from a pick-up truck. That's a sports car, right?"

Janzek nodded. "A very expensive one."

"Sorry, can't say I ever did."

"Back to Jessie, did you ever hear her threaten to kill D-Wayne?"

Samantha almost did a double take. "No, never."

Janzek nodded at a young couple who walked past them.

"What about Saxby?"

Samantha rolled her eyes. "What about him?"

"Well, he and D-Wayne went at it a lot, right? Verbally, I mean."

Samantha pushed a strand of hair out of her eyes. "Yeah, but that was mainly for the show. Like the time D-Wayne and Saxby went outside of Sermet's—" a King Street restaurant "—to duke it out about something. Holly comes up with all that stuff."

"Holly the producer?"

Samantha nodded.

"Yeah, Holly the Hammer."

"And did they?" Janzek asked. "Duke it out."

"Nah, just trash-talked a little. Which they did a lot."

"How did Holly and D-Wayne get along?"

Samantha laughed. "Holly? She doesn't really like anybody," she suddenly looked down at her watch. "Sorry, but I gotta pull some listing sheets and get ready for my appointment." She looked up and smiled. "But I'd be more than happy to answer any more questions you have... say, up at Fuel maybe? Like seven-thirty or so? They got that nice area out back."

He didn't really have any more questions for her. But he wasn't about to tell her that. "Sure, seven-thirty it is?"

"Perfect," she said, "see you then."

She smiled and walked toward her office.

He had plenty of time to come up with more questions.

TWENTY-TWO

Janzek called Leah and asked if he could push back his appointment with her from eight to nine that night. She was okay with it. Then he swung by the police station on Lockwood and picked up Rhett. Next stop was Jessie Lawson's room at the Charleston Place Hotel.

Rhett opened the door of the Crown Vic and got in.

"Hey," Janzek said, "so how'd it go with Greg Burwell?"

Greg, the banker, was the last cast member of *Charleston Buzz* to be interviewed.

"I called it," Rhett said. "I walked into the bank and there he was—in a damn teller's cage."

"He shed any light on anything?" Janzek asked, pulling out onto Lockwood.

"Old news. Jessie and D-Wayne fought on-screen, off-screen, all the time, everywhere," Rhett said. "Oh, and he claimed Saxby is gay and had a thing for D-Wayne."

"The former we've heard and the latter I'm not sure I buy."

"I mean, who gives a shit anyway?" Rhett said. "The guy being gay or not."

Janzek nodded. "So that was all you got out of Greg?"

Rhett nodded. "Pretty slim pickings."

"Samantha Byrd told me about all their fights, too," Janzek said. "So, Jessie's still high on my list."

"Yeah, I'm comin' around a little," Rhett said, "But I'm still not hearin' one hundred percent from you. I mean, not like we're on the verge of reading her Miranda."

"I know, that's 'cause something in my gut's telling me there's someone else out there."

"Your gut's usually pretty good."

Janzek wobbled his right hand. "Yeah, well, better than fifty-

fifty, but not perfect. I just wish we could track down the woman in the car."

*****

They parked in front of the Charleston Place Hotel, went to the front desk, and had the clerk call Jessie Lawson and tell her they were there.

She said to send them up.

She answered the door wearing something quasi see-through and very tight. It was not an article of clothing usually seen on a woman who had been a widow for just a few days.

The hotel room turned out to be a penthouse with water views in three directions.

"Hello again, Detective," she said to Janzek.

"Hello, Ms. Lawson, appreciate you seeing us," Janzek said. "This is my partner, Delvin Rhett."

"Hey, Delvin," she said. "Come on in and make yourselves at home."

"Thank you," said Rhett.

"Mrs. Lawson," Janzek said, pulling the papers out of his breast pocket, "this is a warrant to search your room."

Her expression went from a smile to a squinty-eyed frown then back to a smile. She shrugged. "Hey, what the hell, go crazy. Mi casa es su casa," she said with a sweep of her arm.

Janzek knew that if she ever possessed the murder weapon it was now swimming with the fishes under the Ravenel bridge. Or in one of the many swamps in the area.

Nevertheless, he and Rhett spent the next fifteen minutes going through the large hotel room.

While they did, Jessie Lawson went over, stretched out on her king-sized bed, and watched old *Breaking Bad* shows. Her daughter Eugenie was in the adjoining room with her nursemaid, Yolanda.

Eugenia started wailing when she looked up and saw Janzek.

"You have that effect on women, I've noticed," Rhett said under his breath.

Janzek chuckled, got down on his hands and knees, and looked under a couch.

Fifteen minutes later they had come up with nothing.

After they were done, they walked back over to Jessie's bed. Janzek noted that it was probably about the same position where she would have stood in the Stoll's Alley house if she had shot her husband.

She gestured toward the TV. "This show was so much better than *Buzz*."

No kidding, thought Janzek, the difference between the Charleston RiverDogs and his Boston Red Sox.

"Would you mind turning it off? We have a few more questions."

She hit the clicker. "Sure. Ask away."

"About that carry permit we discussed before," he said. "You said you have a weapon?"

"No."

"No?"

"I have four."

"Really?" Rhett asked, like an excited kid. "Whatcha got?"

"Well, I have a Browning Hi-Power—"

"A P-35?" Rhett sounded envious.

"Uh-huh."

"Far as I'm concerned," Rhett dished, "that was John Browning's masterpiece."

"You might get an argument that it was the Browning Auto-Five shotgun," Jessie said, "but I happen to agree. I also have a Ruger Single Six convertible and a Smith & Wesson 29."

Rhett turned to Janzek. "In case you didn't know, Nick, a Smith 29 is a .44 Magnum. You know, Dirty Harry's piece."

Janzek nodded.

Dirty Harry was a God to Rhett. Janzek actually did know that about the .44 Magnum, even though guns weren't his thing. When he first started out up in Boston, an older cop had told him a Sig Sauer P220 could take out a guy at fifty yards and that was good enough for him.

"And what's your fourth one?" Rhett asked.

"Another Ruger," Jessie said. "A Super Blackhawk."

"Oh, man," Rhett said, turning to Janzek again, "guys shoot bears with those suckers."

91

"Really?" Janzek said.

"*Guys?* Hey, don't be sexist," Jessie said to Rhett, "I bagged a twelve-point buck with it."

"Cool," Rhett said. "So, where do you keep 'em all?"

"In a storage vault out on Seventeen."

Janzek's attention was focused now. "Ms. Lawson," Janzek said, eyeing her hard, "would you mind showing us your guns?"

She laughed. "Really?"

"Your hand guns," he clarified.

"No," she said, "I wouldn't mind at all. When do you want to go?"

"How about right now?"

She laughed again. "No time like the present, huh Nick?"

"That's what they say. Is your baby going to be all right if you leave her for a while?"

"That's sweet of you, Nick. To be so thoughtful. She's in good hands with Yolanda," Jessie said. "Back to guns... I don't get the idea you're that into them?"

"I can take 'em or leave 'em," Janzek said. "But in my line of work, you pretty much gotta take 'em."

"Well said," Jessie said. "But I wouldn't normally expect to hear that from a man who shoots people for a living."

"Well, that's not exactly *all* we do," Janzek said. "You see, people actually call us 'peace officers.' You know, as in 'to serve and protect.'"

"Uh-huh," Jessie said. "You ever kill anybody, Nick?"

Janzek smiled back at her. "Why don't we just follow you out to the storage place."

"Uh-huh," Jessie said, getting up. "I'll take that as a 'yes.'"

TWENTY-THREE

They followed Jessie Lawson in her silver Jag past all the car dealerships on Route 17, also known as Savannah Highway, until she pulled into the driveway at Smart Stop Storage.

They got out of their cars in the parking lot in back.

"That's the building," Jessie said, pointing.

They went inside the brightly lit building and walked past a few storage lockers. The place was new, immaculate, and overly air-conditioned. No more than sixty-five degrees, Janzek figured.

Jessie stopped at a locker and searched her key chain for the right key.

She tried one key. It didn't fit, so she tried another. The second one was the right one. She turned it and the big Master lock opened.

"Here we go," Jessie said, lifting the Master lock off the metal door and opening it.

She walked in and Janzek and Rhett followed.

"I keep them in holsters in the bottom drawer of that bureau," Jessie said, pointing to a mahogany bureau.

Janzek stood over one of her shoulders, Rhett over the other, while she opened the bottom drawer.

In it, Janzek could only see three pistols in dark leather Alessi holsters.

"That's strange," Jessie said.

"That there're only three, you mean?" Janzek asked.

"Yeah."

She bent down, lifted up one of the pistols and put it on top of the bureau. Then she did the same with the one beside it. Then, the third.

"I don't know where the other one could be."

She paused, then opened the drawer above it. It was empty. She did the same with the first and second drawers. They were empty, too.

She turned to Janzek and Rhett. "You might not believe me, but, I swear, last time I was here all four of 'em were here."

"So, Ms. Lawson, the Ruger Single Six is the one missing, right?" Rhett asked.

"Yeah, exactly. I don't know what could have happened to it."

Janzek studied her. "Anyone else have the key?"

She nodded. "That's just what I was thinking. D-Wayne had one. He kept a few of his things here."

"Like what?" Janzek asked.

Jessie pointed to a corner. "Like those polo mallets."

"That it?"

"That file cabinet over there is his; it's got a bunch of real estate stuff in it," Jessie said. "Probably a couple of little black books with his girlfriend's names in 'em, too."

D-Wayne's file cabinet definitely piqued Janzek's curiosity.

"Mind if I have a look," he asked Jessie, pointing to the black cabinet.

"Help yourself."

Janzek and Rhett gave it a very careful look. Unfortunately, it contained nothing but old tax returns and past real estate deals.

Not a little black book to be found anywhere.

TWENTY-FOUR

Janzek and Rhett had just gotten back in the Crown Vic and were following Jessie out of the storage company's parking lot.

"Just drive down to that gas station," Janzek said, pointing, "then pull in."

"Why, what—"

"I want to go back to that place and check something out," Janzek said.

"Okay," Rhett said, putting his blinker on and turning into a Hess gas station.

"What did you make of the missing gun?" Janzek asked.

"You mean the fact that a Ruger Single Six shoots a .22 cartridge, just like the bullet that killed D-Wayne?"

Janzek was nodding. "That's exactly what I mean. We gotta find that thing."

"What do you want to check out back there?" Rhett asked, doing a U-turn in the Hess station.

"There were a bunch of security cameras. Maybe one of 'em caught her walking out of there with the missing gun."

Rhett pulled out of the Hess station, put his foot on the accelerator, and got back onto Route 17.

"Good thinking," Rhett said. "Or maybe D-Wayne?"

Janzek nodded. "Could be."

Rhett drove back into Smart Stop. He parked, and they went into the manager's office. They identified themselves as Charleston detectives.

The manager, whose job seemed to be to sit in an office for nine straight hours as people trickled in and out, seemed excited to have a project. He told them that the facility had twelve different security cameras. They told him all they cared about was the one that monitored the door that went to the storage units in Building E.

95

He motioned to them and they followed him over to a desk that had a black rectangular box, next to a computer. He sat down in a chair in front of the machines.

"Grab those two chairs over there, fellas'," the man said, "and we'll see what we got."

Janzek and Rhett pulled two chairs over and sat on either side of him.

"By the way, name's Al," the man said.

"Detective Janzek and my partner, Detective Rhett."

Al nodded. "So, this little beauty is called a H.264 compression DVR. Baby's state-of-the-art, stores as much as an MPEG or a MPEG5 put together—"

To Janzek, who was tech-challenged, Al could have been speaking Kurdish. He was relying on Rhett to know what the man was talking about.

"What's the hard drive," Rhett asked, "like, one terabyte?"

Al turned to Rhett. "Very good, all the storage you're ever gonna need."

Al was a talker, Janzek could see, who rarely had an audience.

But Al handled his machine like a pro. Within ten minutes, they had what they were looking for: Jessie Lawson arriving at the storage unit at eight p.m. on July 14th and walking out of the door exactly three minutes and eight seconds later. Janzek pointed out to Rhett that the time was approximately five hours before D-Wayne Marion had been shot and it coincided with when Jessie drove up from New Orleans and would have driven right past the storage facility.

The tape showed Jessie carrying some sort of canvas bag in her right hand. They tightened up the focus on the bag but were unable to tell what was in it or what the shape of the object might be.

They thanked Al, who was clearly sad to see them go, and headed back downtown to have one more conversation with Jessie Lawson.

TWENTY-FIVE

This time, Jessie was less accommodating than she had been earlier. "You know," she said, opening the door to her hotel room, "this is starting to get old. You guys are barking up the wrong tree."

"We'll make this brief, Ms. Lawson," Janzek said. "We don't even need to come in. One of the cameras at your storage facility shows you five hours before your husband was killed, removing something from your unit."

She didn't even hesitate. "Yeah, I know," she said, with a scowl. "It was a book of stamps."

Janzek put an arm up on the frame of the door. "Stamps?"

"Stamps," Jessie said. "My father was a collector and had a book of valuable aviation stamps. I had no use for them. I was going to take it to a guy on King Street. You know, a dealer."

"What's his name?"

"I don't remember his name," she said. "But the shop's name was The Philatelic."

Rhett had his iPhone out and was swiping. He showed Janzek his screen: The Philatelic. 510 King St. 2nd floor and a phone number.

Bummer, thought Janzek, who had hoped she might be making it up on the spot. "So, you're saying you had a book of stamps in that bag?"

"Yes, that's exactly what I'm saying," Jessie said. "Sorry to burst your balloon. You can call up the guy. I remember his name now, it's Phil."

"Of course," Janzek said, "what else would it be?"

"And just for the record," Jessie said. "Phil first offered me six thousand dollars for the book. We made a deal at seven and a half thousand. All I can tell you is D-Wayne must have taken that gun."

Janzek glanced over at Rhett. Rhett's face was taut and tense. Janzek had seen the look a lot lately. It was the look of frustration.

Janzek glanced back at Jessie. "Well, Ms. Lawson, thanks for your time... again."

"You're very welcome, Nick," she said. "Now maybe you two will go after someone else for a change. I like our little get-togethers, but two in one day's a little much. Why don't you go rattle Saxby's cage? Or Rip's? Give me a day off."

*****

They had gone back to Leah Reynold's dorm on Warren Street. She was looking through the photos one by one. Janzek got the sense that she was hoping not to find her assailant. Like maybe she had thought through the ramifications of the whole thing and decided it was better not to identify him even if she spotted him in the photos.

She looked through the first few quickly, then hesitated at one of a man with wavy, silvery hair and pencil-thin lips.

"Is that him?" Janzek asked.

"I-I'm not sure," she said, and her hand started to shake.

It was a clear, head-on photo, almost as though the man was looking straight into the elevator camera.

She looked away from the photo and blinked a few times.

"Take another look, will you, please?" Janzek said.

Her eyes flicked down at the photo again, then, just as quickly looked away.

"That's him, isn't it?"

She didn't answer, but the shaking had moved up into her arms and shoulders.

Janzek glanced at Rhett, who nodded imperceptibly. "Ms. Reynolds, if this is the man, he did a terrible thing to you," Janzek said. "I don't need to tell you that."

"He deserves to be brought to justice," Rhett chimed in.

"What he did to you he could do again." Janzek said, "To another woman."

"Please, Ms. Reynolds," Rhett said softly. "We need to make sure that it never happens again."

Then they stopped talking. They didn't want to beat it to death.

After a few moments, she looked up at Rhett, then at Janzek.

"Okay," she said, finally, "that's him."

TWENTY-SIX

They went back to the station and showed the photo again to Ernie Brindle. Brindle said, as he had the first time he saw the photo, that the man's name was Stanton Conger, and that he was a rich, powerful, and—based on everything Brindle knew and had heard—arrogant real-estate developer. Brindle told them that he thought Conger had an office in a building on State Street and they better expect, if they arrested him, that he'd be out on bond five minutes later. As they were talking, Rhett Googled Conger and found out the exact address of his office.

Fifteen minutes later, they pulled up outside Conger's office building, a three-story converted brick house from the 1850s. The receptionist inside eyed them skeptically as they flashed ID.

"So, gentlemen," she said, "how can I help you?"

"I'm Detective Janzek, this is Detective Rhett. We'd like to see Mr. Conger."

"Is he expecting you?"

"No," Janzek said.

The receptionist's face turned stony. She stood and walked toward the back. Apparently, she had decided that two detectives showing up out of the blue was news that needed to be delivered to her boss face to face.

Janzek looked around the reception room. There were pictures of buildings and historic houses on all four walls. Then his eyes shifted to Rhett.

"So, this guy, Conger," Rhett said under his breath, "The local Trump, I guess."

"I guess," Janzek said as the receptionist walked back into the room.

"Mr. Conger's very busy at the moment," she said. "But he can see you in about twenty minutes."

"Ms.—" Rhett looked down at her name plate on the reception desk "—Ms. Blake, we're busy, too, so—"

Janzek held up his hand to Rhett. "That's all right, Del, we can make a few calls, catch up on our magazines."

He smiled at the receptionist. She didn't smile back.

They sat down on a couch facing a table with a brass lamp and some magazines on top of it.

"Asshole," Rhett said under his breath. "Dirtbag's sending us a message."

"Chill," Janzek said. "Beats being outside in the hot sun."

He picked up a Conde Nast Traveler and opened it up to the table of contents. One article was entitled, *Charleston, the Southern Gem.*

"Christ, if I have to see another article about how Charleston is the greatest city in the whole goddamn universe," Janzek said, then, "I mean, it's not all *that* great."

"Yeah, no shit," Rhett said. "Damn horse and buggies everywhere, shittin' up the streets and clogging traffic."

"Tourists all over the place. All the rubber-neckers dumped off the cruise ships," Janzek added.

"No place to fucking park," Rhett piled on.

"Restaurants with eighty-nine-dollar steaks," Janzek groused.

"I wouldn't know," Rhett said. "I'm a Steak n' Shake guy myself. The Cajun steakburger, six dollars and ninety-nine cents."

Janzek shook his head. "How can that possibly be a good combo? A steak and a milk shake. I mean, Christ?"

"You're gonna just have to trust me on this, Nick."

Janzek was not sold. "I don't know," he said, picking up a month-old Sports Illustrated. "I just read something else. How Charleston's the best place in the Southeast for dogs."

Rhett laughed. "How do they come up with shit like that?"

"No clue. I didn't know you could interview dogs," Janzek said. "Still, I gotta say, I do like the place."

Rhett nodded. "Yeah, it's a pretty good town."

*****

Janzek was on his third magazine when Stanton Conger finally came out a half-hour later.

"I am so sorry, guys," he said. "Got tied up on a long call with the Governor."

Already Janzek didn't like him. A name-dropper.

He and Rhett stood up. "That's all right," Janzek said, not initiating a handshake.

"Anyway, come on back," Conger said, turning.

They followed him back to a large wood-paneled office.

It was about what Janzek expected. Pictures of Conger dressed up in expensive, hunting gear, his rifle pointed at some bird not long for this world. Another one of Conger in a dinner jacket, champagne glass in hand, talking to Senator Lindsey Graham like they were old buds from high school. Another one of him talking to the other South Carolina senator, Tim Scott, with his hand on Scott's shoulder, looking as though he was imparting great wisdom. A fourth of him hitting a ball with a croquet mallet on a putting-green-like surface that looked as well-tended as center court at Wimbledon. Conger saw him looking at it. "That one's up in Cashiers. At the Chattooga Club."

Janzek nodded, remembering that's where Sheila Lessing had a place.

He and Rhett did not sit in the two chairs Conger gestured to, but instead stayed on their feet.

"So, what's up, guys?" Conger asked.

Janzek didn't beat around the bush. "Mr. Conger, we're here to arrest you for the sexual assault of Leah Reynolds that occurred on the night of July 15th at Ms. Reynold's room at 69 Bull Street. My partner's going to read you your rights."

Conger reacted like he thought it was some lame practical joke his buddies had put them up to. "You gotta be fucking kidding me?"

Rhett did a quick Miranda read and Conger's eyes shifted back and forth between Janzek and Rhett.

"What the hell is this?" Conger said, eyeing Rhett contemptuously.

"We have a sworn statement from the victim," Rhett said, "And film of you entering the elevator at the building on Bull Street on the date in question."

Conger stood up. "I don't give a fuck what you got, sonny boy. Whatever it is, it won't hold up in court."

"Take it easy," Janzek said. "We're giving you the option of

101

getting in your car and coming down to our station or us handcuffing you right now and perp-walking you out to our car."

"Yeah, it's your call," Rhett said.

Conger turned on Rhett, rage in his sullen eyes.

"That so, Sambo?" Then he swung around to Janzek. "How 'bout tellin' your boy here to shut the fuck up."

Janzek stepped in close to Conger and kept his voice low and under control.

"I suggest you go—right this second—get in your car and go straight to 180 Lockwood Boulevard. Or else Sambo here is gonna slap a pair of handcuffs on you so tight they're gonna cut off your circulation." Janzek leaned in another couple of inches closer to Conger's face. "Did you hear me... *sonny boy*?"

TWENTY-SEVEN

"Guy did everything but call me an 'uppity nigger'," Rhett said as they followed Stanton Conger to 180 Lockwood Boulevard.

"There's still time," Janzek said.

Rhett chuckled as he watched Conger up ahead of them. "Christ, can the guy drive any slower?"

"Doesn't want to get pulled over for speeding," Janzek said.

An hour later they'd booked Conger. And just as Ernie Brindle predicted, Conger's lawyer bonded him out right away. He was back in his office on State Street in record time.

*****

There was nothing Janzek could do about it, so he went into Brindle's office with the photos of Lex Murray and the other man in the elevator. Brindle said the other man, with a cleft chin and beady eyes looked familiar but he couldn't place him. Janzek decided to get on his computer and spend some time looking at mug shots, but when he did, he wasn't able to find anything on the man.

He decided to call Dwayne Embry, the homicide detective in charge of the Lex Murray murder down in Hilton Head to see if the homeless man who'd been at the scene of the crime could make the man in the photo from the Bull Street elevator.

"Hey, Dwayne, it's Nick Janzek, up at CPD. Having any luck on the Murray case? Anything from the homeless guy?"

"Weirdest thing happened," Embry said.

"What?"

"The guy disappeared. Went AWOL on us."

"Oh, shit. You're kidding?"

"Sorry, man," said Embry. "So far we got nada. I'm thinkin' the perp may have followed Murray down from Charleston, so I'm checkin' security cameras along the way. See if one mighta picked up a license plate."

Talk about needles in a haystack. Janzek was wondering how the homeless guy could have just wandered off the reservation. He couldn't be *that* hard to find, but it wasn't like he could tell Embry how to do his job.

"Well, good luck," Janzek said, "Let me know if you find him. I'm gonna send you photos of this guy with Murray in the elevator. They were seen together not long before Murray was killed."

"Thanks," Embrey said. "You'll be the first to know if I get something."

Right after Janzek hung up with Embrey, he got a call on his cell phone.

"Hello."

"Nick, it's Floyd Tyler in the prosecutor's office. Got bad news for you. That assault charge on Stanton Conger was dropped."

"You're kidding? Why?"

"'Cause the girl who accused him changed her tune, said it was consensual."

"Consensual my ass," Janzek said, "That's not what she told us."

"I don't know what to tell you, but that's her story now."

Janzek rapped his knuckles hard on his desk. "Shit," he said. "*Now...* meaning after a goddamn pay-off."

"Sorry. Just felt I oughta let you know."

"Thanks, Floyd, I appreciate it."

Rhett walked in as he hung up.

"Goddamn it," Janzek said. "Leah Reynolds just dropped the charge against Conger."

Rhett shook his head. "Who's surprised? Guy probably stroked a check for Leah Reynold's sophomore year tuition."

Janzek's cell phone rang again.

"Hello."

"Janzek?"

Speak of the devil. It was Stanton Conger.

"Yes," he said.

"I checked you out and found out you just moved down here a little while back," Conger sounded friendly, as if he was shooting the breeze with the governor or a buddy out on the golf course. "So, you made a rookie mistake, got a little overzealous, but I forgive you for it." Then his voice took on a whole new tone. "But if you ever let it happen again, you're gonna have a major fuckin' problem. Understand where I'm comin' from, Nick?"

Janzek counted to ten slowly.

"Yes, sir, Mr. Conger, I totally get where you're coming from, and can assure you, the last thing I want is to have any kind of problem with a man like you."

There was silence on the other end. Like Conger was thrown off his game.

"Just out of curiosity," Janzek asked matter-of-factly, "how much does it cost?"

"How much does what cost?"

"A year's worth of tuition for a girl at the College of Charleston."

Janzek clicked off. Rhett raised his fist and bumped Janzek's.

TWENTY-EIGHT

There were certain words and phrases Janzek never used. "Push back" was one of them. What was wrong with a good, old-fashioned word like "opposition" or "resistance?" Who needed to invent a whole new phrase?

"Optics" was another one of those words. It just sounded so bogus.

But "iconic" was the all-time worst. It was so overused. Was everything in the world iconic?

"Awesome." Now there was a word that had never passed his lips, and never would. To hear people talk, everything and everyone was awesome.

Then, there was the word "hot." It sounded sexist and demeaning somehow. Well, too bad because he did use that one, and Samantha Byrd was indeed "hot." 'Smokin' hot,' was a phrase Delvin Rhett used on more than one occasion.

Samantha wore a simple black cocktail dress with spaghetti straps, not going out of her way to be a sex bomb or anything. Light on the make-up, but long and lean and natural and... elegant. Yes, that was exactly the word for her. *Elegant.*

Of all things, they were playing bocce. Out in the back of Fuel, which was a former Shell station at the corner of Cannon and Rutledge that had been converted into a restaurant/bar that primarily served a college crowd. It was no-frills and basic but had great food and creative drinks. Janzek felt totally relaxed there as opposed to a few overpriced Charleston restaurants that seemed to be trying too hard to be cutting-edge (which was another term he wasn't in love with).

There wasn't much to the game of bocce. Roll one ball—called the jack—down the packed dirt court, then try to roll your other two balls close to it. The closest won. Maybe there were a few subtleties that old Italian guys knew about, which he didn't. In any case, you didn't need to concentrate too hard at it and could carry on a normal conversation as you played.

They were doing the standard backstory stuff. Janzek had told her about moving down from Boston after things went bad up there. Then, of course, she asked him, *what do you mean, what kind of things?* He didn't want to go there, but he did. He told her about his wife being killed by gunshots meant for him. Samantha patted his hand and said she was sorry, then she cocked her head and asked him if he was "still in mourning?" He looked at her funny and said, "No, why? Where'd that come from?"

She shrugged, "I don't know, just a vibe I picked up on." He smiled and patted her hand but didn't deny it.

Then he changed the subject and asked her where she grew up and went to school and how she got on *Charleston Buzz*. She said she came from a little town in South Carolina. He hadn't heard of it, but then he hadn't heard of much other than Charleston, Columbia, and Myrtle Beach, though he still had no clue whether Myrtle Beach was north, south, east, or west. Then Samantha said how she'd gone to the College of Charleston and liked Charleston so much that she decided to stay there. That seemed to be a common story because he had run across more than a few College of Charleston graduates who—among other things—were tending bar and pedaling pedicabs. The refrain he kept hearing from the twenty-somethings was that Charleston was a great place to live but there weren't a lot of good jobs around. And the pay for those jobs was, by all accounts, pretty anemic.

"So, what happened was, I was at Oak one night after showing some people a bunch of houses—" Samantha was describing how she was asked to join *Charleston Buzz* "—and was having a drink with my friend, Jill, and this guy next to me is like glued to our conversation."

"Like that woman in your office?" Janzek said.

"Worse, like leaning in so his ear was practically resting on my shoulder," Samantha said. "Anyway, finally, he said something like, 'Hi, I'm Hudson, how would you like to be on my TV show?' Just like that. So, Jill says to this guy, 'Sure, what do we have to do?' And he looks at her like she's a maggot or something and says, 'Not you... her', and points to me."

Janzek shook his head. "I've had the pleasure of meeting Hudson. He's a real sweetheart."

Samantha laughed. "Well, so then, you know he's basically Holly's lapdog."

"Who's going around calling it 'his' show," Janzek said, rolling his red bocce ball toward the jack.

"Yeah, exactly," Samantha said. "So anyway, I finally said to him, 'No thanks,' and turned away. But he keeps going on with his, 'I could make you a star' BS, and finally I said to him something like, 'What aren't you getting? I'm not interested.' Well, actually, I kinda was, but I felt bad for my friend."

"So, he finally talked you into it?"

"Well, actually, what happened was, we left Oak, and the next day I get this call from him. I guess he found out from the bartender where I worked or something." Samantha said. "Anyway, he's all apologetic about the way he reacted to Jill and wanted to buy me a drink to talk about it. I played hard to get for about three minutes, then finally agreed to meet him and... the rest is history. Jennifer Lawrence, look out, girlfriend!"

Janzek laughed as Samantha rolled her ball up to within a few inches of the jack.

"Nice one," he said. "You some kind of Bocce hustler?"

"Yeah. Wanna play for money?"

"Sure. A nickel a game."

"You're on," Samantha said. "So, you have any more questions for me about D-Wayne?"

"No," he said, "I think we pretty much covered it."

Two young guys came up to Samantha.

"Wow," one said, "you're even more of a smoke show in real life."

Janzek figured that was a compliment though he'd never heard the expression before.

"Uh, thank you," Samantha said.

The other one had his cell phone out. "Can we do a selfie?"

"Sure," said Samantha as the two squeezed in on either side of her and the one snapped off several shots.

"How bout, we buy you a drink?" one of them asked.

"Um, thanks, but in case you hadn't noticed, I've got a date," Samantha said glancing at Janzek.

Their eyes shifted to Janzek. "That guy," one said. "He's way too old for you."

Janzek laughed, but when he got home that night, he spent fifteen minutes pulling out the strands of grey in his hair that had popped up in the last month.

TWENTY-NINE

Janzek had gotten to the office early and was talking to Rhett, who had a photo of the Ruger Single Six, the gun that was missing from Jessie Lawson's storage unit. Janzek had made a discovery when he'd gone through rap sheets of the mutts and miscreants of Charleston County a little earlier. He'd come across a picture of the man in the elevator with Lex Murray. His name was Jim Ray Glover, and he had a few misdemeanor priors, but nothing to indicate he was a cold-blooded killer.

Janzek looked up Glover's number and dialed it, but it just rang and rang. The landline was registered to an address just over the bridge in West Ashley. He was pondering whether it was worth a trip to try to find a guy who was only guilty of being on the same elevator as Lex Murray, when his cell phone rang.

He took it out and recognized it as Sheila Lessing's cell phone number.

He looked up at Rhett. "Hang on a second," he said, then. "Hi, how's everything up in the Blue Ridge mountains?"

"I wouldn't know," Sheila said, "I'm in Columbia."

"What for?"

"Driving through Columbia, that is," Sheila said, "Driving through Columbia at high speed, in fact. Headed to Charleston to see you."

Sheila had told him she planned to be up in her mountain place in Cashiers, North Carolina for the whole summer.

"Well, that's a nice surprise," Janzek said, "but I thought—"

"I'm coming there to spank you, Nick."

"Sounds like fun, but what did I do?"

"In case you haven't noticed," Sheila said, "I have a vast network of spies and one of them told me you were spotted last night with a tall, willowy blonde playing—of all low-life things—*bocce*."

Janzek was blown away. It was only twelve hours ago and at a spot that was pretty far off the beaten path.

"I'm impressed," he said. "But as your spies may or may not have told you, the woman I was with—Samantha Byrd—was on that TV show D-Wayne Marion was on. And, as I know you know, I am the lead homicide detective on D-Wayne's murder. *And*, this won't be news to you either, one of the things I do is go around and badger people with questions."

"Yes, I know all that. But really Nick... *bocce*?"

"Okay, so I don't play polo."

Sheila laughed. "I'm just giving you a hard time. Sort of. Anyway, I just made a reservation for dinner tonight at the Ordinary."

"I can't even afford the crumbs there."

"It's my treat."

Janzek sighed as he glanced up at Rhett. "No, you don't, I'd feel like a gigolo."

"Don't be ridiculous, you can pay for the parking." Sheila said. He could hear an NPR interview on her car radio in the background. "Or maybe you already have plans tonight. With your newfound friend, the tall, willowy blond?"

"You know, I have no clue what willowy even means," Janzek said. "But if I did have plans, I'd cancel them."

"That's the right answer."

"I've gotta go," he said, "I'm in my office with my partner, who's pretending not to be listening—" he looked down at the picture of the Single Six "—checking out a photo of a pistol like one owned by D-Wayne's widow."

"That floozie, Jessie, you mean?"

"Yep."

A pause. "You know something, Nick, you're hanging around too many young women," Sheila said. "So, pick me up at 7:30, will you? I'll be the tall, willowy brunette."

THIRTY

Sheila Lessing sure didn't look fifty.

Janzek had no idea what she did to her face to look so young, but he had studied it pretty closely and knew she hadn't had a face-lift, or any collagen implants. Those things were usually pretty easy to spot, even really good, expensive ones. Most women who had had them, he'd observed, had facial expressions like someone had just snuck up behind them and goosed them. As far as Sheila's body went, he knew she did grueling sessions with a personal trainer at the MUSC gym every day, including Sundays, because she was always grousing about how sore she was from her workouts. In addition to that, she played squash three times a week with the pro up at the Charleston Squash Club on upper King Street.

She was wearing a sleeveless white silk top and there was no trace of jiggly-upper-arm-syndrome, somewhat common in women her age.

They were seated at a table off in a corner and drinks had just arrived.

Janzek had intentionally jumped the conversational gun and asked her what she knew about Stanton Conger before she got a chance to start grilling him about Samantha Byrd. Sheila knew everyone in Charleston, and he felt sure she'd have at least a few paragraphs on the subject of Stanton Conger. And sure enough…

"Here's the thing about him," she said. "He prides himself on being a Southern gentleman blue blood, but underneath he's nothing but a vile snake."

"Wow, that's pretty harsh."

"Yeah, well, I've dealt with him in business, so I know," Sheila said. "He tried to screw me once on a real-estate deal."

"I have a feeling he was unsuccessful," Janzek said, smiling.

"Damn right," Sheila said. "I got the bastard... doubt he'll ever fuck with me again."

Janzek put his hand on his mouth and went into mock-shock mode. "Why, Sheila, you just said the F word."

She laughed. "Yeah, well, when you're talking about Stanton Conger, you can't say it enough. Why you asking about him anyway?"

"He and I had a little disagreement," Janzek said. "So far he's got the upper hand. Let me ask you a question about him."

Sheila leaned back in her chair. "I'm not like the guy's biographer or something, you know."

"I know," Janzek said. "But I have a feeling you'll have an answer to this. There's a house on Bull Street with a big putting green in front of it?"

Sheila laughed and shook her head at the same time. "Say no more: The Boy's Club."

"It's actually got a name?"

"Well, nickname. And Conger is one of the guys who started it."

"He also owns the building," Janzek said. "I know because I tracked him down through an LLC he set up. It was definitely something he was trying to hide."

It had taken a while but the uniform cop Janzek put on it was a real bulldog. He eventually found out that the PO Box in Summerville for Charleston Philanthropies LLC was in Conger's accountant's name.

"Here's something else," Sheila said. "Allegedly, and I use the word very liberally, it's a sorority established to do good deeds in the community. The girls who live there are all on full or partial scholarships. I've never been there but—again allegedly—the bar there donates all of what it makes to the homeless of Charleston."

"What a sham."

"I know, and here's another fun fact," Sheila said. "His latest wife—number four, I believe—he met her there. She was a student at the college. He was around fifty, she was... max, maybe twenty when they got married."

"What's with Charleston?" Janzek asked. "Does anybody in this town go out with anyone their own age? I mean, D-Wayne and his wife, Conger and his..."

He noticed Sheila's wry smile. Then it hit him. She was ten years older than him.

"I'm not including cougars in this," Janzek said, doing his best to recover.

"A cougar, is that what you think I am?"

"It's a term of endearment."

"Yeah, right. Whenever I've heard it used, it's been a term of derision."

"Don't listen to any of that noise," Janzek said, struggling to change the subject. "So back to Conger. What's his child bride's name?"

"I have no clue. I've seen her around but, I'm happy to say, we don't travel in the same circles. I'm guessing she's around thirty now and Conger's probably ready to trade her in for a younger model." Sheila took a sip of wine. "Why is it, Nick, that I always get the feeling our dates are more like fact-finding missions for you?"

"Hey, now, that's so not true," he said. "So, tell me about life up in the Blue Ridge mountains?"

"It's great," Sheila said, "weather's about twenty degrees cooler than here, I do my sports non-stop, tend my garden, read a million books, but..."

"But?"

"You're not there. I get lonely rattling around in that big old house."

"Yeah, unfortunately, murderers don't take the summer off. Actually, there's nothing more I'd like to be doing than going up there. From the way you've described it, it reminds me of summer camp. Tennis, golf, fishing, swimming, hiking--"

"—and the second-best nightly diversion, a bunch of big 'ol cocktails."

"Wait, what's the best—" he started, but then it dawned on him.

"Jesus, Nick, your brain's really bogging down. Is that how you get when you hang out with the young and the vacuous?"

THIRTY-ONE

It was a little past noon when Janzek drove into the parking lot of Leah Reynolds dorm on Warren Street. Numbers and letters were stenciled into the blacktop to mark each parking spot, which he figured corresponded to each room number. Parked in between 5C and 5E was a shiny new BMW. He remembered that Leah's dorm room was 5D.

He went down the list of the buildings tenants and pressed the one that read, 5D-Leah Reynolds.

"Who is it?" Leah asked after a few moments, through the annunciator.

"Buzz me in, please, Leah, it's Detective Janzek."

"What do you want?" Leah asked, less than welcoming.

"Just buzz me in. We need to talk."

He waited a few moments, wondering if she was thinking about ignoring him altogether. But finally, she buzzed him in.

He took the elevator up to the fifth floor, walked down the corridor and knocked on her door.

She came to the door dressed in blue jeans and a short-sleeved shirt with the collar popped. She didn't look happy to see him.

"Hi, I hope you're feeling better."

"Thank you. A little, I guess," she said, her eyes darting around, nervously.

"That new BMW, helps ease the pain, huh?"

Leah frowned. "Why did you come here?" she asked, holding onto the door like she might slam it in his face at any moment.

"I need to talk to you for a second. Could you let me in? I feel like you going to slam that on me."

She broke eye contact and looked over his shoulder.

"Okay, but I have to get to class pretty soon."

"I'll make it short and sweet."

She opened the door and he followed her in.

"I don't need to sit down," he said, as she turned back to him. "I just wanted to tell you; you're playing a very dangerous game. Right now, Stanton Conger thinks he can do anything he wants. All he has to do is pay for it."

"I don't know what you're talking about," Leah said, raking the back of her neck, anxiously.

"Yeah, you do," Janzek said, pointing at the BMW keys in a bowl near the door. "You sent a message to the guy. You're for sale."

Leah put her hands on her hips. "I'm never going to see that man again. Why do you think I moved out of there?"

"'Big deal. He'll just 'see' another girl. And now he's thinking he can do anything he wants. It might be a little expensive but what the hell... he can afford it. Know what I'm saying?"

He looked at her trying to see if it was sinking in. He couldn't tell.

"So, like I said, you sent him a message that was loud and clear. Now here's my message to you: We're gonna close that place down and nail Stanton Conger, with or without your help. We'd prefer with it."

Her expression didn't change. He turned and took a few steps toward the door, then stopped and turned back.

"In case your college advisor didn't tell you, Leah, it's not supposed to be part of the college experience, sleeping with nasty, old men."

He turned and walked out.

As he got into the elevator, his cell phone rang.

He fished it out of his pocket. "Hello."

"Hey, Nick, it's Dwayne Embry, down in Hilton Head."

"Yeah, Dwayne, what's up?"

"We found the homeless guy. And he ID'ed that guy you sent me the picture of as Lex Murray's hitter."

"No shit," Janzek said, opening the elevator door. "And you trust the guy? I mean, he seemed credible?"

"Yeah, he did. I showed him five photos and he picked him out right away. Said he was definitely the guy. No question about it. I got it all on video."

"That's great," Janzek said, going out the front door of Warren Street. "And in the meantime, I got an ID on the guy. Name's Jim Ray Glover. Matter of fact, I was about to go pay him a visit. He lives at 15 Ludwell Street, which is just over the bridge in West Ashley."

"I know the area a little. How 'bout I head up there and we go together?"

Janzek hit the clicker for his car as he went past Leah Reynold's shiny new BMW. "Yeah, you ready to roll now?"

"I'm walking to my car. Takes me about an hour forty-five to get there."

"Tell you what. There's a BP gas station at the corner of Woods Road and Savannah Highway. I'll get my partner and meet you there."

"Sounds good," Embry said, clicking off.

Janzek had started to dial Rhett's number, when his phone rang. He didn't recognize the number.

"Hello?"

"Was it something I said?"

It was Samantha Byrd.

He didn't know she was expecting a follow-up.

"Hi, Samantha. Sorry, I've just been goin' a million miles an hour."

"That's no excuse. You do realize I'm a movie star... well, a TV star... well, a cable star... well, maybe not really even a star. Anyway, is there a second date in this relationship?"

What relationship was that, he wondered?

"The problem is I'm twenty-four-seven at the moment," Janzek said, scrambling.

"You know, Nick, I'm a big girl. You can tell me if you've got a girlfriend."

"Right now, the only girlfriend I got has the initials CPD."

"Okay," Samantha said after a few moments, "well, when CPD gives you a night off, give me a call."

THIRTY-TWO

Dwayne Embry, the Hilton Head homicide guy, and Rhett were in front of the house on Ludwell Street, Janzek around in the back. All three had their guns drawn. Rhett and Janzek were communicating via throat mikes.

"Okay, you guys ring the buzzer," Janzek said from the back. "I'll be here to greet him if he comes out this way."

"Copy that," Rhett said. "I'm hitting the buzzer now."

A minute went by.

"Nothing," Rhett said finally. "How 'bout back there?"

"Nope," Janzek said. "Pretty sure I saw an open window when I came around."

"Hold on a minute," Rhett said. "Don't want you going through any open window with a guy inside."

"My guess is the guy's history," Janzek said.

"How do you know?"

"Just a hunch," Janzek said. "I'm gonna check that window."

"He saw an open window," Janzek heard Rhett say to Embry. "He's gonna try to get inside."

Janzek pushed the six-over-six window up, ducked down, and slid his left leg over the sill. He stuck his head inside and just listened for a few moments.

He didn't hear anything except the tick of a clock. His eyes slowly adjusted to the dark, and he saw he was in a bedroom. It was pretty basic. A bed, a bureau, a lamp on a bedside table next to the clock he heard ticking. The only thing hanging on the four walls was a framed travel poster of Greece.

Embry was posted up front now, while Rhett had gone around to cover the back.

Janzek brought his right leg up, then over the sill and onto the floor inside. He stood up and started walking toward the bedroom door, holding his Sig Sauer straight out in front of him. In a minute, he had cased the entire one-story house. No one was there. It smelled of recent-vintage pizza, and the décor was empty cans of Budweiser and a full bottle of cheap vodka. He walked into the living room again and looked around. Then back into the kitchen. A piece of paper on a kitchen counter caught his attention. He picked it up, read it, then went to the front door.

"It's Janzek," he said, through the locked front door, then he opened it.

Embry lowered his gun. "Not here, huh?"

Janzek shook his head, turned, and walked the length of the house to the back door.

"I'm opening it up, Delvin," he said and opened the door.

Rhett lowered his gun. "Nada?"

"Yup," Janzek said, "but I found this receipt for some repair work on a boat."

He handed the receipt to Rhett.

"A Mako," Rhett said referring to the kind of boat. "This is from yesterday. Maybe he's out on it now."

"You know where this is?" Janzek asked Rhett, pointing to the address.

Rhett looked at it. "Yeah, it's on James Island. Matter of fact, my brother works at a bait shop there. Off the Summerville exit once you get onto the Connector."

Janzek turned to Embry. "What do you think, Dwayne, want to go look at boats?"

"Sure," Embry said, "beats hanging out in this dump."

THIRTY-THREE

When Janzek asked Embry if he wanted to go look at boats, he didn't have in mind burned-out, smoking boats.

They got to the James Island Marina ten minutes later just in time to see a grey-hulled Charleston Police Department boat towing a blackened twenty-six-foot cabin cruiser that had undergone serious fire damage.

"That's a Mako," Rhett said, pointing at the burned-out boat.

Janzek, Rhett, and Embry hurried down to the dock, where the police boat was towing the Mako.

The police boat nudged up to the dock and a uniform hopped out.

He was a guy Janzek knew named Ron Demaris.

"Hey, boys," Demaris said, tying a rope to the dock. "What are you doin' here?"

"Got a perp we're looking for," Janzek said. "Guy by the name of Jim Ray Glover."

The uniform turned toward the boat he was towing. "Just so happens he's in the back of that boat we're towing. With a big-ass bullet hole in his head."

*****

Janzek, Rhett, and Embry spent the better part of the next two hours in the back of Jim Ray Glover's Mako, speculating about what could have happened that resulted in his death. CPD had gotten a call from a boater saying he saw a boat on fire and had gone to try to put it out and rescue whomever was on board. The man and two friends with him had been successful in only one out of two of their objectives. Their fire extinguishers had been able to smother the fire.

There were seven men and one woman aboard the fire-scarred twenty-six-foot Mako now, including Janzek and Rhett. One of the men was the medical examiner Jack Martin, who gave Janzek his usual frosty greeting.

Janzek responded with his best plastic smile.

Ron Demaris and the other uniform had stuck around, not talking much but keeping the curious—of which there were many—away from the boat. Ruthie Mueller, the CSI who'd covered the D-Wayne Marion scene, arrived at the dock just after Janzek, Rhett and Embry.

The three of them had been tossing scenarios back and forth, then poking holes in them, and refining a few.

At the moment, the two that made most sense were: One, Jim Ray Glover and his killer had met in two different boats out in Charleston Harbor, or two, that Glover and his killer had both been in Glover's boat. Then, possibly to steal the millions that Glover had recovered from Lex Murray and which he might have been carrying aboard the Mako, the killer had shot Glover and, to cover it all up, started the fire. At which point, the killer had either taken off in his own boat, or—they theorized—dived over the side of Glover's boat and swum to shore. The latter, though, didn't make much sense, because it would mean the killer would be toting $12 million in cash.

Demaris had showed Janzek a piece of paper with the names and cell phone numbers of the men who had put out the fire on Glovers boat. Janzek then had called the rescuers and asked whether they had seen either a swimmer in the water or another boat leaving the vicinity of the burning Mako. The answer was no to both questions.

After he got off the phone with them, Janzek walked over to Jack Martin, who had a very unscientific-looking pocket-knife in hand and was poking it into the side of the boat in short jabs.

"You got a slug there?" Janzek asked.

Martin didn't look up or say anything. He just kept poking with the pocket-knife. Then finally, he reached down and pulled something out.

Janzek could see that it was indeed a slug.

He crouched down next to Martin to get a closer look.

Martin turned and eyed him like he was a trespasser "Can I help you?"

121

"Looks like a .22, huh?"

Martin squinted. "Oh, so now you're a ballistics expert, too?"

"Nah. Just been around a few slugs in my day."

The double entendre was unintentional, but if the shoe fit…

With that, Janzek got up and walked away. He went over to Rhett and Embry, who were talking near the bow of the boat.

"Mr. Personality found the slug," he said to Rhett. "Looked like a .22 to me."

Rhett started to nod, then turned to Embry. "Which, just so happens, is the same caliber that killed D-Wayne Marion."

"No shit," Embry said. "That guy on the TV show."

Janzek and Rhett both nodded.

"You think the two killings could be…" Embrey asked.

"Could be," Janzek said.

*****

A few minutes later, Rhett made a discovery in the cabin down below. It was an empty five-gallon gas can with its top off, shoved off to one corner of the cabin, and covered by a dirty black T-shirt.

The three detectives figured that whoever started the fire had doused as much of the boat as he could, then hid the can in the cabin and struck a match. Their theory was that the killer figured once the flames got to the gas tank of the boat the Mako would blow up and there'd be a blazing inferno within seconds. But because the three men on the other boat got there in time to put out the fire, that never happened.

Janzek, wearing plastic gloves, brought the gas can up to Ruthie Mueller and asked her to dust it for prints when she got it back to the lab at the station. She thanked him and said she would. She'd already lifted a lot of other prints from various parts of the boat.

A few minutes later, Dwayne Embry went up to Janzek. "You don't need me anymore," he said. "Think I'll hit the road back to Hilton Head where—I gotta tell ya—things are *way* slower than around here."

"What are you talking about," Janzek said. "You had yourself a murder."

"Yeah, first one in six years."

THIRTY-FOUR

Janzek and Rhett were back at the station when Janzek's cell phone rang. He looked down at the caller ID. It said Saxby Wentworth-Kuhn.

"Hey, Saxby," Janzek said, "what's up?"

"I been thinkin' about D-Wayne's murder and, being the civic-minded citizen I am, think I got something for you."

"Are you at your house? Because I'm headed in your direction in a half hour."

"I'm here. It's Moses's day off, so I'll leave the front door open. Just come on in and go to the library. You remember where that is, right?"

"Yeah, I do. See you in a little while."

*****

When Janzek got there, Saxby was sitting in the same chintz-covered chair he was in last time Janzek was there.

Penelope Kuhn had her same seat, too.

She gave Janzek a big smile. "I promise to be very quiet. I'm just going to be reading my book over here."

Janzek got the feeling she was very involved in her son's life. The proverbial helicopter-mother. Probably wanted to tag along with her thirty-six-year-old son on dates. But hopefully not to the stabbin' cabin.

"That's fine, Mrs. Kuhn," Janzek said to her.

"Penelope," she said.

"So, Saxby, what did you call about?"

"Well, no doubt you've come across my esteemed producer, Holly Barrow, in the course of your investigation."

"Yes, I have. We met a little while ago. Why?"

"Well, I'm sure she didn't volunteer this, and I don't know whether you've heard it before, but she had a thing with D-Wayne that didn't have a particularly happy ending."

Janzek pictured the horsey Holly Barrow and handsome-in-a-smarmy-kind-of-way D-Wayne and had difficulty putting them together as a romantic duo.

"Really? This is the first I've heard of it."

"Yeah, girl plays her cards pretty close to the vest, but D-Wayne told me once—" Saxby glanced over at his mother and lowered his voice "—that he had tossed her a mercy fuck once or twice."

"I heard that, Saxby," Penelope said, "and that's absolutely disgusting."

"Mom, just read your book and stay out of this, will you please."

"So how long did this 'affair' go on for?"

"As far as I know, it was infrequent. But the guy who works for her told me she carried the torch for a while."

"Hudson Rock told you that?"

"Yeah," Saxby said, shaking his head. "So, you've had the pleasure, huh?"

"Ah-huh. But I'm having a hard time seeing how this makes her a suspect."

"Okay, so the story's got a few more chapters. Juicy one's, too. So, what happens is, all of a sudden, rumor starts going around that D-Wayne wasn't going to come back for the third season."

"Really? Why was that? I thought he was the big draw."

Saxby's frown covered the whole lower half of his face. "That's highly debatable."

"People watch the show because of Saxby," Penelope said, putting her book down and her two cents in. "A woman came up to me at Whole Foods yesterday and said how much she loved him."

"Okay, Mom, I'm really serious, either read your book in peace or you're going to have to leave the room."

Penelope's eyebrow's shot up. "May I remind you whose house this is?"

Saxby sighed.

"So, are you saying D-Wayne maybe not coming back for a third season had something to do with Holly Barrow?" Janzek asked.

"Everything to do with Holly Barrow. The old spurned-lover revenge motive."

Janzek nodded and thought for a second. "Sounds like—"

"I know what you're gonna say, cutting off your nose to spite your face. If he was so vital to the show why would she cut him loose. Is that what you were thinking?"

"Yeah, something like that. Why would you get rid of one of the stars of the show?"

Saxby shrugged. "I don't really have an answer to that."

It still seemed like a leap across the Grand Canyon to Janzek: Holly Barrow killing D-Wayne.

"So, 'spurned lover'... that's the long and the short of it?"

"I told you this thing had a bunch of chapters," Saxby said, glancing over at his mother, then lowering his voice again. "So, one time when D-Wayne was drunk in this restaurant scene he blurted out something about how doing Holly was like doing a paraplegic—"

Penelope hopped to her feet. "That is the last straw, Saxby, I've heard just about enough."

"Jesus, Mom. I wasn't talking to you."

Penelope glanced over at Janzek. "Detective, I apologize for my son. I can assure you he was not brought up to talk like this."

Janzek didn't know how to respond. "It's okay, Mrs. Kuhn, he's just... trying to be helpful."

"I'm just glad his father isn't around to hear him talk like this. He'd be horrified," Penelope said and stormed out.

"Good riddance," Saxby muttered. "So anyway, I looked over at Holly right after D-Wayne said that—she was directing a scene at the time—and there was nothing but pure hatred in her eyes. If she had a gun, guarantee you, she would have pulled the trigger."

Janzek chewed on that for a few moments. "Did she say anything?"

"Nah, Holly's the 'controlled-burn' type. The scene just kept rolling. But—surprise, surprise—that segment ended up on what we call the cutting-room floor."

"I'm familiar with the expression."

"So, you ready for the last chapter?" Saxby asked, rubbing his hands together and grinning. "Talk about juicy."

"Sure. Bring it on."

"You gotta fasten your seat belt for this."

Janzek just waited.

"So, take a guess how Holly got her start in the film business."

Janzek shrugged. "No clue."

Saxby's voice took on a conspiratorial tone. "Know what a snuff film is?"

THIRTY-FIVE

It was true.

Janzek had gone back to his office and Googled Holly Barrow after Saxby told him the story.

An industry web site called IMDb showed Barrow's name, then Director/Producer, and after that listed seven credits to her name—all TV shows or movies she's been involved with. Most recently it showed *Charleston Buzz* (TV series) (executive producer and director-7 episodes) 2018-2019. After that, in descending chronological order, were other shows—only one of which he had ever heard of. But it was one from 2007 that caught his attention. It was a movie called, *Someone Really Gets Killed in this Movie.* A bit of an unwieldy title, for sure, but one that you couldn't ignore. He Googled the movie.

It popped up in Wikipedia. At the top was a graphic illustration of a headless woman. Above it, it read: 'The picture they said could never be shown.' And below the illustration, more hype: 'It could only be made in South America, where life is cheap.'

Janzek read on.

The movie, according to Wikipedia, was originally called *Carnage* and plotlessly followed the gruesome murders carried out by a band of Manson-style misfits in a remote region of Chile. The movie opened to horrendous reviews and grossed under $300,000. Three years later, the article went on, Killjoy Productions re-shot the ending after, "Executive Vice President, Holly Barrow," read an article about a movie called *Snuff,* where an actress allegedly was killed. Killjoy then shot a new, cinema-verité-style ending in which a woman was brutally murdered by members of the film crew. The new footage allegedly showed an actual murder and was spliced onto the end of *Carnage* with an abrupt cut suggesting that the footage was unplanned and the murder authentic. Then it was released for a second time.

Barrow had apparently learned considerably more about movie promotion since the time *Carnage* had first come out. Because the first thing she did, according to Wikipedia, was to hire fake protesters to picket movie theaters showing the film. She also was able to land a front-page article in *Variety* and a thirty-second teaser for it went viral on Facebook. But apparently people were more willing to tweet about it than shell out ten bucks to see it. Still it did about $800,000 in box-office revenue the second go around.

Janzek's first reaction was that somehow his hands had gotten really filthy just reading about the movie. His instinct was to go take a long shower and use lots of lye soap. His second reaction was how often the words "alleged" and "allegedly" were sprinkled in the various accounts of the "snuff".

He decided to have another conversation with Holly Barrow. Right after he met with Rhett and Brindle.

*****

They met in Brindle's office and Janzek got right to it.

"Know what a 'snuff-flick' is?" he asked first eyeing Rhett, then Brindle.

"Yeah, sure," Brindle said, "Supposedly, they kill someone in the course of shooting a movie."

"Exactly, so turns out the first movie the executive producer of *Charleston Buzz* ever made was—supposedly—a snuff flick." Janzek said. "A little beauty called, *Somebody Really Gets Killed in this Movie.*

"That's a mouthful," Brindle said.

"Yeah, so follow me here," Janzek said, "D-Wayne and the *Buzz* producer Holly Barrow had a one- maybe two-night stand."

"Jesus Christ," Rhett said. "The guy didn't miss anything in a skirt, did he?"

"Yeah, and apparently Holly was hoping it was going to go somewhere," Janzek said. "D-Wayne, on the other hand, acted like it never happened. Totally ignored her afterwards."

"Sounds like that dirtbag," Rhett said.

"So, Holly, who as producer-director calls the shots on the show, apparently decides not to have D-Wayne come back for the third season."

"Vindictive little bitch," Rhett said.

"Okay, Delvin, enough with the peanut gallery shit," Brindle said.

"So, a little bit later," Janzek went on, "they're filming a segment and D-Wayne figures he's got nothing to lose plus, apparently, he's drunk—"

"As usual," Rhett said.

Brindle shot a glare at Rhett.

"And when the cameras are rolling, he blurts out something about how Holly's a shitty lay—"

"Class act, that D-Wayne." Brindle interrupted. "So, you're saying that him saying that—humiliating her in front of everyone—plus this whole snuff flick thing gives her motive to qualify as a suspect?"

"I'm saying it's something worth looking into," Janzek said. "Even though I'm not sure I'm buying this snuff flick thing."

Brindle scratched his head and thought for a second. "Jesus, I think I need a playbook for this whole clusterfuck."

THIRTY-SIX

It was gnawing at him.

Janzek had a seriously guilty conscience. So, he called Samantha Byrd on his way to meet with Holly Barrow.

"So," she answered, "is CPD giving you a breather?"

He laughed. "Actually, Samantha, I gotta come clean with you."

"Okay?"

"See, truth is," he said. "I'm kind of seeing another woman."

In the old days, he probably would have attempted a juggling act. Seen both Samantha and Sheila at the same time. But that could get complicated. And besides, he always got caught. Not to mention, someone might get hurt, and he really didn't want that to happen.

"You know, Nick, I gotta say, that's pretty decent of you. Unlike most guys out there."

Janzek stifled a sigh. "I just didn't want—"

"You don't need to explain," she said. "I appreciate it. If things ever change..."

"I'm sure I'll see you around," he said.

"Okay, well, take it easy. And thanks for being straight with me."

Short and sweet… it was the right thing to do.

*****

Hudson Rock reminded Janzek of a pit bull. One who sat at Holly Barrow's feet, ready to sic Janzek when she gave him the word. He had a rabid attack-dog look to him, too: nasty, hard eyes, his body all tensed up.

Holly, on the other hand, was mellow and cooperative. Janzek had asked her about her "relationship" with D-Wayne Marion and

130

while acknowledging it, she downplayed it. She even joked about it, saying she could barely keep track of all the men she had sex with. But yes, one had been D-Wayne. And, as far as she was concerned, it had not been "memorable."

When Janzek came right out and asked her if she had cried at D-Wayne's funeral, she made another joke, saying she had always been emotional. How she went into a major tailspin when her hamster died at age six.

Meanwhile, Hudson Rock just nodded a lot, looked surly and laughed at his boss's jokes.

When Janzek asked Holly how she felt when D-Wayne commented about her "sexual performance" in one of the show's scenes, she tackled it head on.

"You mean the paraplegic thing?'" Holly said, "Yeah, that stung a little, but I mean, I do live in Hollywood and work in a pretty brutal business. Harvey Weinstein and all."

She went on to say that, contrary to what Saxby claimed, she'd actually wanted to air the segment in which D-Wayne made the drunken comment and bleep out the most offensive parts. It made for good TV, she said, but she had been talked out of it. At that point, Hudson Rock volunteered something about how the show had a higher purpose than being, "a carnal rating service by D-Wayne Marion." He looked very proud of his turn of phrase.

Janzek just nodded, unable to put his finger on what that higher purpose might be.

Holly, on the other hand, was all-pro at being frank and blunt. Like she was going to give you a direct, honest answer no matter what you asked her. Back on the subject of D-Wayne, she smiled wistfully and called him, 'just a drunk.' A handsome drunk, for sure she quickly added, but—bottom line—'drunks get boring and repeat themselves after a while.'

"It's like this old show I used to watch in reruns when I was a kid," she said. "It was called 'The Dean Martin Show.' You ever watch it?"

"Yeah, a couple of times," Janzek said, not quite sure where she was going, "He was Frank Sinatra's sidekick, right?"

"Yeah, one of 'em," Holly said. "Anyway, old Dino's schtick was that he was this good-time drunk. It was pretty funny for a while, but it didn't take long for it to get old. I mean, how many falling down jokes can you do?"

Janzek nodded. All he could remember was Martin's slicked-back, duck's-ass hairdo and the fact that he was always smoking cigarettes that he'd suck down to his toes.

That's the way it was with D-Wayne, Holly explained, and why she'd decided to cut back on his airtime. Drunks have a limited shelf life. Ultimately, it had been a business decision.

Then she told him how all of the characters on *Charleston Buzz* were rated—episode by episode—by focus groups for their popularity with fans. And, it turned out, D-Wayne's popularity had been sliding, while Rip's and Samantha's were both going up. Saxby, despite what he might be thinking, she said, was basically treading water.

Holly paused. It was time for Janzek to lob in his big question. "About ten years ago you shot a movie," he asked, matter-of-factly. *"Someone Really Gets Killed in this Movie."*

"'*Somebody*,'" she said.

"Okay, '*Somebody*'."

She was nodding cheerfully. "I see where you're going. Well, fact is, nobody actually did get killed. It was a very convincing fake. But, did you really think that somehow connected me to D-Wayne's murder?"

Hudson Rock snorted a laugh at the absolute absurdity of the idea.

"So, you're saying that actress was not actually killed?"

"Yes, that's exactly what I'm saying. In fact, she wasn't even nicked up a little," Holly said. "You can ask her. Last time I heard she was alive and well, waitressing at some dump in Pasadena. Sherry Betts is her name. But, I'm pretty amused at the idea of you thinking I might be a murderer."

Janzek nodded for a second. "I look at it this way: everybody who knew D-Wayne might be his murderer. Unless, of course, they have an iron-clad alibi. Which is what I haven't heard from you yet. Why don't you look at this as an opportunity to convince me why I should take you off my shortlist?"

Holly smiled. "That's very good, detective."

"Thank you. So, here's the question," Janzek asked. "Where were you between the hours of eight p.m. and three a.m. on July thirteenth?"

Holly smiled demurely. "I was watching TV for half of that

132

time, sleeping the other half. I'm an early-to-bed kind of gal," she said. "Let me ask you this, Nick: Why aren't you giving Jessie Lawson the third-degree? That's what you call it, right?"

"Well, yeah, that's a little dated, but it still works. Answer is, I've spoken to Ms. Lawson plenty. But let's stick with you for now. So, tell me a little more about that movie, I'm curious. You figured if people thought someone actually got killed, they'd want to go see it."

"Of course. Why do you think you see people hanging out their windows when they drive by a car wreck?" Holly leaned forward. "So, what's the verdict on Jessie? Not that I want to see any of my former cast members in jail, but—"

Hudson followed his boss's lead. "Yeah, you do know that D-Wayne was trying to make her sign something that said she'd get bupkis if he divorced her. Plus, the fact the girl could shoot like a sniper. Hello, detective..."

Janzek looked over at Rock and smiled. "Thank you, Mr. Rock, for weighing in." *You smarmy little weasel, you.*

"Just sayin'."

"Yup," Janzek said, "and don't think I don't appreciate it. While you're both so busy helping me out, who else do you suggest I talk to?" He turned to Holly "Since you've now convinced me to rule you out."

"You say that," Holly said, "but have you really?"

"Well, now, that's a good question. Because if I was any good, I'd probably want you to think that I ruled you out even if you were my prime suspect."

"Exactly," said Holly.

"Well, on that note, I'm going to end our little interview. Thank you very much, both of you, for all your cooperation."

"That's the way you're going to leave it?" Holly said, her brow knit tightly.

"Yeah, you know, kind of a cliffhanger. Like *who shot J.R.*"

But Holly Barrow was a woman not to be outdone. "Oh, by the way, detective, how's it going with Samantha?"

Janzek could only play it one way. "Who?"

"Samantha Byrd," Holly said with a snicker. "You know, the cute blonde from my show you played bocce with the other night."

"Oh, her." Janzek said, "Yes, well, she and I had a very nice interview. And she's a hell of a Bocce player too."

THIRTY-SEVEN

He was on his way back to the station when he got a call on his cell.

"Hello."

"It's Jessie Lawson, Nick. I just saw that girl. You know, the one I spat at."

Janzek pulled over to the side of Calhoun Street. "Where are you?"

"Cypress restaurant. On Bay Street."

Janzek hit the accelerator and did a wide, tire-burning U-turn. "I'm on my way."

"See you in a few. I'm at a window table, near the front door."

"Five minutes," he said.

*****

He made it in four, double-parked, walked into Cypress, and saw Jessie sitting at a window table wearing Ray-Bans.

"Hel-lo, Nick. You got here fast," she said, taking off the Ray-Bans.

"Hello, Ms. Lawson," Janzek said, pulling out the chair and sitting down.

"Can you please just call me Jessie," she said, leaning back in her chair. "Do you call Samantha Byrd, 'Ms. Byrd?'"

Jesus, was there a news bulletin about their bocce date or something?

"Where exactly did you see the woman?"

She pointed at the window.

"She walked past here, ten minutes ago."

Janzek leaned forward so close he could see a tiny scar on her chin. "Which way was she going?"

134

Jessie pointed to her left. "That way. Up the street."

"What did she look like?" he asked, reaching into his jacket pocket, and pulling out a pad and pen. "And what was she wearing?"

Jessie looked away for a second, then back at Janzek. "Come on. Do I really need to describe her again?"

"Blonde, big hair, trampy, that's what you said before," Janzek said. "But what else? That doesn't exactly paint a full picture."

"Okay, then. Kind of slutty, lots of make-up—"

"Can you be more specific?"

"Sure, a bunch of pancake like she's hiding acne or something," Jessie said. "Looked like false eyelashes. Think queen of the trailer park."

"And what was she wearing?"

"A sleeveless beige T-shirt, heels, and a pencil skirt."

"I don't know what a pencil skirt is."

"Hookers wear them."

"No help."

"Okay," Jessie said, "a tight skirt—straight, narrow cut—stops right above the knee."

"Got it."

Out of the corner of his eye, Janzek suddenly saw a man on the sidewalk whose nose was practically pressed up to the window, aiming a big, black camera.

Janzek held up a hand to cover his face.

"Don't worry," Jessie said. "He's aiming it at me. One of my paparazzi."

Janzek put down his hand as the man snapped away.

"How can you stand it?"

"The price of stardom," she said with a shrug.

"What color was this pencil thing?"

"Yellow," she said, smiling.

"That was a joke, right?"

"Yes. It was black actually."

"And how tall would you say she is?"

"About five-eight or nine."

He pushed back his chair and stood. The man with the camera was still there. This time he aimed it at Janzek.

"Where are you going?" Jessie asked.

"Try to find her."

"Happy slut-hunting."

"That's a little harsh."

"But accurate."

The man with the camera was still snapping away.

"Thanks for all the help," Janzek said, looking over at the man with the camera. "I'm going to let your admirer have you all to himself."

Janzek hoofed it all the way up East Bay almost to Calhoun Street, glancing into shops and restaurants as he went by them. Then he turned around, crossed the street, and went back down East Bay on the other side. But he didn't see anyone who came close to matching Jessie Lawson's description of the woman.

As he got into his car parked in front of Cypress, he made a mental note to give the description of the woman Jessie Lawson had given him to the department's sketch artist. Maybe have him talk to Jessie. He intended to then make copies and send out a handful of uniforms to go door-to-door and see if anybody recognized her.

Charleston was a small town; somebody ought to know who she was.

Janzek was getting sick of dead ends and suspects he couldn't nail down. The only solace was that he had been in this position plenty of times before and, most of the time anyway, found something that broke a case.

Seventy-nine per cent of the time, to be exact. That was his clearance rate up in Boston—meaning the percentage of killers caught and convicted on the cases he worked. The average clearance in Boston was somewhere in the low sixties. So, his rate was close to twenty per cent better than the average and he'd been proud of that. So far in South Carolina, he had a hundred per cent clearance rate— two for two—and he wanted to keep it that way. Ernie Brindle had told him once that the statewide rate in South Carolina was seventy-seven per cent.

Maybe, Janzek had mused, the South Carolina rate was so much higher than the Boston one because murderers in Boston were smarter. There were a million colleges up there after all. He hadn't shared that conclusion with Brindle, who'd advanced a quite different theory: that the reason the clearance rate was so high in South

Carolina was because cops were more intelligent and better trained here than other states.

Janzek wasn't sure he bought that.

He got back to the station, parked, and went into his office. The department's sketch artist was out, so he left him a note to call him.

Having Jessie Lawson's more complete description of the woman in bed with D-Wayne gave him hope that he might be getting closer—and soon would be three for three.

But maybe he was deluding himself.

THIRTY-EIGHT

Janzek got a call from Ruthie Mueller in CSI shortly after he returned to the station.

She said she had a few good sets of prints from the crime scene on the burned-out boat and was hopeful that soon she'd have a print or two off the gas can.

She had identified the person whose prints had been found so far. His name was Galen Parris and he had been arrested for assault with a deadly weapon ten years before, but never convicted.

Janzek went straight to Ernie Brindle's office. Brindle pointed to the chair across from his desk.

Janzek sat down. "I need to run a few things by you, Ernie."

"Sure. Go ahead."

"A guy named Galen Parris. You ever hear of him?"

Brindle scowled. "Sure have. Good 'ol Gay Paree, son of a bitch is the biggest slum lord in Charleston."

Janzek laughed. "Gay Paree, that's what they call him?"

"Yeah, if they want to lose a few teeth," Brindle said. "Guy's one nasty piece of work. Why you askin'?"

"CSI lifted his prints off of that torched boat of Jim Ray Glover's, the guy who took out Lex Murray. I'm hoping they're gonna be on the gas can we found, too."

"So, you're thinking Parris did Glover?"

"I don't know. He's the only candidate we got so far."

"Okay," Brindle said, "here's a quick rundown on the guy. Owns a bunch of piece-of-shit, dilapidated houses over on the east side. I heard back before the crash he owned like twenty of them, but a lot of them got foreclosed on and the bank ended up with 'em. He still owns quite a few and manages a bunch for other people. Story goes that he shows up with a .44 if you're late on your rent. That's what he got busted for, as I remember. Taking the butt of his gun to a delinquent tenant. Poor bastard spent a week in Roper Hospital."

"Think I'll go pay the guy a visit. Any idea where he hangs his hat?"

"I think he's got a fleabag office somewhere up in the hood. Upper St. Philip maybe."

"Thanks, man," Janzek said, getting up.

"Hey, Nick," Brindle said, clicking on his computer. "I know you're doin' all you can and maybe are a little frustrated. But hey, it takes time. I'm Googling Parris now."

"Thanks," Janzek said. "If this was up in Boston, chief would be on my ass twenty times a day."

"What can I tell you? Things move a little slower down here," Brindle said, looking at his screen. "Here you go, here's his phone number. 7-2-3-7-2-3-7. Give that jack-off my worst, will you?"

*****

Janzek left three messages in three hours and finally got Parris on his fourth try.

He sounded gruff and imposed-upon but agreed to meet with Janzek at his office on upper St. Philip Street. The office was bare bones and smelled like a combination of tobacco and vomit. Parris was dressed in chinos and a dark blue T-shirt that emphasized his barrel chest and slab-like arms. He was six-three, somewhere around two fifty.

Janzek started out by asking him if he had ever been on Jim Ray Glover's boat before. He said he had, a bunch of times. They were fishing buddies, Parris said, and added, drinking buddies, too. He'd just heard about Glover's death and said he was really gonna miss 'ol Jim Ray. The guy had a knack for finding the fish, he said, and always had a cooler full of Bud.

Next Janzek asked Parris if he had been on Jim Ray's boat the day before. Parris cocked his head and said, "You talkin' about the day he got shot?" Janzek said, yes, and Parris said, no. Said he was working on a house up on Hanover Street all day, and if Janzek didn't believe him he could talk to a carpenter named Rusty, who'd back him up.

Then Janzek asked Parris if Jim Ray had ever mentioned anyone who might have threatened him or given Jim Ray reason to believe his life might be in danger. Parris's eyes circled the room, then came back to Janzek's. "Jim Ray was a nice fella," Galen said finally. 'Wouldn't hurt a flea. Can't imagine why anybody would want to pop him."

Janzek told him that there was an ex-drug dealer named Lex Murray who would beg to differ. If he could.

THIRTY-NINE

After a few more questions that didn't go anywhere, Janzek thanked Galen Parris and headed back to his office, buying a paper along the way.

Despite Brindle's remark about being patient, Janzek wasn't. He couldn't remember a case—well, cases—where he had a million leads, with none of them close to being solved. He realized that he had been getting short and testy with people. Snapping at them like a high-strung poodle. Rhett was his most frequent target and Delvin had so far told him to, 'go fuck himself' twice and another time to, 'quit being such a bitch.'

Maybe he needed a break since he had been working sixteen- to eighteen-hour days. He was thinking about calling up Sheila and asking her out for dinner, but he was worried that he wouldn't be much fun in his present state of mind. He wanted to see her, but not if he was going to mope, be a downer, and be preoccupied with work.

He walked into his office, sat down at his desk, opened up the paper, and read an article about how the mayor was proposing to have new bars in Charleston close at twelve o'clock. *Twelve o'clock...* that was crazy. Hell, that was when he and his band of ne'er-do-wells back in college twenty years ago were just getting started.

What was really absurd about the mayor's proposal was that Charleston bars that were already in business were grandfathered in— they could stay open until two. Hardly fair, to say the least. Plus, two o'clock? That seemed ridiculously early to be putting down the highball glass and calling it a night—by his Boston standards anyway.

There wasn't much more in the main section worth reading so he turned to the next section called "People".

It took a few moments to register.

There—in a big three-by-five-inch series of photos—he was.

Three pictures of himself with, from left to right, Sheila Lessing, Samantha Byrd, and Jessie Lawson.

The headline read: NEW DETECTIVE ON *BUZZ* CASE.

"Shit," he said and started reading the article.

Detective Nick Janzek who solved the murder of Mayor James McCann last March has been assigned the D-Wayne Marion homicide with his partner, Delvin Rhett. Janzek, formerly a highly decorated homicide detective in Boston, joined the Charleston Police Department shortly before Mayor McCann's murder. Detective Janzek has been variously described as "the hardest working cop in Charleston" by one of his colleagues and as "a man who could charm a fox out of a tree" by a woman admirer, who asked to remain anonymous."

There was more, but he'd read enough.

He hurled the paper into the trash and yelled, "Je-sus fucking Christ!" at the ceiling.

A few moments later, Delvin Rhett stuck his head in. "Saw that article, huh?" He shrugged. "Hey, at least they're good pics of you."

FORTY

Thad Whaley was wearing nothing but Brooks Brothers white boxers as he lined up a two-foot putt on the green in front of the sorority house on Bull St. He jabbed at the golf ball and it went past the hole by about ten feet.

"Don't know your own strength, bro," William Kidd said, sarcastically.

Kidd had a bottle of Makers Mark in one hand and a Cohiba Behike cigar in the other. Unlike his opponent, he was completely dressed. He and Whaley were playing for the usual $1,000 a hole. Jolene was Whaley's caddie and another girl, Brooke, was Kidd's. It was not a job that required heavy lifting: just holding the men's putters when they were drinking and smoking, then their drinks and cigars when they were putting.

The pay was good, too. The custom was that the girls were tipped twenty per cent of their player's winnings. So far Brooke had made $400 and Jolene $600. The girls—naturally—encouraged the men to play for as long as they could stand up.

Whaley walked over to his ball and studied it. He'd had so much to drink that he saw three balls. The hole, ten feet away now, looked like a round, fuzzy blur.

"I'll give you three to one odds if you make it," Kidd said.

"On a grand?" Whaley slurred.

"Yeah," Kidd said, "should be a routine putt for a guy like you with a five-handicap."

"Four to one and you're on," Whaley said.

Kidd looked at Jolene. She smiled and nodded, doing the math on what her cut would be.

"Okay, you got it."

Whaley moved into position facing his ball. He took a few practice putts and squinted down at the ball.

143

"I can hardly see the goddamn thing," Whaley said.

Kidd laughed, just as Whaley dropped down to his knees

"What the hell you doin'?" Kidd asked.

On his knees now, Whaley turned the putter around, so the grip end was facing the ball. He held it like a pool cue, sliding it through two fingers of his left hand on the putting green, billiards-style.

Then he flopped down in a prone position, like a sniper lining up a kill shot two hundred yards away.

He smiled up at Kidd.

"What are my odds this way?" Whaley asked.

"I've seen you play pool," Kidd said. "Six to one."

"Book it," said Whaley.

He sighted in the dimpled white ball. "Shit," he said, "thing's a whole lot smaller than a cue ball."

He quickly slid the putter forward. It caught the golf ball on one side and the ball spun left and careened into one of Brooke's feet.

Kidd roared with laughter.

"Interference... on your caddie," Whaley said. "That was gonna go in."

"Yeah, right. You mean, ricochet off her ankle and go in?" Kidd put out a hand to help him to his feet. "Pay up, old buddy."

Whaley took his checkbook out of the breast pocket of the jacket that Jolene was holding and, in barely legible penmanship, stroked a check for a thousand dollars.

He handed it to Kidd as Kidd was taking out his wallet.

"Thanks, man, you'll probably win it all back tomorrow night—" then turning to Brooke and handing her two hundred-dollar bills "—thanks, honey, good job."

*****

An hour later, Whaley and Kidd—alias Mr. Jones and Mr. Johnson—were playing another sport. If you could call it that. It was a game called Beirut that the girls had taught them. There was a four-piece band playing oldies at the opposite end of the bar in the cavernous room on the second floor of the Boy's Club. Three men in their late fifties to early sixties were dancing with three girls in their late teens or early twenties. The men were doing a bad shag, and the girls were twerking.

Whaley took a ping-pong ball that had just been tossed into a cup in front of him and took a quick pull on a sixteen-ounce plastic cup of beer.

"Come on, man," said Raleigh Dunn—alias Mr. Williams—a short man in his fifties, "gotta chug it, not sip it."

Whaley tilted back the cup and took a long pull.

"That's more like it," Dunn said, then pointing at the band. "Remember a band back in the day called, "Maurice Williams and the Zodiacs?"

Whaley, about to try to toss his ping-pong ball into one of the cups at the other end of the table, stopped and turned to Dunn.

"Fuck, yeah," he said, "old Maurice wrote that song, 'Stay.' They were right up there with Doug Clark and the Hot Nuts. 'Member those guys?"

"Who could forget 'em?" Dunn said. "The kings of X-rated doo-whop."

Whaley nodded and tossed the ping-pong ball. It bounced off the rim of a Dixie cup. He took another pull.

FORTY-ONE

Meantime, Jessie Lawson was going full speed ahead. A girl in a hurry to make her mark in society.

She had wangled an invitation to Dede Wiedeman's capacious house on Legare St. and in the course of a boozy, two-hour lunch told Dede about her childhood growing up in Charlottesville, Virginia. How she had gotten shipped off to Foxcroft School at sixteen and made her debut at eighteen under two big tents in the backyard of their twenty-two-room, white brick Georgian. Then how she had gone off to Hollins to become an English major and meet a man who was marriage material.

The only true part of the story was that she had grown up in Virginia, but it was a dumpy two-bedroom bungalow in Virginia Beach.

She told Dede that she was looking for a cause now, something to dedicate her time, energy, and—yes—money to.

Dede threw out a few ideas. She mentioned that the Gibbes Art Museum was having a huge fundraiser in two months and volunteered that none of the locals ever stepped up and gave much more than a few hundred dollars. Jessie was surprised to hear that and asked about several society women she thought were prominent and active. Dede laughed and explained that those women were indeed prominent and active, and had good family names, but struggled to pay the grocery bill. She went on to explain how the husbands of those women were tight-fisted, except when it came to their own pleasures.

Jessie saw her opening and volunteered to donate $20,000 to the Gibbes fundraiser.

"Good God, girl," Dede said. "You can buy the whole museum for that. You don't need to give anywhere near that much. For five thousand dollars you can become the major sponsor and along with that they'll throw in Honorary Chair."

"Really?" Jessie figured she was getting off cheap and wondered how else she should strategically sprinkle her money around.

"Next step is," Dede continued, "you get on the Committee for the annual antiques-show benefit coming up this winter. That's the Preservation Society's big wingding. It'll cost you another five thousand dollars but it's well worth it."

Jessie was thinking so far this was all pretty much just a bunch of chump change.

"Then what you do is get one of those anti-cruise-ship flags and hang it on your house."

"A what?"

"One of those grey flags, you've seen 'em on houses South of Broad," Dede said. "With the red ship, you know, and the big X through it?"

Jessie thought hard. "Oh, is that what those things are? I thought that was just some cheesy abstract art. You know, like how people stick some tacky steel sculpture in their back yard."

Dede burst out laughing. "That's too funny. Then after that what you need to do is get an anti-cruise-ship bumper sticker. Mary Jennings's gallery has them. Then, like I said, get one of those banners. Costs around twenty-five bucks, I think."

"Okay, so I hang the banner on my house," Jessie said. "What exactly is the message I'm trying to convey?"

"That you want the mayor to tell the cruise ship people to park their big ugly ships somewhere else," Dede said. "Like Myrtle Beach or Columbia maybe."

"Ah, last time I checked, Dede, Columbia's not on the water," Jessie said.

"Good point. Then Savannah. Let them disgorge the great unwashed, strappy T-shirt crowd on the streets down there instead of here. I mean, seriously, have you looked at those people?"

"Yeah, pretty hideous," Jessie said.

"I mean, the other night Lucien and I were having dinner and I look up and there was this fat couple, from New Jersey or some such place, with their noses pressed up against our window. I mean, *pul-lease*! Get the hell out of here."

"Time to get out the shotgun, right?"

"Exactly. So anyway, after that you need to start going to St. Michael's church, and sign up for the flower guild there."

"But I don't know the difference between a rose and a dandelion," Jessie said. "Horticulture is hardly my strong suit. And besides, I go to Church of the Apostle."

"Oh, my God, are you kidding? That's the absolute kiss of death. In case you haven't noticed, that's where the poor white trash goes. Gotta go to St. Michaels, honey. As far as flowers, we'll go out to my garden and in an hour, I'll make you an expert on everything from podocarpus to pittosporum."

Jessie cringed. "My God, those sound like diseases or something. So then, after that, what's next?" She was quickly adding it all up in her head. For $12,000 or so she was on her way to becoming an instant, prominent member of Charleston society.

"That's all you really need to do. But if you want to be creme de la creme, there are two more steps. One, you need to buy a Hutty and, two, join Yeamans."

Jessie had no idea who or what a Hutty was but knew all about Yeamans. It was called Yeamans Hall and was the country club for the rich and prominent located just north of Charleston.

"I don't play golf, though."

"You don't need to. Can you play croquet?"

Jessie cocked her head. "You mean where you go through those little wickets and try to knock the other guys ball into the bushes?"

"Yeah, well, it's gotten a little more... refined."

"Okay, so what's a Hutty then? A kind of boat or something?"

Dede laughed hysterically. "You're a stitch. That's the name of a painter. Very, very popular at the moment. He did paintings of sharecroppers and slaves picking cotton. Big baskets on their heads and stuff."

"Baskets on their heads?"

Dede nodded. "Yeah, that's the way they carried cotton around, I guess."

"So how much for one of those?"

"Between fifteen and twenty thousand dollars," Dede said. "People drool over them. And to have one hanging in your living room means you're definitely in the know."

"And to join Yeamans?"

"Initiation is fifty thousand. Then about twelve thousand a year in dues."

"That's a lot of money," Jessie said, "I mean, for a couple of games of croquet and a bunch of picaninnies picking cotton—" she paused and killed the last of her white wine "—I don't think I need to be creme de la creme right away. Maybe just... creme de la lait. So, let's go out to your garden, take a look at your pitocarpus."

Dede laughed. "Come on, honey, get with the program... *pittosporum.*"

FORTY-TWO

Janzek put in a call to Sherry Glover, who was Jim Ray Glover's ex-wife. He wanted to pick her brain and see if she could be of help in trying to nail Glover's killer. He got her message machine and just as he hung up, got a call from a uniform cop who said he had just arrested Saxby Wentworth-Kuhn. Or, "that squirrely little dude from the TV show," as he described him. The cop went on to say that Saxby told him Janzek could put in a good word for him. Act as a "character witness" were Saxby's exact words.

Janzek said he wasn't about to go that far, then asked the cop what Saxby had been arrested for.

Trying to drive one of the horse and buggies downtown off the road, the cop responded. "I guess you could call it a bad case of road rage."

The cop said he had just brought Saxby into the station and Janzek, who was in his office, said he'd be down there in two minutes.

When Janzek got there, he found a knot of gawkers, all trying to look like they were just going about their business. Two women uniforms, a traffic cop who rode a Segway, and one of the girls from dispatch, were pretending like they were conducting some official task, when, in fact, they were actually checking out TV star and local A-list celebrity, Saxby Wentworth-Kuhn.

Janzek walked up to Saxby and the uniform. Saxby looked relieved to see him.

"Hey, Nick, thanks for coming," Saxby said, thrusting out his hand.

Janzek shook it less than enthusiastically. "Hi, Saxby," he said, glancing at Zack Nelson, the uniform, and nodding.

"What exactly's this about?" Janzek asked. "Officer Nelson said you tried to run a carriage off the road down on Tradd Street."

Saxby raised his hands. "Let me tell you what happened, Nick." Janzek wished he'd call him detective, not comfortable with the implied closeness of their relationship. "This guy, driving the carriage, packed with a buncha rubes from a cruise ship, wouldn't pull over. So, I gave him a friendly honk—" Janzek wasn't aware there was such a thing "—and he still wouldn't pull over, so I went around him and that was that."

Officer Nelson smiled and shook his head. "Wait a second. I got eight eyewitnesses saying you went around the carriage, then cut it off, and spooked the horse so bad it plowed into a hedge."

"Look, Officer," Saxby said, "there was a car coming in the opposite direction, so I had to cut back pretty fast."

"And what about the gun?" Nelson asked.

Janzek who had been eyeing Saxby, swung his head around at Nelson.

"Gun?"

"There was no gun," Saxby said, vehemently.

Nelson turned to Janzek. "A couple of the passengers, and the driver, said they saw Mr. Wentworth-Kuhn aim a gun at the driver."

Saxby shook his head violently. "Goddamnit, I said there was no gun. All I did was this—" he raised his arm, made a fist, and pointed his index finger "—so it was perfectly harmless."

"My eyewitnesses said you had an actual gun," Nelson repeated.

Janzek flicked his head at Nelson. "Let me talk to you for a second, Zack."

Nelson nodded and followed Janzek to a corner of the room out of earshot of Saxby. Janzek looked back at Saxby, whose darting eyes suggested he'd much rather be quaffing a cocktail in the salon de the. Anywhere but here.

"What happened?" Janzek asked. "Did someone get Saxby's plate number and call it in?"

"Yeah, exactly, then I went to his house and arrested him."

"I'm assuming you looked for a gun in his car?"

"Not yet, haven't had a chance," Nelson said. "I was thinking about getting a warrant to go through his house—"

"You really think he did it? Aimed a pistol at the driver?"

"I don't know. The driver seemed to think so. But he might have seen what he wanted to see."

"Yeah, I hear you," Janzek said. "But, if it really was a gun, I want to pursue it. That would be a big find."

Nelson thought for a second. "'Cause you're thinking, if there was a gun, maybe he'd be a possible in that D-Wayne shooting?"

Janzek shrugged. "Yeah, maybe. Even though I don't really see it."

"I hear you."

"What's the charge? Vehicular endangerment or something?"

"Yeah, exactly."

"Okay," Janzek said. "We could get a warrant to search his entire house, but I don't think that's necessary. And the reality is, if he did have a gun and wanted to hide it there, we'd have a hell of a hard time finding it."

"So, what do you want to do?"

Janzek turned, flicked his head and he and Nelson walked back to Saxby.

"You got the key to your car, Saxby?" Janzek asked, approaching him.

Saxby reached in his pocket.

"You don't really believe that gun bullshit, do you?"

"It's a serious charge," Janzek said, "so we have to check it out."

Saxby handed him his keys.

"Total waste of time," he said.

*****

Turned out, it was.

In fact, Saxby's car was immaculate. Janzek suggested that Nelson go interview as many of the people as he could who were on the carriage and grill the driver again. See if they were really sure that it was an actual gun that Saxby was brandishing. Nelson said he'd take care of it and they released Saxby, still unsure whether to file a charge or not.

Janzek went back to his office and found a sketch on his desk, depicting the woman Jessie Lawson had seen in bed with D-Wayne Marion. At the top of the drawing was a yellow sticky that said, 'Nick. Hope this helps. Just to make sure I got it right, I went and spent a half hour listening to Jessie Lawson describe the woman. Wow, she's a trip!' It was signed by the sketch artist Rick Dodge.

Janzek had previously asked Jessie if she would be okay with Dodge getting in touch and describing the mystery woman to him. She'd said it was fine with her. Janzek's one experience with Dodge had been a few months before when he had rendered a decent likeness of a suspected perp.

The woman in this sketch, however, looked more like one of those blow-up sex dolls with blonde hair, a button nose, and a prominent chin. Nevertheless, Janzek ran off a hundred copies and distributed them to everyone on the Charleston Police Department, figuring it couldn't hurt.

Just as he got back to his office, he got a call on his cell. He didn't recognize the number.

"Hello, Janzek," he said.

"Yes, this is Sherry Glover," she said. "You called and left a message about my ex-husband, Jim Ray?"

"Yes, thanks for getting back to me, Ms Glover," Janzek said. "First, let me express my condolences about what happened to your former husband."

Her terse 'thank you' indicated that maybe she hadn't taken it so hard.

"Can you tell me how long ago you got divorced from Jim Ray?"

"About a year and a half."

"And did he ever talk about anybody who might want to do harm to him?" Janzek said, "Any enemies, someone he might have had a problem with, anyone at all like that?"

"Not really, but then Jim Ray never talked about much of anything with me."

"But did he ever mention anybody he may have had a dispute with? Business or personal?"

"No, not that I can remember."

"And he and his friend, Galen Parris, did they do a lot of things together? I understand they went fishing pretty often?"

There was a pause. Then finally. "Galen who?"

"Parris."

"Never heard of him."

FORTY-THREE

An overweight cop named Alvin Deaver, who Janzek had seen around, came charging into Janzek's office like an eighteen-wheeler whose brakes had gone out.

"I think I know who the girl in the sketch is," Deaver said, catching his breath.

"Who is she?"

"Cotton Kelly. She's got a gallery downtown, on my beat," Deaver said. "Same chin, high cheekbones, big hair, the whole nine. Hell of a flashy dresser, too; ain't shy about showin' off her equipment."

"Is that right?" Janzek said. "Big question is, did she show off her equipment to D-Wayne Marion?"

"Wouldn't know about that. Girl doesn't share a lotta intimate shit with me. But that's definitely her."

"Well, thanks, man, I'll go talk to her. What's the address of her gallery?"

"Corner of State Street and Church. The Cotton Kelly Gallery."

*****

But by the end of the day, four other cops positively ID'd the sketch as women other than Cotton Kelly. One thought she was the mother of a kid who went to school with his kid out in Mt. Pleasant. Another was pretty sure she was a waitress at the restaurant, Slightly North of Broad. A third thought she sold jewelry at one of the Market Street shops, and a fourth was absolutely certain she was a stripper up in some North Charleston dive.

That watered down Janzek's hope that Cotton Kelly was the woman who might be able to shed light on D-Wayne Marion's murder.

154

But because Alvin Deaver was so sure, he decided to go see her anyway. The other four sounded sketchy but he'd check them out too.

First of all, it seemed pretty unlikely that a waitress or a stripper was going to be behind the wheel of a flashy Aston Martin, even though he had heard some strippers made pretty good money. Ditto a mom in Mt. Pleasant—unlikely. Though Cotton Kelly certainly seemed more likely, the car didn't exactly fit the profile of a gallery owner either. Unless, of course, she'd sold a wall full of Picasso's lately.

In any case, he decided to drop in at the gallery, but before he did, he wanted to talk to Galen Parris again.

Once more, he found Parris in his office up on St. Philip Street.

"Well, Detective, awful nice of you to drop by again," he said, bursting with insincerity. "What can I do for you this time?"

Janzek walked up to the grey metal desk Parris was parked behind.

"Got a few more questions," Janzek said, not sitting down.

"I figured as much," Parris said, folding his meaty hands together. "So, let 'er rip."

"How come your fishing buddy's ex-wife never heard of you?"

Parris' smile faded fast. "Probably same reason she never heard of Sunny Porcher," Parris said. "Until it was too late."

"Who's Sunny Porcher?"

"Chick Jim Ray was bangin'. They were an item for a while," Parris said. "So, you thinkin' I might have had something to do with what happened to Jim Ray?"

"You're on my list."

Parris just chuckled. "And just what do you think my motive was?"

"I don't know. I'm still workin' on that."

Parris nodded again. Then he stood up. He had about three inches on Janzek. Parris came around his desk and got face to forehead with him.

"Well, I gotta get goin', hoss," Parris said. "Collect me some rent. Why don't you come back when you got things figured out a little better?"

Janzek had been called a lot of things, but never "hoss".

*****

155

It didn't go much better at Cotton Kelly's gallery. But at least she was more welcoming. In real life, she looked much better than how Jessie Lawson described her... and Rick Dodge sketched her.

To him she didn't look either trampy or slutty. In fact, she looked pretty damn good.

She was sitting at a desk in the back of the gallery when he walked in, talking to a woman who he figured to be in her early twenties. Her assistant, he guessed. Cotton Kelly got up and walked toward him.

"Welcome," she said, from a few feet away. "I'm Cotton. We're having a special exhibit of Alfred Hutty's paintings and etchings. The man was an extraordinary talent—maybe you're familiar with his work?"

Janzek shook his head. "Sorry, can't say I am. My name is Detective Janzek, Charleston Police, I actually stopped by to ask you a few questions, if that's okay."

She slipped into a frown. "Sure, I guess so. Questions about what?"

He had rehearsed on the trip down from Parris' office.

"About David Marion. He was called D-Wayne on that TV show, *Charleston Buzz.*"

She nodded. "Oh, sure, the poor man who was killed."

"Exactly, I'm guessing from your reaction that you didn't know him."

"No, I didn't," she said. "I knew of him... but probably most people in Charleston did. Why did you think I might know him?"

"Well, because his widow described a woman she met, ah, in the presence of Mr. Marion, and you kind of fit the description."

Cotton Kelly raised her arms and smiled. "Sorry, wrong girl, detective. But while you're here, maybe you want to take a look at my Hutty's?"

Somehow the invitation seemed more than a little suggestive.

*****

When he got back in his car, he dialed Jessie Lawson's number and asked her if she knew a woman named Cotton Kelly. She said no, she didn't, but she knew of her gallery. Janzek explained that she might be the woman Jessie had seen walk by the restaurant and, before that, in bed with her husband the night he was killed. Then he asked if she would mind walking by the woman's gallery to see if she was the one. Jessie said she wouldn't mind. In fact, she had been meaning to go to the gallery anyway. There was a certain artist there whose paintings she wanted to see.

"Alfred Hutty?"

"That's him," she said enthusiastically. "They have any of black women with big baskets of cotton on their heads?"

FORTY-FOUR

It was two incidents that took place in rapid succession that had Janzek in a funk.

The first occurred while he was in his office, trying to see if he could dig up anything more on Galen Parris via the internet.

He got a call from the front desk.

"Hey, Nick," the receptionist said, "got a celebrity up here wants to see you."

"A celebrity?"

"Penelope Kuhn."

"Oh, Christ, what does she want?"

"Didn't say," the woman whispered. "Want me to ask her?"

Janzek stood up. "No, that's all right. I'll be right out."

Penelope Kuhn was wearing a black, low-cut dress that reeked of a pricey Fifth Avenue boutique. It clashed mightily with Janzek's Costco shirt and Old Navy tie.

She also seemed to be swaying slightly.

"Hello, Mrs. Kuhn," he said, putting out his hand. "What can I do for you?"

She shook his hand limply and gave him a smile he suspected she might have cribbed from a soap opera.

"Hello, Nick." He could hear the booze.

He waited for her to tell him what was on her mind, but she just kept smiling that smile.

"Want to come inside and sit down?"

"Sure."

"Follow me," he said, and walked down to the musty soft room with its plastic flowers and burnt-orange couch. "Sorry, I'm afraid it's not exactly the salon du thé."

She laughed as she sat down on the couch. "You mean, Kathleen Rivers wasn't your decorator?"

"Who?"

Penelope laughed. "A big decorator in town."

"I don't think so," he said, sitting across from her. "So, tell me why you stopped by, Mrs. Kuhn?"

"You," she said, fluttering her eyelashes.

"Excuse me?"

"I saw that newspaper article about you, Nick," Penelope said. "You and Sheila Lessing. The two of you looked pretty... chummy."

Janzek judged it a three sloe gin fizz slur. "I'm not sure what you mean."

"I figured that if you were interested in older women, well, then maybe I'd throw my hat into the ring--" *Jesus, please,* Janzek thought, *someone please put a bullet between my eyes right this minute!*

He stood quickly. "Mrs. Kuhn, I appreciate your stopping by. I was hoping you were maybe going to volunteer something about the D-Wayne Marion murder."

Penelope Kuhn's eyes dropped.

Janzek suddenly felt sorry for her and patted her shoulder lightly. "Well, anyway, thanks for stopping by. It's always nice seeing you."

*****

After walking Penelope out, Janzek went back to his office and saw something on his desk that had not been there ten minutes before. It was the picture from the newspaper of himself and the three women, now housed in a cheap plastic frame. On the upper left-hand corner, a Post-it was stuck there. Janzek leaned down and read it. It said, "Nick the Chick Magnet."

He picked it up and stormed into Rhett's cubicle, where Delvin was munching on an oversized blueberry muffin.

"Not funny, asshole," Janzek said, flashing the picture at Rhett. Then he lobbed it into Rhett's wastebasket.

"Come on, man, where's your sense of humor?" Rhett said. "Christ, that thing set me back three whole bucks."

"Hey, look," Janzek said, "that whole thing embarrassed the shit out of me, okay?"

159

"O-kay, okay. Don't have to bite my head off. Just a lame attempt at humor."

Janzek sighed and held up a hand. "Sorry, guess I'm just taking my frustration out on you."

"You mean, the fact that we're nowhere on anything?"

"Yeah," Janzek said, sitting down on a corner of Rhett's desk. "That's exactly what I mean."

"Hey, I hear you. I feel the same way."

"I don't know about you. But I feel like I'm running around in circles, chasing my tail."

"Me, too."

"You know what it is," Janzek said. "On Marion, we got three suspects. Anyone could have done it, but none of 'em strike me as the one who *did* do it."

"Jessie, Saxby, and Holly being the third?"

"Yeah, but I have to say, a distant third."

"So, who you got as front runner?"

"I don't know, still Jessie, I guess," Janzek said. "She's got the strongest motive. I'm just not feeling it."

"And Saxby?"

Janzek nodded. "Dude needs a little work in the anger management department, but I don't see him as a killer."

"Me neither. So, you're saying... none of the above?"

"I'm still thinking the woman in bed with D-Wayne is the key. Only problem is, we can't find her. I went and saw someone who I thought might be her, but she denied it."

"You believe her?"

"I don't know, man. People in this town—I'm finding out—lie like they majored in it in college. No *tells* or anything."

Rhett laughed as Janzek caught him up on going to see Cotton Kelly, then his call with Jim Ray Glover's ex-wife and, lastly, the one with Jessie Lawson, who was going to check out Cotton Kelly on the sly.

"So, Jim Ray's ex had never heard of Galen Parris even though Parris made it seem like they were best buddies?"

"Yeah. Not exactly sure where that leads us. If anywhere."

Rhett shrugged.

"It'd make things a whole lot easier if Jessie Lawson tells us Cotton's the person she saw that night," Janzek said.

Rhett leaned back in his chair. "So, if it *was* her in the sack with D-Wayne, she could have done it, you mean?"

"Could have, but I strongly doubt it. Doesn't really add up," Janzek said. "My guess is, if it was her, she knew the actual shooter, though."

"So, like a husband or jealous lover?"

"Yeah, they're the most obvious."

"Well, you're gonna find out pretty soon, I guess," said Rhett. "If Cotton was the girl Jessie spat at."

FORTY-FIVE

The next morning, Rhett walked into Janzek's office, looking as grim as Janzek had ever seen him.

"Jesus, what's the problem?" Janzek said. "You're almost as white as.... me."

Rhett didn't laugh or even crack a smile. "Big problem."

"What is it?"

"Know how I told you about my younger brother, Leon?" Rhett said. "Did a three-year bit at Northside Correctional?"

"Yeah, some kind of arson thing, right?"

"This guy was messin' with his girlfriend, so Leon burned down his house."

Janzek nodded. "Yeah, I always thought that was a bit of an overreaction."

Again, Rhett didn't crack a smile. "Well, Ruthie the tech called and gave me a heads-up. Told me it was Leon's prints on that gas can at the boat fire that killed Jim Ray Glover."

"Jesus Christ," said Janzek, "you gotta be kidding."

Rhett shook his head grimly.

Janzek's cell phone rang. "Hang on," he said and looked down at the number. It was Jessie Lawson. He let it go to voice mail, then looked up at Rhett. "What the hell would Leon's prints be doing on the gas can?"

"'Cause he works at that marina. Remember, I told you. At the bait and tackle shop there."

"But what do you think—"

"I have no idea, man. No fucking clue," Rhett said. "Except I gotta go talk to him. Right now. Will you go with me?"

Janzek nodded and got to his feet. "Sure. Where you think he is?"

"His place. He doesn't start work until nine-thirty."

*****

162

Leon Rhett lived in a converted two-car garage behind his parents' house on Sumter Street. It was probably illegal and certainly small, but Leon had it fixed up pretty nice. Janzek guessed that Leon did a lot of his shopping at Goodwill, but everything was neat and orderly and surprisingly bright, since there were windows on all four sides of the little white shed-like building.

Delvin knocked.

Leon came to the door with a piece of toast in one hand.

"Hey, man," Leon said to his brother, "what's up?"

"That's what I want to know," Delvin said with a deep frown, pushing his way past his brother. "This is my partner Nick Janzek. I got a bunch of questions for you."

"Hey, Leon, how ya doin,'" Janzek said.

Leon nodded. "Good, man." Then he turned to his grim-faced brother and mumbled. "Or maybe not... questions about what, Del?"

Delvin bore down on Leon. "About what your fingerprints were doin' on a gas can on that boat from your marina that got torched. The one that guy got shot on."

It took Leon Rhett a few moments to wrap his head around the question.

"A guy called me up," Leon said slowly. "Told me he'd give me twenty bucks to bring a can of gas out to him on a boat that was docked there. Hey, I figured the can costs three bucks and the gas another two--that was a pretty good profit."

"So, where'd you take it?" Rhett asked.

"Guy was out on Mr. Glover's boat."

"With Glover?" Rhett asked.

"No, Mr. Glover wasn't there. I figured it was cool, though, 'cause they went fishin' together. Only weird thing was he had these gloves on when I handed him the can."

Rhett exhaled, looked at Janzek, then back at his brother. "Jesus, Leon, the guy was settin' you up. Who the fuck is this guy?"

"Some big guy. I don't know his name. Nice fella. We talked a couple times when he came into the shop."

"So, he's a friend of Jim Ray's?" Janzek asked. "And they go fishin' together?"

"Yeah," Leon said.

"Was his name Galen Parris?" Janzek asked.

"Don't know, I never heard a name," Leon said.

Delvin was eyeing his brother like big brothers do. "Leon, for Chrissakes, tell me the truth. Did you have anything to do with that fire on Glover's boat?"

Leon's eyes went wide with fright. "Hell, no, man. I told you. Guy paid me to take the can out to him. That's all there was to it."

Delvin didn't look sold. "Did you ever wonder why some guy would give you twenty bucks to do something that would cost him five bucks to do himself?"

Leon shrugged. "Well, I did deliver it out to him."

Rhett rolled his eyes. "Big fuckin' deal! Two minutes of work to make fifteen bucks. Didn't that get you suspicious?"

Leon's head dropped and he dug into his beard with his fingers, then scratched it nervously.

"I don't know, I just figured..."

"Just figured what?"

"I don't know," Leon said quietly.

"Describe this guy, will you, Leon?" Janzek asked.

"Like I said, he was a big guy--"

"For Chrissakes," Delvin said, losing it. "'Big guy' isn't any goddamn help! What color hair? Beard? Mustache? Fat? Skinny? Come on, man, give us something to work with!"

Leon looked at his brother sullenly, like Rhett was showing a side that scared him. "Chill, I was gettin' to it. The guy's got brown hair that's kind of combed forward, a little grey on the side. Big, muscular guy. And tall, like six-three, six-four. Late fifties, maybe. Couple times I saw him he was wearing shades."

Janzek was nodding. "That's Galen Parris," he said to Rhett. "Ruthie lifted his fingerprints from the boat. Guy I went and talked to a couple of times."

"So, Parris definitely set him up," Rhett said, flicking his head in Leon's direction. Then, to his brother, "When you were having one of your friendly little chats with this guy, did you ever mention anything about what happened with Jonzeeta to him?"

"You mean, the fire?"

"Yeah, 'course I mean the fire," Rhett said, turning to Janzek. "Jonzeeta was his old girlfriend—"

164

"Got it," Janzek said.

Leon was looking at the floor again.

"Leon, for Chrissakes," Rhett said. "You told him about starting that fire, didn't you?"

Leon blew out a lungful of air. "Yeah, guess I mighta," he said, almost inaudibly.

Rhett shook his head so hard his hair moved.

"Dumb fuckin' moron." He turned for the door. "Come on, Nick."

Janzek nodded to Leon. "Take it easy, man."

Leon nodded back.

Rhett went out the door and Janzek followed him.

Rhett turned. "Something tells me this guy Parris is gonna have a very different version of this story."

"Something tells me you're right."

"I know my brother," Rhett said. "When I asked him if he had anything to do with it, and he said no, he was tellin' the truth. He's just not the sharpest tool in the... whatever the hell that expression is..."

"Bait shop?"

FORTY-SIX

The name that popped up on Janzek's cell phone as he walked into the station after coming back from Leon Rhett's house was Jolene Roberts, the girl from the sorority house.

"Janzek," he answered as he walked into his office.

She got right to it. "This is Jolene. I need to know that if I tell you something it will be completely confidential," Jolene said in a nervous tone. "Will you promise me that?"

"Yes, I will."

Jolene sighed, like she was assessing whether to believe him or not.

"Okay," she said finally. "A bunch of men just took some of the girls here out on their boat."

"Who were the men?"

"I don't know their real names," Jolene said. "But one of them was the man who assaulted Leah."

Stanton Conger.

"Thanks for telling me," Janzek said. "Problem is... unless they're underage, it's not illegal."

Jolene inhaled dramatically. "That's the thing, see, the reason I'm telling you this is 'cause two of the girls who went with 'em are in high school."

"Really?" Janzek said, patting his pockets for a notepad and pen. "Who are they?"

"Well, see, one of the girls here, Sierra, has a sister in high school. The sister is interested in going to school here after she graduates. So, she came to take a look at the College, you know, sit in on a class, get the tour and everything. She came with a friend and the friend's younger sister. They're crashing in Sierra's room on an air mattress and a couple of sleeping bags."

"So, how'd they meet the men?" Janzek was chomping at the bit.

"Well, sometimes the men just come up to our rooms. Drop in, you know," Jolene said. "So, Mr. Smith, Mr. Jones, and Mr. Brown asked the girls if they wanted to go out on Mr. Smith's boat. I think maybe they slipped 'em some money to entice 'em."

"You think?"

"Okay, I know. You have to promise that you didn't hear this from me?"

"Don't worry, I'm not going to tell anyone. So how old are these girls?"

"I don't know exactly. The sister of the one was really young, I think. Like only a sophomore."

"In high school?"

"Yes."

"How long ago did they leave the house?"

"About half an hour ago. I think they were going to a shop on King Street first."

"What for?"

"Get bathing suits or something."

"Have you ever been out on the boat, Jolene?"

"Uh, once. Why?"

"What marina is it at?"

"That big one you see coming into town, with all the huge boats."

Which meant not the marina where Rhett's brother worked. Delvin, however, did keep a small boat at the marina Jolene had just described. Probably the smallest one there. Delvin called it the *S.S. Minnow*. He and Delvin had been out on it a couple of times together. Ostensibly, to catch fish, but really to drink beer, shoot the breeze and chill out. It had a 25-HP-Evinrude engine and was screaming for a paint job.

"What kind of a boat is it? Do you remember?"

"I just know it's a really big one. The name is the *High Cotton*."

"Thanks. You did the right thing. And we never had this conversation."

"Thank you."

Janzek clicked off and went into Rhett's office.

"What's up?" Rhett asked, looking up.

"We're gonna take a little ride on your boat. This time the city's paying for the gas."

"What's the plan?"

"We're gonna catch something other than fish. I'll fill you in on the way. Gotta go right now. We're putting a tail on our buddy Stanton Conger and the *High Cotton*."

"He owns that one?"

"Yeah, supposed to be pretty big, I hear."

"'Pretty big?' How 'bout a coupla football fields big. Only one that's bigger is Sheila Lessing's."

FORTY-SEVEN

Janzek played back seven messages he had on his voicemail as he watched Rhett start the engine of his boat. The third one was from Jessie Lawson:

"Nick," she said. "I went to that gallery. Call me right back."

That sounded promising. Like maybe she was going to tell him Cotton Kelly was the girl in bed with D-Wayne. He dialed Jessie's number. It went to voicemail.

Janzek clicked off and turned to Rhett.

"You know, Delvin, I been thinkin' about your brother."

Rhett rolled his eyes. "Yeah? And?"

"I think you gotta get out in front of it. I'd go to Brindle and tell him the whole thing. It beats the hell out of him finding out from Ruthie the tech or some other way."

"Yeah, you're probably right."

"Yeah, I definitely am. I'd go in there right after this boat thing, tell him the whole deal. It's obvious Leon had nothing to do with what happened to Jim Ray Glover. You know it, and I know it, but you just gotta head it off."

Rhett patted Janzek on the shoulder. "Thanks, Nick, I appreciate it."

*****

Twenty minutes later Janzek and Rhett watched four men and four girls board the *High Cotton*. A few of the girls looked as though they'd already had a cocktail or two. Their balance looked a little off and they seemed to be giggling and laughing too much.

"Jesus Christ, man," Rhett said, "talk about robbing the cradle."

"Yeah, those two in front look like they just got out of Girl Scouts."

"Buncha creepy old lechers."

A few minutes later the boat started slowly steaming out of the harbor.

"How many in the crew, you suppose?" Janzek asked.

Rhett guided his sixteen-foot Bayliner Capri out of its slip. "Boat that size... I'm guessing, twenty-five, thirty maybe. For a little ride like this, only half that."

Janzek nodded. "The question is, how long is it going to take for these lowlifes to try to peel off with the girls down to a cabin below?"

"Probably gonna wanna tune 'em up a little, you know, couple vodka and OJ's."

Janzek pointed to the stern of the *High Cotton*. "So, I'd say our play is to sneak up and tie the *Minnow* to that swimming platform in back of the boat."

Rhett laughed. "Hey, Nick, if you're gonna be on board the *Minnow*, you gotta talk like a sailor. The back of the boat is called the stern."

"Fine, tie up to the swimming platform at the goddamn stern then. Thing I worry about is the crew packin' guns maybe."

"Yeah, I hear you. We gotta flash 'em ID fast if we see 'em."

Janzek nodded. "You got a bullhorn on the *Minnow*, by any chance?"

"Yeah," Rhett pointed, "over there."

"Good, let's bring it along."

"What are you thinking the charge is gonna be?" Rhett asked. "Statutory?"

"Yeah, soliciting, too. I Googled the definition on the way here. It's something like, "Solicitation of prostitution is a crime involving a person's agreement to exchange money for sex. The kicker is, this agreement does not have to be explicit. A person's actions can be enough to demonstrate agreement."

"So, what exactly are we trying to prove?"

"Well, I'd say if we catch one of the girls in bed with one of these sleazeballs it's 'cause she's getting paid, not 'cause he's Bradley Cooper."

"So, it's implicit, you're saying..."

"Yeah, exactly."

"You figure we might need to break a door down or something?"

"Yeah, then snap off a few shots with our phones."

"What if we don't catch 'em in the act?"

"I'm not worried," Janzek said. "We're gonna get 'em on something. That girl Jolene told me one of these girls was just a high-school freshman. Aren't freshman like fifteen?"

"Yeah, fourteen or fifteen."

"So, under sixteen is statutory rape," Janzek said. "That was another thing I Googled."

"This could get our buddy Conger ten years."

"Yup," Janzek smiled. "Couldn't happen to a nicer guy."

FORTY-EIGHT

Janzek was wearing a floppy hat with earflaps on it, the kind fishermen wear to protect themselves from the sun and rain. In one hand, he had a fishing pole, which had no bait on it. He didn't want to have the distraction of reeling in a fish and unhooking it. In the other hand, he had his cell phone.

He hadn't heard back from Jessie Lawson, so he called her again. Again, it went straight to voicemail.

"Jessie, call me. It's Nick Janzek."

He looked over at Rhett. "She left me a voicemail after going to the gallery. Said we needed to talk."

"Shit, if she IDs Cotton Kelly, that could bust this whole thing wide open."

"I know."

Rhett, wearing a baseball cap and shades, was also holding a fishing rod. Also unbaited.

The *High Cotton* hadn't gone very far out before dropping anchor. Apparently, Stanton Conger didn't want to waste gas. Janzek could see Fort Sumter about a half mile away. He could also see that no one remained on the deck of the *High Cotton.*

After a while, Rhett nudged the *Minnow* toward the stern of the *High Cotton.* It was like a gnat creeping up on an elephant.

Rhett cut the engine and coasted up noiselessly to the swimming platform.

Janzek grabbed the side of the platform and jumped out. He tied Rhett's boat to it and Rhett climbed over the side and got aboard.

"Ready to rock?"

"Ready," Rhett said, bullhorn in hand.

"Only use it if you have to," Janzek said, pointing.

Rhett handed it to Janzek. "I'm going to let you make the call."

172

Janzek started up the steps to the main deck of the *High Cotton*, Rhett right behind him.

There was rock music playing in the background.

"These guys are a little old for Hootie," Rhett whispered, right behind Janzek.

They inched down the port side of the ship toward the middle, the music and laughter getting louder.

"Where do you figure the master cabin is on a boat like this?" Janzek whispered, turning to Rhett behind him.

"Normally I'd say one flight down," Rhett said. "But I checked out this rig on the internet. It's on the same level we're on. I know because those windows on the foredeck with the 180-degree views are the master."

Janzek chewed that over.

"I'm guessing where the music is coming from," Rhett went on, "is the main salon on this deck."

"And the master would be on the other side of the main salon, you're saying?"

"Yeah, that's my guess," Rhett said. "With another smaller salon or two in between."

"So, I figure after dropping anchor, Conger told the captain and crew to make themselves scarce."

"I agree." Rhett said. "The fewer eyes the better."

"So, none of the crew will be on look out?"

Rhett stifled a laugh.

"What?" Janzek said

"It's not like we're cruising past Somalia or something," Rhett said. "Haven't been any pirates in these water for like three hundred years. But you're right about one thing: these guys aren't gonna want the crew anywhere near 'em. No eyewitnesses."

Janzek took a few steps forward and looked through a frosted-glass window at a lavishly appointed living room. It wasn't what he expected at all. Seated in the deeply cushioned grass-green chairs and divans, centered around a huge, low glass coffee table, were two girls and two men. The room had an Art Deco look to it, but the thing that caught Janzek's attention were massive floor to ceiling bookshelves made from what looked like cherrywood with ebony inlays.

The last thing Janzek figured Stanton Conger for was a guy who

173

read books. Then he looked again and noticed that that books were all bound in leather and figured that Conger might have bought them by the pound at some upscale garage sale.

"Where's Conger?" Rhett whispered, as he crept up to Janzek's side.

Janzek pointed.

Conger had his arm around a girl and was standing over near the bar.

"Fuckin' pig," Rhett said. "Age difference has to be close to fifty years."

"Let's just wait until he goes somewhere," Janzek said.

"Looks like one couple already has," Rhett said.

Janzek just nodded as he watched Conger with the girl.

God, how he hoped she was the freshman. The way he read the law, the difference between fifteen years old and sixteen could be the difference between a wrist slap and doing hard time.

Conger had slipped his hand around the girl shoulder and slid it down onto one of her breasts.

Janzek had a hard time watching.

"Guy's a fuckin' pig," Rhett whispered. "Case you didn't hear me the first time."

Then Conger leaned down and kissed her. It wasn't pretty and her natural instinct was to turn away, so he just caught her on the ear. Then he said something to her. She hesitated for a second, so he reached down and grabbed her hand. He started walking. It seemed like he was almost puling her. She looked scared. As if the reality of the situation had suddenly struck her.

"Okay, looks like showtime," Janzek said, as Conger and the girl stepped through a door and disappeared. "I'll follow them. We both don't need to. You go down below after we go into the salon, see if you can catch another couple in the act."

"Roger that," Rhett said.

Janzek went around to a mahogany door, shoved it open, and they walked into the salon. None of the four sitting there looked happy to see them.

"Charleston Police," he said, holding up ID. "Stay right where you are and don't move—" he said, then to Rhett. "Take a few pictures."

Then Janzek walked quickly toward the door that Conger and the girl had just gone through. He went down a narrow hallway, then saw a closed door. He turned the knob, but it was locked. He took a step back, lowered his shoulder and took a short run at it.

It crashed open and Janzek burst into a darkened room.

"What the fuck?" came a man's voice.

Janzek recognized the voice as he hit the button on his Maglite.

He shined it straight ahead and saw the girl, in bra and panties, at the side of the massive bed at the far end of the spacious cabin. She looked relieved to see him. Then he saw Stanton Conger in black boxers, just to the left of the bed.

Conger stared at Janzek in disbelief.

"You're totally fucked," Conger said. "Should have learned your lesson the first time."

Janzek looked at the girl. "Charleston police. Put your clothes on and get out of here."

The girl looked tentative. "Go on," Janzek said, turning away from her.

Janzek eyed Conger. "You, too, Conger. Get your clothes on."

Conger just stared back. "You're in way over your head, pal."

"Hurry the hell up," Janzek snapped.

Conger reached for his pants on the floor.

Janzek looked over at the girl, she was buttoning up her blouse. She looked closer to fifteen than eighteen.

"Show me your ID," he said to the girl.

"What for?" Conger said.

Janzek kept his eyes on the girl. The girl didn't move.

"Right now," Janzek said, "show me your ID."

She walked over to a purse that was on a couch in a seating arrangement off to one side of the room. She picked it up.

"You don't have to show him anything," Conger said, walking toward her.

She had her wallet out but stopped.

"Shut the hell up, Conger." Then to the girl. "I'm not going to say it again," then walking toward her. "I need you to take out your ID and show it to me."

"Don't do it," Conger said.

Janzek was just a few feet away from the girl. So was Conger.

The girl reached into her wallet.

Conger grabbed for her wallet with his right hand.

Janzek reached out and slapped the older man's hand with his fist.

"Back away, Conger."

But Conger didn't move.

"Let me see it," Janzek said to the girl.

She pulled out her driver's license and handed it to Janzek.

It was a Florida driver's license.

Kayla Hillary West had turned sixteen five days before.

FORTY-NINE

Stanton Conger's first reaction was to get on the phone with his attorney and try to get Janzek and Rhett fired from the Charleston Police force. Hang them on whatever charges his cutthroat barracuda lawyer could come up with. Harassment, false arrest, whatever. Then he thought about it a little more and realized it didn't pass the smell test. The appearance of the whole thing wouldn't be good. How would it look if the word got out and it hit the papers? That he was out on his boat, plying a bunch of teenage girls with adult beverages? Sketchy, at best. A very expensive divorce at worst. He didn't need another one of those.

Bottom line, it was best simply to just make it quietly go away.

*****

So, after Conger got his clothes on and his temper under control, he told Janzek, with a straight face, that the girls were part of his crew, and that accounted for any cash Janzek might find in the girls' possession. They were part-time "hostesses," he explained, who served drinks, showed his guests where their cabins were, and gave them a hand with their bags and suitcases. He even got a little creative and claimed one of them was an assistant sous-chef.

Janzek just looked at Conger, nodded and thought, *ah-huh, so that's your story and you're stickin' to it?* He ordered Conger and the girl up to the main salon. He noticed that one of the men who had been there before was not there now and asked the girls where he'd gone. One of them finally explained that the man had jumped overboard. Janzek assumed that he had a wife who might get a little upset if she found out what actually went on out on Congers boat.

Rhett walked into the main salon with a couple he had barged in on in a cabin down below. He held up five crisp hundred-dollar bills that he'd found in one of the girls' purses when he was checking her ID.

Conger quickly explained that was her pay for working on his boat. Janzek cut him off and said he didn't want to hear it.

The big disappointment was that none of the girls were under the age of sixteen. There went the statutory rape charge. Solicitation of prostitution was the remaining option.

Janzek called Ernie Brindle and hit the high points with him about what had just taken place on Conger's boat. After listening to every detail, Brindle told him it wasn't worth it. The downside was too big—a possible lawsuit against the department and a lot of negative publicity accusing them of being overzealous cops, invasion of privacy and yada, yada, yada.

Janzek and Rhett went into the main salon.

Stanton Conger had a sneer on his face. As if he knew merely by their walk and how their shoulders were slumped what the situation was.

"Okay, Mr. Conger, the party's over," Janzek said. "Take these girls home right now and we won't charge you."

Conger's sneer got bigger and his brazenness amped up a notch. "Don't tell me what to do. I told you, these girls work for me," he said, putting his arm around Kayla. "I'll take them home when they've finished their jobs."

Janzek had never felt so powerless.

Knowing he held all the cards, Conger got to his feet.

He walked up to Janzek.

"Good night, Detective," he said, getting in Janzek's face. "Time for you to hop onto that pathetic little boat of yours and run along now."

FIFTY

Jessie Lawson's midnight blue Mercedes was found on the side of a scarcely traveled road in North Charleston early on Sunday morning. Her body was in the back seat. She had been stabbed repeatedly, leaving a half-inch pool of blood in the right rear footwell.

Four hours after the body was discovered, Ernie Brindle was contacted by the North Charleston police chief because of the connection between Jessie's murder and that of her husband, which, of course, the North Charleston chief knew Brindle's department was investigating.

Brindle immediately contacted Janzek.

"Jesus, that poor kid," was Janzek's first reaction.

"What?" Brindle asked.

"Jessie's daughter. I mean first her father, then her mother."

"Never thought of that," Brindle said.

"Kid's probably with the nanny," Janzek sighed, shaking his head. "Did they find any evidence? In the car or the area around where they found her."

"I don't know. I didn't get a lot of details," Brindle said. "You and Rhett oughta take a ride up there right away."

*****

Janzek's second reaction was that he wished he had tried a little harder to contact Jessie about whether Cotton Kelly was the woman Jessie had seen in her husband's bed.

Rhett was doing ninety on their way up to North Charleston.

"Okay, so this is just speculation," Janzek said. "Jessie goes to Cotton Kelly's gallery. She walks in, recognizes Cotton as the woman who was in bed with D-Wayne, and they have a confrontation."

179

"Yeah," Rhett said, "I could see it getting ugly."

"So then, Cotton's obviously not too thrilled, knowing Jessie can ID her as the woman who was in bed with D-Wayne."

"Yeah," Rhett said. "But you're not thinkin' Cotton would have done Jessie herself?"

"Nah, no way," Janzek said as Rhett flipped his blinker on and slowed down to exit off Route 26. "I'm guessing she called some guy to take care of business."

Rhett nodded as he got onto Dorchester Avenue. "And the guy… probably a jealous husband or boyfriend of hers?"

"Yeah, I'd say so," Janzek said. "So, it's time to dig real deep on Cotton. Find out if she's got a husband or a boyfriend, for starters. If so, how handy with a knife he is."

FIFTY-ONE

Janzek was in his office, having just gotten back from the murder scene in North Charleston. Jessie Lawson had been stabbed over twenty times with a knife that had a long, narrow blade. She had been dead for approximately twenty hours before being discovered.

The North Charleston detective who caught the case hadn't found any physical evidence that pointed in the direction of a killer. The crime scene techs had lifted four sets of prints but weren't particularly hopeful that any of them were the killer's. It had all the earmarks of being a neat, professional hit, where the killer wore gloves and wasn't about to leave any incriminating DNA behind. The knife used in the murder was, of course, nowhere to be found.

Janzek had a million questions: What was Jessie doing in North Charleston? How did the killer know how to find her? Or did the murder happen somewhere else and the killer drove her car to the remote North Charleston location? Those were just a few. He and the North Charleston detective in charge, Randy Mellor, agreed to stay in close contact. Mellor had located Jessie's parents and given them the news, and Janzek had volunteered to speak to Yolanda, the nanny. At first Yolanda seemed uncomprehending, then as it sunk in, she started to get hysterical and peppered Janzek with questions. What do I do with the baby? Who's going to take her? Janzek tried to calm her down and explained that the baby's grandparents were on their way to Charleston.

After he hung up with her, he thought again… *if only*.

If only he had spoken to Jessie. If only he hadn't been out on Stanton Conger's yacht wasting his time, as it turned out.

He went to his office to pick up his digital recorder. His next stop was Cotton Kelly's gallery, but as he was about to leave, he got a call on his landline.

"Nick, your celebrity friend is back," said the woman at the front desk. "Penelope... I forget her last name."

Oh, for Chrissakes. Talk about a waste of time. She was turning into a stalker.

He walked out to the front desk. Penelope Kuhn looked so totally out of place. She was wearing a cream-colored silk top, lots of Fifth Avenue bling, and a skirt that was way too short for a woman who claimed to be sixty but probably was closer to seventy-five. That was part of the problem, Janzek suspected: the woman couldn't accept the fact that she was no longer a mini-skirt girl.

"Hello, Nick," she said, extending her long, skinny arm like she was a member of the royal family, and he should bow to her. "How divine to see you again."

One of the beat cops behind him snickered.

"Hi, Penelope, yes, divine to see you again, too," Janzek said for the cop's benefit. "Come back to my office, but I have to leave in a few minutes."

They walked into his office and he motioned to the chair across from his desk. She brushed the seat of the chair with her hand as if she suspected germs, which was understandable, then sat down.

"Nick, I know you're busy, so I'll get right to the point," she said, stealing his line. "You know who Rip Engel is, right?" she asked. "On Saxby's TV show?"

So now it was Saxby's TV show. "Yes, sure, I've talked to Rip several times."

Penelope's face went ripe tomato red.

"Well—"

Oh, God, Janzek thought, was it possible they were an item? Another January-December affair.

"Well, Rip and I recently had a relationship," she said. "But I think he was just using me. He's a very attractive young man, but I think the only money he has is the little bit he gets from the show."

"Mrs. Kuhn, does this have anything to do with the murder of D-Wayne Marion?"

"It has to do with Rip stealing my jewelry," Penelope said.

Janzek pushed his chair back and stood up. "Mrs. Kuhn, I'm sorry to hear about that, and I'd be happy to take you down to a detective who specializes in burglary. He's a good man and the best at what he does."

Penelope didn't move.

"There's a little twist to the story, which I think might be of interest to you."

Janzek suppressed a sigh. "Okay, what is it?"

"Actually... two twists, come to think of it."

Janzek put his hands on his desk. "What exactly do you mean by twists, Mrs. Kuhn?"

"Well, the first one is the fact that Rip has a pistol at his apartment that he got from Jessie Lawson."

Janzek sat back in his chair and said slowly. "You have my full, undivided attention, Mrs. Kuhn."

FIFTY-TWO

He listened to Penelope for the next ten minutes. Occasionally, he asked a question, but mainly he just paid very close attention.

Penelope had been "intimate," as she described it, with Rip for a few days when she noticed—just yesterday morning, in fact—that her best jewelry had disappeared. Specifically, a pair of 14-carat diamond studs, a pearl necklace, and a very pricey emerald brooch.

She confronted Rip and he vehemently denied knowing anything about it. The only other possible suspects, she said, were Moses Gronowski, her butler, and her cleaning lady, Hermina. But Moses had been with her for more than twenty years and Hermina, close to fifteen. There was no way either one was about to start stealing from her. They had too good a gig going.

It had to be Rip.

Penelope explained how she had gone to his apartment building yesterday afternoon, when she knew Rip would be shooting an episode of, *Charleston Buzz*. She pressed the buzzer of the building superintendent on the first floor, handed him a hundred-dollar bill and said she needed to get in to Rip's apartment. The super didn't hesitate.

It didn't take her long to find her stolen jewelry. It was in a top-drawer underneath Rip's socks. Right next to it was the pistol. Penelope took the jewelry and left the pistol.

Shortly after she left, she called Rip and told him about going to his apartment and finding her jewelry. She told him she was going to call the police and report it. At that point, Rip got extremely upset and poured out a long tale of woe.

He told her about his lifelong desire to run a restaurant. How it was his one dream in life. He told her about how he had broached the idea with D-Wayne Marion late one night, hoping that D-Wayne might back him in the venture.

While not agreeing to do so, D-Wayne apparently did not close the door to the possibility. He also told Rip that he would be happy to introduce him to his banker, who might be a possible source of funding. Rip put on his best suit and met with the banker, who was encouraging and gave Rip an application for a loan and various other paperwork. Rip called the banker a few days later and the banker gave him a verbal green light. He said the loan committee would meet the next day, but the banker was going to recommend that they approve the loan, and they always went along with what he recommended.

Then, Rip screwed up.

Big time.

He slept with Jessie, who had been going out with D-Wayne for a couple of weeks. D-Wayne found out because Rip had a big mouth and D-Wayne immediately put in a call to his banker friend and told him to pull the plug on Rip's restaurant loan.

The banker did not return Rip's calls, and when Rip finally went to his bank on Meeting Street, the banker apologized but told him that the loan committee had turned down his loan.

Rip was devastated. His restaurant dream had gone up in smoke.

So, after telling Penelope the story, Rip pleaded with her until she finally promised she wouldn't call the police. But, she said, she was curious: What was he doing with a pistol that—she observed— had real bullets in it? He explained that it wasn't his but was in fact Jessie Lawson's. When she asked him what he was doing with Jessie Lawson's pistol, he hemmed and hawed and changed the subject, admitting he had stolen Penelope's jewelry with the intent of selling it and getting the money he needed to stake a restaurant.

Penelope explained to Janzek that she had taken pity on Rip. To the point where she actually thought about lending him money to help finance the restaurant.

"I brought it up with my son," Penelope said.

"What did he say?" Janzek asked, not expecting Saxby to be too keen on the idea.

"He said, 'Not in a million years. You're not going to go blow my inheritance on that loser' were his exact words."

"So, what happened?"

"I told Rip that I had a friend who I know sometimes finances start-up companies," Penelope said. "The only problem was that I

185

heard he charges a very high interest rate or else wants a piece of the business."

"So, what did Rip say?"

"He said he didn't care," Penelope said. "He was so sure it was going to be successful that he didn't mind giving up a piece of it to get it off the ground."

Janzek was only paying half attention to her now. What he zeroed in on was Rip's motive to kill D-Wayne. And the gun.

D-Wayne had destroyed Rip's lifelong dream. Not only that, Rip had the pistol in his possession, which might have been the murder weapon in D-Wayne's death.

Janzek was amped up now. Between Cotton Kelly possibly being the woman in bed with D-Wayne and Rip being the possible shooter of D-Wayne, he was finally getting somewhere.

Penelope continued to drone on as Janzek's mind raced ahead.

"So, I gave Rip his phone number...."

It was a toss-up now. Who to go talk to next? Rip or Cotton Kelly.

He thought about calling Rhett and splitting them up but decided to handle both himself.

He looked back at Penelope. "I'm sorry, what were you saying? About a phone number?"

"Yes, I gave Rip my friend's phone number," Penelope said. "And Rip called him and thanked me; he said he had scheduled a meeting with him."

Janzek nodded, still trying to decide who to see first. "That's nice... and who is this person?"

"His name is Stanton Conger," she said. "Rip's going to meet with him tomorrow."

FIFTY-THREE

Based on Stanton Conger being in the mix, Janzek decided to see Rip first. He had read that *Charleston Buzz* was being shot on location now. And the location was—surprise, surprise—a bar.

Janzek parked, flashed ID to a man standing in his way at the front door of the bar and barreled right up to Holly Barrow. She was standing next to a cameraman, who was recording the scene from behind the bar.

"Hi, Holly," Janzek said.

She swung around. "This is a closed set," she said angrily. "In case you didn't notice, we're shooting a scene here."

He looked across the bar and saw Rip, the girl with the purple hair, Greg the bank teller, and Samantha Byrd all staring back at him.

Samantha winked and Rip shot him his goofy grin. "Hey, Nick."

Nick nodded at him, then turned back to Holly. "I need to talk to Rip."

"Are you crazy?" Holly said. "We're right in the middle of this."

"I'm sorry, but this is important police business."

"And this is important show business," Holly said.

"It won't take long."

"You'll have to wait until we've shot the scene."

Nick reached down and pulled the plug on the bank of camera lights.

"What the hell are you doing?" cried Holly, close to hysterical.

Janzek looked up at Rip. "Rip, I need to see you," he said, looking back at Holly. "Just five minutes."

Unless, of course, he arrested Rip for murder and took him down to the station. In which case, she'd have to find herself a new actor.

Rip looked caught between his boss and the law. "What do I do?" he asked Holly.

"Go with him," Holly said with a sigh.

Her angry-looking, pit bull assistant, Hudson Rock, had come up beside her now.

"But for Chrissakes, make it short," said Holly. "I'm paying fifteen people here union scale."

"This is totally outrageous," Hudson Rock piped in.

Janzek fought the urge to tell Hudson to go fuck himself and led Rip to a far corner of the room.

Janzek stopped, turned, and faced Rip. "My partner is at your apartment right now confiscating that Ruger Single Six you got from Jessie Lawson."

The goofy grin slid off Rip's face.

"O-kay,"

"I want to tell you a quick story that ends with a question."

"O-kay," Rip repeated.

"This guy was getting a friend to help get him a loan so he could fulfill his lifelong dream of opening a restaurant. Then the guy who wants to open the restaurant sleeps with the other guy's girlfriend, i.e., the girlfriend of the guy who's helping him get the loan. With me so far?"

Rip nodded.

"Not surprisingly, that guy puts the kibosh on the loan. So, the question is, is that a motive for the guy who wants to open the restaurant to kill the guy who killed his dream?"

Rip was blinking a lot. "I guess you might come to that conclusion, Nick," he said, "but here's the truth. I admit it, I was so pissed at D-Wayne maybe I *did* want to kill him. But then I go, hey, it was me who screwed-up, not him. I fuckin' well deserved it." He shrugged and tried hard to smile. "But also, do I really strike you as a guy capable of killing somebody? I mean, really?"

Janzek had pondered that on the way over, and no, he didn't.

"Then what the hell were you doing with that pistol? Jessie Lawson had it in a storage place... did you go there and steal it? Just like you stole Penelope Kuhn's jewels?"

Rip's head drooped. "You know about that, too?"

"Yeah, I know about it, but what about the gun? What were you doing with it?"

"Jessie gave it to me," he said slowly. "After we went shooting down on my plantation and I saw how good a shot she was. I asked her to teach me and she offered to lend me the pistol. You know, to practice with."

"Wait a minute, she told me she didn't know what happened to it," Janzek said. "Why would she lie about that?"

Rip shrugged. "I don't know, maybe... I really don't know..."

"Come on, you're holding out on me, Rip. You want me to take you in for burglary and suspicion of murder?"

Rip's eyes were darting around like he wanted to make a run for it.

Janzek leaned in close. "Hey, Rip, look at me. Tell me what's going on here. Did Jessie ever talk to you about killing D-Wayne? That's a yes or no question."

Reluctantly, Rip's eyes wandered back to his, fear and panic in them. Then he looked down again

"I said look at me," Janzek said again. "Did she, or didn't she?"

Rip's eyes tilted up.

"Once, at my place. We were kind of drunk and she brought it up,"

"Was she married to D-Wayne at the time?"

"Yes, it was when that whole thing about the post-nup came up."

"For God's sake," Janzek said, shaking his head, "You started up with her again, after she got married?"

Rip looked like a dog that had just been booted across a room.

"Yeah, it was kind of my way of getting back at D-Wayne, I guess."

"So, what did you say when she brought it up? About taking out D-Wayne."

"I said, 'no, are you crazy?' I mean, the whole idea was nuts. I just figured she was drunk and had no idea what she was saying."

Janzek was processing it slowly. But then, suddenly, it all made sense. It was something Jessie considered, but never acted on. Maybe because someone else beat her to it. Or maybe because she just didn't have it in her. But she no doubt figured, that if she dangled enough cash in front of Rip, he might consider doing it.

"Can we just keep this between us, Nick. I mean, I never seriously considered... Please don't bring it up with Jessie, will you?"

Obviously, Rip hadn't heard. Which meant nobody else on the set had either.

"I've got bad news for you," Janzek lowered his voice, "Jessie was found dead in her car earlier this morning."

Rip looked as though he wasn't sure he heard right. "Wait. What?"

"Somebody stabbed Jessie to death."

Rip's eyes got huge. "Are you kidding?" he blurted loudly.

Everyone on the other side of the room suddenly swung around and looked over at them.

"Jesus Christ, Jessie's dead!" Rip shouted so all could hear.

He slowly turned back to Janzek. "Christ. First D-Wayne, then Jessie..."

Janzek kept his voice low. "Tell you what I'm gonna do. I'm gonna forget I ever heard anything about the gun and the stolen jewelry, but only if you do something for me."

"Okay. What's that?"

"There's a gallery at State and Church. The Cotton Kelly Galley it's called. Take a look in there, see if the woman who runs the place is the same one you saw drop D-Wayne at the set that day."

"The one in the green convertible?"

Janzek nodded.

"I'll go there right after we're finished here."

"Don't let her see you, though."

Rip nodded as Holly approached them, her hand up to her mouth. "Oh, my God. What happened to her?" she asked Janzek.

"She was found stabbed to death in her car."

"Oh my God..." Holly said again. "Any idea who...?"

Janzek shook his head. "No, not yet."

Holly turned and walked away slowly, her head down. It looked like her clothes weighed a thousand pounds.

Janzek and Rip followed her.

Holly walked up to the cast and crew who were huddled together. "Okay, everybody, we're done for the day."

Hudson Rock looked alarmed. "But, Holly, you can't—"

"Shut up, Hudson," she said. "I just did."

FIFTY-FOUR

Cotton Kelly looked up from her desk at the back of her gallery as Janzek walked in.

"We're getting to be old friends, Detective," Cotton said. "I saw your picture in the paper."

Janzek had hoped he had put that behind him. "Ms. Kelly, I need to ask you a few more questions."

She started to roll her eyes but caught herself.

"Okay, go ahead."

He pulled a picture out the breast pocket of his jacket.

"First, have you ever watched *Charleston Buzz*?"

This time she did roll her eyes. "No, I haven't. It's on the same time as *Downton Abbey*, so it wasn't a tough decision to make."

Janzek nodded and handed her the picture of Jessie he had taken off the *Buzz* website. "Have you ever seen this woman before?"

Cotton took a fast glance and handed it back. "No."

"Never?"

"Never."

"You're absolutely sure? And she never came into your galley?"

"I'm absolutely sure, she did not."

Janzek eyed her closely for a few moments.

"Okay, Ms. Kelly," he said, putting the picture back in his jacket pocket, "thanks for your time."

$$*****$$

As Janzek was pulling into the police department parking lot, his phone rang.

"That's the woman, Nick, the one in the green convertible," Rip said. "I looked through the front door of the gallery. She didn't see me, but it definitely was her."

191

Janzek took a deep breath and pounded his steering wheel in triumph. "Thank you, Rip. Now try to keep your nose clean in the future, will ya?"

"I will."

"You'd better," he said, then remembering. "Hey, Penelope Kuhn told me you were going to be talking to a man named Stanton Conger about a business loan?"

"Yeah, I'm going to see him tomorrow. Why?"

"'Cause Stanton Conger is bad news. You should stay as far away from him as possible."

"Hey, man, money is money. And if he's the only guy who's gonna lend it, then I'm gonna at least talk to him."

"Look, I'm not your goddamn father, but I'm warning you. A guy like him gets his hooks into you, he might end up owning you."

"Thanks, but I gotta do what I gotta do."

Janzek hung up.

Something told him that Rip's meeting with Stanton Conger would have a bad ending.

FIFTY-FIVE

First thing he decided to do was check Cotton Kelly's Facebook page. As of about five years ago that had become a routine part of his job, part of his basic investigation technique. Cotton, he found out, had gone to Gethersburg High School in Gethersburg, Kentucky, then to the College of Charleston where she got a degree in Communications back in 2005. Her main picture on Facebook was a Warhol of three Elvises' drawing a gun. Janzek was pretty sure he read something about it selling for a gazillion dollars recently.

He scrolled down. He was looking for something in particular: a shot of Cotton with D-Wayne Marion maybe. Or something to make a liar out of her. But he didn't see D-Wayne in any of her photos or in her friend's pictures below.

He almost stopped at that point but scrolled a little further. Fact was, even though Janzek didn't have a Facebook page, he knew they could be pretty useful at getting a glimpse into someone else's head. Under her favorite Places, she had put down Asheville, North Carolina, St. Barths, and New York City—three places that seemed to have absolutely nothing in common.

Under Sports, nothing.

Under Music, Taylor Swift, James Taylor, and a band he'd never heard of called Shovels and Ropes. Under TV shows, *Big Little Lies, Dead to Me*, and *Euphoria*. Then he flipped over to Instagram and saw a photo of Cotton and an old man with a bow tie posed in her gallery. Alfred Hutty maybe? And another one of her with four women her age holding up half-empty wine glasses to the camera.

Then he looked down and saw another one of her posing with a man with wavy grey hair and a mole on his cheek.

Stanton Conger.

Janzek looked closer.

No doubt about it, Conger had his arm around her in more than a casual way. Possessive was more like it.

The light bulb popped on. What Sheila Lessing had told him.

About a woman who Stanton Conger met at the Boy's Club ten years before and married. He was ninety-five per cent sure that had to be Cotton Kelly. No ninety-nine per cent.

He called up Sheila and she answered right away. "Hello, Nick."

He was expecting her to answer the way she usually did. "Well, well, the prodigal son." Or, "he's alive," or some other wiseass way of pointing out that he either didn't call enough or only when he wanted something.

He decided to mix business with pleasure. He could use a break anyway. "So, I was thinking, don't I owe you a drink or dinner?"

"You owe me so much more than that, but I'll settle for a drink *and* dinner," she said. "Why don't you just come to my house, though. I'll cook you a steak. You being such a red-meat guy and all."

"I would love that... tonight?" he asked, even though he wasn't sure he could wait that long.

"Sure," she said, "say about seven?"

"Perfect," he said. "I'll bring a bottle of Whispering Angel rosé."

She had pretty simple tastes, despite the fact that she could afford a cellar full of Chateau Lafite Rothschild.

"Yes, that would be great," she said. "I'll see you then. I'm going to put you in charge of shucking the corn."

"Works for me," he said, "best damn shucker in South Carolina."

FIFTY-SIX

He had shucked the corn and made sure that there was not even one single strand of corn silk left on all four ears. His mother had been a real stickler about that. Still was, actually.

They were in Sheila's kitchen, which probably cost more than most houses in Charleston. Sheila was not ostentatious in any way, but she did like to cook and had a kitchen that featured every bell and whistle known to culinary science.

Janzek had decided he was going to lay low in the weeds and, he hoped anyway, slowly reel Sheila in. He wasn't about to come right out and ask his first burning question: Was Cotton Kelly... Mrs. Stanton Conger?'

She had a glass of white wine in her hand as she approached Janzek. He had just put the four ears of corn down on a serving plate.

"Good, job," she said. "But I'm only going to have one. Think you can eat three."

"Umm, I've been known to eat six. Sure you're not going to want a second?"

"No, thanks, one's plenty. So, what's new on the D-Wayne front? I haven't read anything new lately." He crept out of the reeds, thinking, 'so glad you asked.'

"Well, we're making progress, but we're not quite there yet," he said. "That guy we talked about last time, Stanton Conger? What's his wife's name?"

"Same as his yacht," Sheila said. "High Cotton."

Of course, he hadn't made the connection. How'd he miss that? He was really slipping.

"And she's the one he met at the Boy's Club?"

"Yup, at the time he was married to a friend of mine, LeeLee Limehouse. I remember her coming to me one morning and saying

195

Stanton wanted a divorce. I said she was better off without that sleazeball and gave her the name of a scrappy attorney."

"And what happened?"

"It was bloody. Stanton turned the tables and accused her of having an affair with this guy who was giving her riding lessons. The guy testified they used to ride naked in the woods.... on the same horse."

"That's creative."

"Yeah, can you believe it? I think he was just another guy Stanton paid to say what he told him to say. Anyway, so LeeLee went way back and dredged up Stanton's past. Starting with when he was back at Chapel Hill and supposedly selling dope with that guy who just got killed."

"Whoa, whoa, slow down," Janzek said, leaning forward and putting both hands on her shoulders. "What guy who just got killed?"

"I forget his name. It was in the paper. Down in Hilton Head."

"Lex Murray?"

"Yeah, that's him. He and Stanton were in the same fraternity together. LeeLee told me Lex Murray was this wild guy who got into drugs, then started selling them to friends. Next thing you know he dropped out, went down to Miami, and a couple years later was this major dealer."

"Yeah, okay, but what did Conger have to do with it?"

"Well, so the story goes anyway, he inherited some money from his grandfather when he turned twenty-one. And Murray talked him into blowing grandpa's dough on a big shipment of pot. The way I heard it, it was enough to keep both the Chapel Hill and Duke campuses high for a whole semester."

Janzek shook his head. "Wow, no kidding?"

"So eventually, like ten years later, Lex Murray finally got caught and went to jail for a long time."

"By then, I'm guessing, Conger had cut his ties with him?"

"Yes, that's what LeeLee said. But Stanton was his original backer. Made it possible for Murray to go from small time to big time in a hurry. Supposedly Murray bought a boat with some of the money Stanton fronted him. After a while he had a whole fleet of boats. Planes, too."

"You got all this from his ex-wife?"

"Yup," Sheila said. "Then, later on, I heard pretty much the same story from a guy who was on the board of one of my companies. He was in the same fraternity as Stanton. Place was pretty infamous for bad boys. A few of them who grew up to be bad men, by the way. Supposedly they all got into the cocaine pretty good back then. Stanton included, I heard."

"Is he in Charleston, the guy on your board? I'd like to talk to him."

"Charlie Peck, yeah, I'll give you his number. He lives just a couple blocks from here."

"So, okay, back to Stanton's divorce from LeeLee Limehouse…"

"What do you want to know about it?"

"Well, did anything else come out?"

"Not really," Sheila said, raising her hand. "Hold on, wait a sec, that's not true. It came out that Stanton tried to hide a lot of the real estate he owned in LLC's. LeeLee's badger dug around and tracked it all down, though. She made out all right in the end… after both of them had chalked up a million or so in legal fees that is."

"So, then Stanton married Cotton and I'm guessing set her up with the gallery?"

"Yes, exactly. To her credit, she wanted to do something more than join the ladies-who-lunch bunch, aka, the Charleston gossip queens. I guess she's not exactly a sit-around-the-house kind of gal."

"So then, what kind of a *gal* is she?"

"One who likes men," Sheila shook her head. "Okay, enough. You got me gossiping and nothing I hate more than a gossip."

"Come on, what else?"

Sheila smiled and shook her head.

"This is really important," Janzek said. "You told me about the Charleston rumor mill. How it gets the news before it even happens. She ever on its radar screen?"

Sheila stood. "Come on, let's eat," she said. "That's really all I know about her. She likes men… so do I. So, shoot us."

"That's all I'm getting, huh?"

She smiled and nodded as if she was dealing with a naughty boy.

"You're bad," she said. "Here's my final statement on the matter: I just heard a thing or two, but my impression is Cotton's pretty discreet. And if you're discreet in this town, sometimes you can slip under the radar. I did notice at a cocktail party once that Stanton watched her like a hawk. Like if she talked to another man, he'd shoot right over. You know, practically muscle in between 'em."

Janzek wanted to call up Delvin Rhett and fill him in on the two bombshells right away. His instinct was he needed to get together with Rhett as soon as possible and work on a plan to try to take down Conger. Once and for all.

But it was eight o'clock at night and he was sitting at a table with an incredible dinner and one of the best-looking woman in Charleston sitting across from him.

Janzek didn't want to press his luck with Sheila, push the Stanton Conger Q & A too far. Because pretty soon Sheila, a famously smart woman, was going to catch on and realize the primary purpose of him coming there was to pump her for information. But the fact was, he enjoyed her company and there was no one he'd rather be with.

"So, enough about Stanton Conger, tell me about your day?" he asked.

*****

After dinner, they decided to watch a movie on HBO. Janzek was almost certain they'd never get to the end of it. They had been down this road before. As Sheila played around with the clicker next to him on the sofa, Janzek told her he had to make a quick call. He couldn't help himself. He got Rhett on the second ring and asked him to meet him the next morning at seven o'clock at the office. He told him they had a lot to talk about and left it at that.

Fifteen minutes into the movie, Janzek put his arm around Sheila's shoulder. Ten minutes later he leaned in and kissed her. Three minutes after that they were going at it like two teenagers at a drive-in. Three minutes after that Janzek was unhooking her bra. A minute later she was helping him off with his pants. Forty-five seconds after that they were both naked and back to kissing—with a vengeance.

Then Sheila pulled back and looked him in the eyes. "Right here?" was all she said.

"Sure, why not."

*****

Usually after three drinks or so Janzek had no problem nodding off. And usually when he threw sex into the mix, he went right out. But not tonight, or more accurately, not at this early morning hour. Too much was slamming around in his head—Cotton and Stanton Conger being married, Conger and Lex Murray being former business partners, the brutal murder of Jessie Lawson, just for starters.

Finally, Janzek slipped quietly out of Sheila's bed and walked downstairs. He went into her library, which had books from floor to ceiling on one entire wall, then he plunked down in his favorite chair and just let his mind go.

In addition to everything else swirling around, it was a damn good bet that Galen Parris was behind the killing of Jim Ray Glover. His prints all over Glover's boat could be explained away because he and Glover fished a lot. But not the full gas can that Leon Rhett had delivered to Parris. No, that was definitely all about covering up the murder of Glover. So, the question was... was Parris a guy who Stanton Conger went to for his dirty work. It sure looked that way.

An hour and a half later Janzek crept back upstairs, having mapped out a plan of attack in his head. He pulled the covers up and slid back under the sheets.

"Got everything all figured out?" Sheila asked.

"You're a light sleeper."

"No," she said. "I just wake up when it's time for more fooling around."

FIFTY-SEVEN

Even with three hours of sleep, Janzek felt better than he had in a while. Well-fed and, well, well-satisfied.

He slipped out of the bed without waking Sheila, took a quick shower, got dressed, and was in his office at the station by seven.

Rhett showed up at 7:10, his usual container of Black Tap coffee glued to his hand.

"Morning, Nick," he said. "So, today's the day?"

"Yeah, time to wrap it up."

He proceeded to tell Rhett about Conger and Cotton, and Conger and Lex Murray.

"Okay," Rhett said, "so Conger and Murray is easy. Conger knew Murray had stashed a bunch of drug money before he got shipped off to a six-by-ten at MacDougall. Figured he had a right to it since he bankrolled Murray in the first place. So, after Murray gets out, Conger puts his guy Jim Ray on it, then when Murray digs up the buried treasure, Jim Ray says, 'thank you very much,' pops him, takes the money, and fills in the hole."

Rhett nodded. "Okay, but what's your read on why Galen Parris hit the hitter—his old fishing buddy, Jim Ray?"

"That's easy," Janzek said. "First, 'cause Parris knows Conger, and Conger hires him to do his dirty work. Second 'cause Jim Ray maybe got greedy when he got his hands on the twelve mill. Almost like it was his."

Rhett started nodding. "I'm with you. So, Jim Ray sees it all and thinks, based on all Conger's gonna get, 'it's time to renegotiate my contract'."

"Something like that," Janzek said. "Conger's probably paying him the standard hit rate—whatever the hell that might be, twenty-five K or so—but Jim Ray figures he should get a hell of a lot more than that. He's like, 'I'm getting this guy twelve mill and all I get is a measly twenty-five K. That ain't right.'"

200

"Or maybe," Rhett said, "he could have gotten even more ambitious. Know what I mean?"

Janzek nodded. "You mean, tried to take it all?"

"Yeah," Rhett said. "Wouldn't you be tempted?"

Janzek nodded. "Damn right I would. I'd be on the first plane out of there, suitcase full of cash."

"Yeah, but Jim Ray's a little slower than you," Rhett said. "So, anyway, Parris and Jim Ray end up in the boat together."

"Yeah, probably right after Conger calls Parris and says, get rid of this guy, he's getting greedy. And the rest, as they say, is history."

"So, what do you think the Conger-Parris relationship is?"

"Don't know. My guess is he's done stuff for Conger before. Maybe his go-to for big jobs. But as far as killin' D-Wayne goes, I figure that was Conger solo."

Rhett was nodding. "So, Conger walked in on D-Wayne and Cotton doing the nasty. Put one between his eyes?"

Janzek pointed a finger at Rhett. "Yup. Exactly."

Rhett nodded and gazed out the window.

"A friend of mine told me Stanton's got a big-time jealous streak," Janzek leaned back in his chair and looked up at the ceiling. "Ever notice how the ones who fuck around the most are always the most jealous ones."

"Yeah, 'cause they figure everyone's just like them. They don't trust a fuckin' soul."

"Bingo," Janzek said. "So, while we're floating all these theories, here's an obvious one: Jessie shows up at Cotton's galley to ID Cotton. Cotton sees she recognizes her, calls Stanton in a panic, and Stanton gets his guy to crawl on out of that roach motel of his."

"So, you figure that was Parris, too?"

"Probably," Janzek said. "Though maybe Conger has a couple of guys."

Rhett shook his head. "Seems like Conger and his lowlifes had a pretty busy couple of days."

Janzek rapped his hand on his desk and eyeballed Rhett. "Yeah, and now it's time to put 'em all out of business."

Rhett leaned toward him, itching for action. "So, you got a plan?"

"Just so happens, I do."

FIFTY-EIGHT

Janzek's next stop was the office of Charlie Peck, the man who'd served on the board of Sheila Lessing's company. He went alone because Rhett was meeting with the North Charleston crime-scene techs in charge of the Jessie Lawson homicide scene. Janzek had called Peck from his office at nine o'clock that morning and said that Sheila Lessing suggested he call. Peck said he'd be happy to make time for Janzek.

It was a little before eleven when Janzek got to the stockbroker's office on Broad Street. Peck looked to be in his late fifties, had bushy salt and pepper hair, and wore a seersucker suit with a bow tie. He stood out from the other men in the office who looked younger and didn't wear jackets or ties.

Janzek followed Peck back to his office. "How do you know Sheila?" Peck asked.

Janzek had never been asked the question before—mainly because he kept their relationship tightly under wraps—and was unprepared.

"Oh, ah, we belong to the same… book club."

Lame, he thought, disappointed at not being able to do better.

"Really?" was all Peck said as he sat down behind his desk. He gestured to the chair in front of him. "So, Detective, how can I help you?"

Janzek dived right in, wanting to put the book-club reference as far as possible behind him.

"As I'm sure you heard, or read maybe, a man named Lex Murray was killed in Hilton Head a few days ago. Ms. Lessing said you went to college with him."

"Yeah, poor old Lex. King of the party boys at Chapel Hill."

"She mentioned you were in the same fraternity."

Peck shook his head. "No, actually, I was a Phi Delta, Lex was a Deke. But, still, we crossed paths a lot."

"And Stanton Conger," Janzek said, "what about him?"

"He was a Deke, too. I guess Sheila told you he and Lex were roommates."

Janzek leaned forward and put a hand on Peck's desk. "Mr. Peck, what can you tell me about Murray and Conger dealing drugs back then?"

Peck exhaled loudly and thought for a second.

"Well, I prefer not to talk about Stanton. Seeing how he's an acquaintance of mine—" Janzek noticed he didn't say 'friend'—"but I can tell you about Lex. I think it started out as a lark for him. Girls kind of went for the outlaw thing. Know what I mean?"

"I think so. The way I heard it was Conger put up the initial money, but wasn't really involved in the day-to-day. Is that accurate?"

"Like, I said, I don't really want to talk about Stan—"

"Then maybe you can just confirm this for me. Ms. Lessing told me Conger funded Murray's little endeavor."

Peck leaned back. "Well, Sheila's a pretty reliable source. You might say unimpeachable."

"So, it's true then, about Conger fronting the money?"

"I would never contradict anything Sheila Lessing said. But far as Lex goes, he started skipping classes after a while. He was totally into his new... endeavor. Like I said, he liked playing the outlaw. First guy with a motorcycle, first guy to grow his hair long. You know, one of those kind of guys."

"And what about Conger?"

"You are persistent," Peck said, leaning forward, and putting his hands together.

"None of this is for attribution, is that understood?" Peck said, sitting down again.

"Of course."

"Okay, well, Stan kind of liked to think of himself as the brains behind the operation. The big-picture guy, the guy who came up with the thing in the first place. Which, as I recall, wasn't the case. I think it was pretty much Murray's baby from the git-go. Anyway, within a couple of months they owned the UNC and Duke campuses. You wanted a nickel bag; you went to Lex. You wanted to do a few lines of coke; you went to Lex."

"So, what was Conger doing?"

"Not much," Peck said. "The way I remember it, he still got a cut. But Lex was doing all the heavy lifting, taking all the risk, and after a while I think he just thought, 'What the hell do I need Stan for?'"

"But Conger felt that since he was there in the beginning," Janzek said, "he should get half? Is that kind of—"

"—Yeah, I'd say that's about right. Before Lex got big, there was this other dealer, who was doin' it before them. Not a college guy." Peck shook his head and his eyes narrowed as he remembered.

"So, what happened to him?" Janzek asked.

"I don't know exactly. Story was the guy got beat up really bad. Way I remember it, a broken arm, stitches all over his face, and a dislocated jaw or something. That kind of curtailed his activities. Put him out of business for good, actually. Word was that Stan got his football player friend to do it."

"The football player friend? He got a name?"

"Yeah. Sheila didn't tell you about him?"

"No. I'm not sure she knew about him."

"Well, anyway, he was a guy on scholarship, played half back for the Tarheels. Got to be friends with Murray and Conger, but, like Lex, never graduated," Peck said. "Ended up here in Charleston. I see him around every once in a while. Works for Conger actually. Has for a long time. Manages a bunch of his buildings."

"What's his name?" Janzek knew the answer.

Peck scratched his chin and blinked a few times. "Parris," he said, "Galen Parris."

FIFTY-NINE

The connection between Stanton Conger and Galen Parris filled in a lot of holes. Janzek punched in Rhett's number on his cell.

"Yeah, Nick, what's up?"

"Just got a game-changer. Talked to a guy who went to college with Conger. Turns out Conger and Galen Parris went to college together."

"Parris?" Rhett said. "He seems more like reform-school material from what you told me."

"Yeah, well, he never got his sheepskin. Guy told me he spent his junior year in a foreign-exchange program. In Columbia. Running dope."

Rhett laughed. "Sounds about right."

"Turns out Conger and Lex Murray, another classmate of theirs, started this little drug operation their sophomore year."

"Ho-ly shit!"

"Yeah, Conger was the money man and Murray did the work. This guy told me what he heard was that at some point Murray cut Conger loose; said he didn't need him anymore. Apparently, that didn't go down too well with Conger."

"Wow, this guy was a gold mine."

"Yeah, sure was," Janzek said. "So, I need you to take a photo of Parris to your brother. Confirm that's the guy he took the gas can to."

"Yeah, okay. It's all starting to fall into place now. Conger got Parris to hire Jim Ray to take out their old college buddy, Murray. Then Jim Ray tried to hold them up for more money. Either that or tried to take off with the whole twelve mill—"

"Or, another possibility, maybe Conger just got nervous having Jim Ray know he was the guy who ordered the hit. Worried Jim Ray might let it slip after a couple of drinks or something."

"I hear you," Rhett said. "Why take a chance? So much easier just to pop the guy, torch his boat and be done with it."

*****

Janzek had decided he needed to *wander off the reservation.* That was Rhett's description for when Janzek resorted to something not quite by the book and definitely not in the police manual. First, he called Rip Engel and got him on board, then he went and dropped in on Holly Barrow at the SLAM! Offices on upper King Street. They went into the conference room and sat down. He explained that he was sorry to tell her but because of a certain occurrence—which he said he couldn't go into because it was a police matter—he needed to keep Rip in custody for at least a few days.

Her reaction was everything he hoped for and more. She flew off the handle and said he couldn't do that because Rip was integral to several scenes that were being shot in the next few days. It would cost thousands of dollars to postpone the shooting of those scenes, she said.

"Come on, Nick, gimme a break," she implored, her hands together as if in prayer.

He paused, long and dramatically.

"Please," she said.

"I don't know, Holly, I'd like to help you out but—"

"Please," she said again, then, like a light bulb clicked on over her head. "What if... how 'bout if I paid you to let Rip work, then you can put him in police custody next week. How would that be?"

Janzek cocked his head and smiled. "Holly, I'm shocked. What you've just suggested, sounds like a textbook description of a bribe."

"I-I didn't mean the money would go to you, maybe to the police department or, you know, the South Carolina Film Commission or—"

Janzek held up his hands. "Tell you what—" Holly's eyes sparkled with hope. "If you can do something for me, maybe I can return the favor."

"Oh, yes, just name it."

"Better not say that until you hear what it is."

"What is it?"

"Well, you know how you and Hudson planted that story in the paper about the cameras in your cast member's bedrooms?"

"That was Hudson."

"Okay, whatever, I need you—or Hudson, I don't care—to do the same thing again."

At that point Hudson walked into the conference room. He took one look at his boss' face and knew something was wrong.

"Everything okay?"

"Yeah, yeah, fine," Holly said impatiently, "keep going Nick."

"So anyway, it's just an innocent little story—" Janzek pulled a piece of paper out of his jacket pocket and slid it over to Holly.

Holly started reading it, Hudson craning his neck over her shoulder.

"I'm sure your source at the *City Paper* might find it newsworthy. Maybe add a few of his own touches."

"It's a she," Holly said, looking up from reading what Janzek had written.

"You can't tell me she won't love to have this scoop," Janzek said.

"But it's not true," said Holly.

"Details," said Janzek.

Rock looked outraged. "We can't have our names associated with—"

"Shut up, Hudson," Holly said.

"You got a real short memory, Hud," Janzek said.

Hudson bit his lip.

Holly smiled at Janzek. "I've got to hand it to you detective. You have a very devious side to you."

"Thank you," Janzek said. "Coming from you, that's a huge compliment."

"You came in to horse-trade from the git-go, didn't you?"

Janzek thought for a second. "I prefer to call it making a mutual accommodation."

"As in I scratch your back, you scratch mine?'

"If that's what you want to call it, I'm good with that."

Hudson just scowled.

*****

From the SLAM! offices on King Street, Janzek went to Cotton Kelly's gallery on State and Church. By now, he could almost get there blindfolded. He walked in at just past one. The other times he'd been there, he'd yet to see a paying customer. Obviously, Cotton didn't have to rely on the gallery to put food on her table.

Cotton was straightening out an Alfred Hutty painting of three black women talking in the foreground with what he guessed was a cotton field in the background. Janzek came up behind her, and she swung around and eyed him with a combination of irritation and weariness.

"You've become quite the regular, Detective. Sure wish I could foist off a few paintings on you."

"Sorry, not on my pay check," he said with a smile. "I just have two questions, Ms. Kelly. By the way, do you ever go by Mrs. Conger?"

She frowned. "Is that one of them?"

"No."

"Okay, the answer is sometimes I do. Why?"

"Just curious," he said. "The first question is, do you have a green Maserati convertible?"

He knew the answer, having called Motor Vehicle on his way over. The woman there said a green Maserati convertible was registered to Cotton Kelly. Right after that, he called Rip Engel and asked him if he was sure that the car he saw was an Aston Martin? Rip answered that he wasn't sure. *Could it have been a Maserati?* Janzek had asked. *Maserati… Aston Martin*, Rip had said. *What's the diff?*

"Yes, as a matter of fact, I do," Cotton said. "Why do you ask?"

"Because you were seen driving it to the set of *Charleston Buzz* last week, dropping off D-Wayne Marion."

"Je-sus, that again? You're wearing me out. I told you before I never met the man."

"I have an eyewitness who says it definitely was you."

She put her hands on her hips and dialed up a frosty, belligerent look. Eyes, squinty, her lower lip was rolled up over her upper one. "Well, I gotta tell you, your eyewitness has really shitty eyesight, my friend."

For the first time, Janzek could hear the coal-country Kentucky twang in her voice.

"And you still deny knowing Marion, or having spent time with him?"

"Absolutely."

"And you've never been to his house on Stolls Alley?"

She shook her head. "You got the wrong girl, detective. And that was your third question," she said, her eyes burning. "I understand you went and accused my husband of something he never did, too."

"Trust me, he did it. That and a whole lot more."

She set her jaw and gave him a nasty smirk. "You're heavy on accusations, but real light on proof."

Janzek was tempted to pull out his camera and show Cotton her husband and his sixteen-year-old friend on the *High Cotton*. But he didn't see what it would gain him.

Cotton just shook her head. "Almost seems like you got a thing against the Conger family."

He smiled. "I just have a thing against murder."

At first, she just shook her head very slowly, then she summoned up a look she might fix on a cockroach that had just skittered across the floor.

God, he was sick of all her headshaking and pained looks. He cautioned himself... *be professional, don't react.*

Fuck it, he thought. *Not today.* "Mrs. Conger, I understand you met your husband back when you were a student at the College of Charleston," he said. "And I understand you belonged to a sorority on Bull Street. I think they call it the Boy's Club."

`The headshaking stopped. She ratcheted up her look from mere belligerent to pure, unadulterated hatred.

"Get out of my gallery," she growled, reaching for her cell phone. "I'm gonna call my husband and tell him all about this."

"Good," Janzek said, "saves me the call."

SIXTY

One of Janzek's morning rituals was to go to the Krispy Kreme on Meeting Street, get coffee and a couple of doughnuts then grab a copy of the *Post & Courier* and the *City Paper* on his way out. It was a little out of the way, but he liked the people who worked there, and it had a very comfortable, albeit colossally ugly, green sofa to read the paper on.

Today, he varied his routine. Forgoing coffee and doughnuts, he went straight to the stack of daily newspapers and sat down in the ugly, green sofa.

And there—in screaming, twelve-point type—it was. As welcome to him as the picture of him with the three women had been unwelcome a few days before.

He took great pride in making the front page of the *City Paper* in his first attempt as a ghost reporter. The paper hadn't changed a word of his headline: *Who Shot D-Wayne*? it asked. But the reporter, Holly Barrow's contact at the paper, had made several changes that, Janzek had to admit, improved the article. *The producers of the SLAM! Network reality TV show, Charleston Buzz, have made an interesting discovery: they may hold the key to who murdered David Wayne Marion, one of the shows principal characters. A producer of the show, who requested anonymity, disclosed that SLAM! had a stationary camera mounted in a corner of the living room of Marion's apartment at the time of his death. Footage from the camera shows a man walking into the house on the night Marion was killed, although the camera angle is from the side and the resolution is somewhat grainy. According to the producer, the twenty-second segment of film will appear in the next episode of the show. As they say in show business, stay tuned.*

That last line was his, too. Damn, he was proud.

Janzek stood up and went and got his coffee, but this time, got six donuts to go with it.

Delvin Rhett was at the station when Janzek got there. He had the *City Paper* on his desk.

He raised his container of coffee in a toast. "Guess you know what you can do if you ever get sick of catching killers."

"You mean, look out Woodward and Bernstein."

"Were you a journalism major at Boston College, Nick?"

"History... which got me far," Janzek said. "Learned stuff like when the War of 1812 took place."

It took Rhett a second, then he smiled. "Good one."

Janzek sat down across from Rhett. "So, we better get ready for the blow back on the story."

"What do you mean?"

"Everyone sayin', 'how come you guys haven't caught the killer when there's a tape of him goin' into the house?'"

"We better tell Ernie it was bogus." Rhett pointed at the newspaper.

"Already did."

"What did he say?"

"I tried to sell him that it was a way to flush out the killer."

"And he bought it?"

"Let's just say... he didn't fire me. I kind of wore him down. I think he's got a problem with some of my crime-solving techniques."

"What exactly did he say?"

"Threw around the word 'rogue' a lot," Janzek said. "I been called worse."

Rhett smiled wide. You could see a gold tooth way back in there. "By the way, I stationed a guy outside the SLAM! office, like you suggested. Told him a little while ago we'd be coming over to relieve him pretty soon."

"Good," Janzek said. "Hopefully Conger's gonna send a couple of guys to get the tape. Bust into the office, grab 'n go."

"You don't think he'll read the article and think it's too late?"

"Why?"

"Well, 'cause he'll probably figure we read the article, too. And we're on our way to get the tape?"

"I thought about that," Janzek said. "Way I see it is, he'll figure they'll be a step ahead of us. Figure we'll read it, but then we gotta go to a judge, get a warrant to confiscate the tape."

Rhett nodded. "I'm with you," he said. "And maybe the judge is out on the golf course or something, so it's not 'til tomorrow 'til we get our asses over there."

"Yeah, something like that," Janzek said. "We're like the big tanker that takes a couple miles to turn around."

"So, you're guessin' they'll swing into action fast."

"Yeah," Janzek said, standing up, "which means we should get our asses over there."

Rhett stood up, too. "Only question I got is, if we catch 'em in the act, where's that really get us? Not like we can put 'em away for long on just a B&E."

"Agreed. We catch 'em, max we got is armed robbery. But what we really have is confirmation. Confirmation Conger's our guy. Then we gotta figure out a way to take him down. Most obvious way is to get the guys we catch to flip. Tell 'em they're looking at five years, then throw 'em a plea. Guys have been known to flip for a whole lot less than that."

"Assuming we catch 'em," Rhett said.

Janzek looked at his watch. "Hey, there's no guarantee. If this doesn't work, then it's your turn to come up with something," he said, grabbing the box of donuts. "All right. Let's head over there, knock back a few donuts, see who shows up."

SIXTY-ONE

Janzek finished off a jelly donut on the way over and had a tiny burgundy stain on his blue shirt to show for it. Rhett parked in an alley off Liberty Street, from which they had a perfect view of SLAM!'s second-story office.

From 7:45 to 8:50, all they saw was a three-legged cat snoop around a trio of garbage cans that were sealed too tightly for the feline's liking. Janzek watched it finally skulk off and go up a fire escape looking for other nourishment possibilities.

Janzek looked at his watch a few minutes later. 9:05.

"I don't know, Delvin, it was a good try but—"

Suddenly, the cat arched its back and flew back down the fire escape, disappearing behind the garbage cans. Janzek looked higher up on the fire escape and saw what had startled the cat: a man crouching on the metal structure, his back to them. He was a big man and wore a black T-shirt and beige-colored gloves, which contrasted with his tanned arms.

Janzek touched Rhett's shoulder and pointed.

Rhett looked up, nodded. "What's he got in his hand?"

"Looks like a gas can."

On cue, the man lifted the red can and, with both hands, splashed it on the wooden back wall of the building. Still in a crouch, he moved a few steps to his right and splashed more gas on the wall in front of him. Then he set the gas can down and reached into his pocket.

"Let's go!" Janzek flung open the car door and drew his Sig Sauer.

The man heard the noise and swung around. He had a nylon stocking over his face under a black baseball cap.

"Hold it right there," Janzek said. "Hands up and get down here."

The man, a wooden match in his hand, stood up and started running up the fire escape.

"Shit," Janzek said, sprinting towards the fire escape, "I'm too old for this."

He got onto the fire escape, with Rhett right behind him. The man jumped to the roof of the building next door and disappeared from sight.

Janzek and Rhett ran up along the fire escape, then, following the man's lead, jumped onto the roof next door.

As Janzek landed, his ankle twisted, and he winced in pain. "Shit!" He stood and put some weight on it, but he wasn't going anywhere.

"Gotta sit this out, Del. Go get the son of a bitch."

Rhett was off like a shot.

"Hold it!" Janzek heard Rhett yell from the other side of the peaked roof.

Janzek slowly inched his way up to the top of the roof and looked down. At the far end of a long slope of black tar roofing, he saw Rhett dive at the man. It was a tackle worthy of a linebacker on the football team of the Citadel, Rhett's alma mater. The man went down and his face skidded along the roof's surface. The pair stopped just short of the roof's edge, and Rhett had his handcuffs out in a flash.

He cuffed the man's right hand, then yanked back his left one and slid the other cuff onto it and clicked it shut. Quick and neat.

Janzek heard Rhett recite the Miranda as the man remained facedown and silent. Then Rhett reached up, pulled off the man's baseball cap, then tugged at his neck and yanked up the torn nylon.

"Know this dude?" Rhett shouted up to Janzek.

"Sure do," Janzek said. "Goes by name of Gay Paree, to his friends."

SIXTY-TWO

Janzek had a twisted ankle but still felt pretty good.

He was sitting across from Galen Parris in the soft room. Parris had a skinned nose and seriously wounded pride—the natural reaction of a six-foot-four, two hundred sixty-pound redneck being taken down by a five-eight, one hundred seventy-pound black man.

Delvin Rhett was sitting next to Janzek, just to rub it in Parris's face who was responsible for him being in custody. Janzek was surprised Parris hadn't demanded to make his phone call yet.

"You're not gonna be able to torch anything for a long time," Janzek said.

"Hey, I was trespassing," Parris growled, "a fuckin' wrist-slap."

"I don't think so, Galen," Janzek said. "Try attempted arson. Then I expect we can tie you to the fire on your buddy, Jim Ray Glover's boat. I noticed you used the same kind of gas can. Jury'd see a lot of similarities. We also got a photo of you swimming away from Jim Ray's boat. One of the guys who put out the fire took it. Swimmer had the exact same Dumb and Dumber haircut as you."

Rhett didn't react to his partner's ad lib. He was getting used to Janzek making it up on the fly. Rhett just kept staring at Parris, who was blinking more than usual.

"I don't know what you're talking about," Parris said.

"Hey, man," Janzek said, holding up his cell phone. "You can keep denying everything, but pictures don't lie."

Parris eyed him long and hard.

"You want to see it?" Janzek bluffed.

"Nah," Parris said, turning away. "Big fuckin' deal, so you got a picture."

"Not just any picture," Janzek said. "Guarantee you a jury's gonna find it a 'big fuckin' deal.' A guy trying to torch a building on King Street in broad daylight?"

215

"I figure the DA's gonna throw in attempted murder, too," Rhett said.

"What the hell you talkin' about?" Parris said.

"There were people in that building," Rhett said, "People you could have burned up."

"That's such bull—"

"So, long story short," said Rhett. "You're screwed, my brutha."

Parris scowled. "I got no clue what you're talking about."

"Talking about offering you a plea," Janzek said. "You give up somebody, we go easy on you. I think you know who we mean."

"Yeah, guy from your old alma mater," Rhett said. "Lex Murray's former drug-running partner and, by the way, a guy who doesn't like people who can finger him."

Parris just sighed and looked away.

"May be too subtle for you, but what my partner is pointing out is what happens to people who get on the wrong side of Stanton Conger," Janzek said.

"Four people, in particular," Rhett said. "First D-Wayne Marion, then Lex Murray, then Jim Ray, and, finally, Jessie Lawson."

"It's a long list," Rhett said. "And, for all we know, there may be a few more we don't know about yet."

Parris glared at him.

"Let me make it real clear to you," Janzek said. "You're next on Stanton's hit parade. See the pattern is, he doesn't like it when people have secrets on him."

"Just being here with us is a big problem for you," said Rhett. "Conger tends to believe in that old adage, loose lips sink ships."

"Imagine what he'll do to a guy who can point a finger at him," Janzek said.

"Imagine? He doesn't need to imagine," Rhett said. "Galen's seen this movie a couple of times."

"Good point," Janzek said. "Doing a long bit in jail's probably the safest place to be."

"Unless, of course, Conger gets to a guy inside."

Janzek nodded. "Gee, I never thought of that."

Parris rubbed the side of his head, then looked hard at Janzek. "Are you assholes done?"

"Yeah, just about," Janzek said. "One last question, how's it feel to be on deck?"

"The hell you talkin' about?"

"Next on Conger's list?"

Parris glared at Janzek. "I want to call my lawyer."

*****

"Shit," Janzek said, pounding his desk, forty-five minutes later.

Galen Parris had just bonded out. The same lawyer who had sprung Stanton Conger a few days before.

"Hey, it's not so bad, man. We got the bug in his car," Rhett said, sitting across from Janzek in his office. "I thought the thing about the photo of Parris swimming away from the boat was an inspired touch."

"Yeah, well, look where it got me," Janzek said. "The guy still bonded out."

"But I guarantee you he's got a lot more to think about now."

Janzek looked up and smiled. "I liked your attempted-murder thing, too. Why didn't I think of that?"

"You can't have all the good ideas."

Janzek smiled. "And, by the way, I didn't have a chance to mention it, but that was one helluva tackle on the roof top."

"Thanks," Rhett said. "So, we didn't get Parris, but we still got Conger wondering whether we can make him on that tape you invented."

"Yeah, I know," Janzek said, nodding.

"You think he's gonna try again... to get the tape?"

"Nah," Janzek said, staring out his window. "I figure right now he's workin' on his story. Like maybe he'll say he went to D-Wayne's house 'cause he suspected D-Wayne was sleeping with his wife. Goes there, find them in bed together, cusses out D-Wayne, grabbed his wife, and goes home. End of story."

"Sounds about right," Rhett said.

Janzek didn't say anything for a few moments.

"What are you thinkin'?" Asked Rhett.

"I don't know, the more I think about it, the more Galen looks like the ticket. Between us and the prosecutor, we just gotta keep the heat on him. Make him think we're gonna go after him hard with what we got. Throw everything at him. Also, keep reminding him what Conger does to people who try to screw him over."

217

SIXTY-THREE

The bug in Parris's car paid off.

Parris called Conger an hour later. The bug only caught Parris's side of the conversation. But it was enough.

"Fuckin' caught me in the act," Parris said.

Pause.

"Easy for you to say," Parris said. "Plus, Janzek claims some guy took a picture of me swimming away from Glover's boat after the fire."

Pause.

"Yeah, I don't know either," Parris said. "I just know I've gone this far in life without ever doing time, and I ain't about to start now."

Long pause.

"Yeah, I hear you," Parris said. "But even the best lawyer in the world can't get me off if they connect me to Glover. Let me tell you, this guy Janzek is like a dog with a fuckin' bone."

Pause.

"Okay, check ya later," Parris said, and he clicked off.

"Sounds like he's a little more nervous than he let on," Rhett said, sitting across from Janzek.

"Yeah, but how else was he gonna play it," Janzek said, swinging his feet up onto his desk. "So now imagine for a second, you're Conger, and you just had that conversation with Parris."

Rhett didn't say anything for a few moments. "If I'm Conger, I'm hearing a guy who's scared. A guy who wants no part of goin' to the fun house for twenty years. And, if I'm him, I'm thinking that Parris flipping is a good possibility."

"Yeah, me, too," Janzek said. "You know what might help our cause?"

"What's that?"

"Like I said, get the prosecutor to turn up the heat so Parris sweats a little more. Get him to push that 'attempted' charge you dreamed up."

*****

Assistant Solicitor, Carl Sampson, agreed that the attempted murder charge—though it might be something of a stretch—had merit.

After spending a half hour with Sampson, Janzek and Rhett drove up to Parris's office on St. Philip St.

"Now what?" Parris said, rolling his eyes and fidgeting with a pen as Janzek and Rhett walked in.

"We're gonna make you the same offer as before," Janzek said, sitting down across from him as Rhett stayed on his feet. "Tell us all about Stanton Conger. If you don't, we gonna take you in for attempted murder, just as soon as we get the paperwork."

"Gotta be shittin' me," Parris said, more annoyance than fear.

"No, we're not. Got anything to drink in this rat hole, Galen? Throat's parched from talking to the solicitor so long."

Parris turned to his right and reached down. He had a small, brown microwave-size refrigerator on the floor. He opened its door, and as he did, Janzek slid something out of his pants pocket and stuck it under the lip of Parris's desk.

"I got water," Parris said, "or I got Budweiser."

"I'll take a water," Janzek said.

"Two waters," Rhett said.

"Only got one," Parris said.

"Okay," Rhett said, "gimme the Bud."

Parris handed Janzek a water and Rhett the Budweiser.

"Thanks, Galen, that's awful kind of you," Janzek said.

Rhett nodded, popped the top of the Bud, and took a pull.

"So, what's the verdict?" Janzek asked.

Parris looked up at him and his eyes got hard and squinty. "The verdict is you guys are just blowin' smoke up my ass. None of this shit's gonna stick."

"Whatever you say," Janzek said, getting up. "Don't say we never gave you a chance. Maybe you want to check the conviction

219

record of this solicitor. Sampson's his name. Got a record way better than your Carolina Tarheels football team."

"What?"

"That's a football reference," Janzek said. "Seein' as how you used to run the ball for the 'Heels. Back when you and Conger were college chums, budding young entrepreneurs and all."

Parris started to say something but thought better of it.

"Well, we'll be seeing you, Galen," Janzek said, going toward the door.

Rhett killed the rest of the Bud and put it down on Parris' desk. "Thanks for the beer."

They walked out the door and got into the Charger. Rhett stuck the key into the ignition and turned to Janzek. "Nice goin'," he said with a smile. "Next place we gotta bug is the cell he ends up in. Hear how he likes the food."

"Yeah, and his roommate, Bubba."

SIXTY-FOUR

It didn't take long until Janzek and Rhett heard Galen Parris sound a lot less relaxed than he sounded with them earlier.

"We gotta talk," Parris said on the phone, five minutes after they left. "Janzek and the other guy just left. They're threatening an attempted murder charge. Solicitor's writing it up."

Pause.

"Yeah, well, better make it quick," Parris said. "Cause I'm not likin' what's goin' on down here."

Next, they listened as Parris made a threatening call to a tenant in one of his buildings. Right after that Parris's cell phone rang.

"Yeah, Stan?"

Long pause.

"That's not enough," Parris said. "You gotta make it five mill. If I'm gonna skip forever, I sure as hell don't want to run out of money. And you're not gonna want to get a call from me in a couple years, hittin' you up again."

Short pause.

Groan. "Okay, three it is," Parris said.

Another short pause.

"That's not a bad idea," Parris said, "I hear they got some pretty hot broads over there."

Pause.

"Okay, so where do you want to meet?" he said. "And the big question, how the hell am I gonna get out of the country with the cash?"

Long pause.

Finally, Parris guffawed a long, horsey laugh. "I love it," he said. "A little business with pleasure. Yeah, I know, same way Lex smuggled in ten kilos of coke once."

221

Pause.

"I warn you, though, I really suck," Parris said. "No keepin' score, huh?"

Short pause.

"Yeah, okay I understand," Parris said, "I don't want to talk about it on the phone either. Yeah, you never know."

He clicked off.

Janzek raised his coffee mug to Rhett. "You never know, do you, Del?"

SIXTY-FIVE

Janzek and Rhett were in Ernie Brindle's office. Brindle's eyes were darting back and forth between the two of them as they filled him in.

"You do know, of course, none of that's admissible?" Brindle said.

"Yeah, we know," Janzek said. "But God knows where we'd be without it."

Brindle nodded slowly. "So, bottom line, Parris plans to skip town with three million bucks."

"Yeah, the 'how' part is what we're just guessing at," Janzek said. "But the tip-off was when Parris said three things. One, 'mixing business with pleasure.' Two and three were when he said he really 'sucked' at it and 'no keeping score.'"

"We figured he's talking about playing golf," Rhett said to Brindle. "What else do guys do where they keep score? Bowling maybe, but Conger doesn't strike us as a bowler."

"I don't know," Brindle said. "Makes sense, I guess. Except why would they go play a leisurely game of golf when you just threw an attempted murder charge at Parris and he plans on skipping the country?"

"Hang on, we'll get to that," Janzek said. "But first, Parris asks Conger how he's gonna get the money out of the country, then says in response to something Conger says, 'Yeah, same way Lex smuggled in five kilos of coke once.'"

"It was ten, actually," Rhett said.

"Yeah, okay ten," Janzek said. "So, we had our guy Wayne Embrey down in Hilton Head check the transcript of Lex Murray's trial from twenty years back. Told us about a witness who flipped on Murray who said Murray smuggled in coke in those bigass metal golf bag carriers."

"I'll be damned," Brindle said, shaking his head. "One of those things with the rollers?"

Janzek nodded. "We're guessing you can jam a hell of a lot of cash in one of those."

"Maybe all three mill," Rhett said.

"Yeah, I hear you," Brindle said, still shaking his head. "Je-sus Christ, these guys, I gotta admit, pretty goddamn smart."

"And if I was Parris, I'd buy the whole set-up," Janzek said.

"What do you mean?" Brindle asked.

"I mean, my sense is Parris trusts Conger. Been doing his scut work forever," Janzek said. "But I got no doubt Conger's planning to take him out. No way in hell he's gonna let Parris ride off into the sunset."

Brindle thrummed his desk with his fingers.

"See," Janzek said. "It's not that Conger wouldn't pay Parris three mill to go away and disappear forever, but there are too many 'what-ifs.' What if Parris doesn't like Thailand or Tahiti or wherever the hell he's going? What if he gets homesick, or runs out of money, and wants to come back with all the secrets he's got on Conger?"

"Or, what if we track him down wherever he goes?" Rhett said. "Or what if we catch him at the airport?"

Brindle was nodding. "You're right. Or what if he's taping Conger?"

"Yeah, or that. There are just too many things that could go wrong. Too many what-ifs," Janzek said. "It's so much easier just to kill the guy. Dead men tell no tales."

"Still," Brindle said, "just in case, we're gonna want to cover our bases. Put a team at the airport, for one thing."

"Yeah, absolutely," Janzek said. "There's no guarantee Conger's gonna take him out. I mean, I think it's a long shot, but he could just be looking to help Parris make a run for it."

"But you doubt it," Brindle said.

"I *seriously* doubt it," Janzek said. "Still we should also put another team up at the private aviation place. Landmark it's called. I checked; Conger has a G2."

"What's that?"

"Come on, Ernie, get with the program," Rhett said, "A Gulfstream 2, private metal, the only way to go."

"Thanks, Delvin," Brindle said. "Appreciate you keeping me up on rich men's toys."

Rhett shrugged and smiled.

"We should also send a team up to Charlotte," Janzek said. "Just in case Parris decides to drive up there. Charlotte flies to a hell of a lot more foreign destinations."

Brindle nodded.

"Like you said, we gotta cover our bases," Janzek said. "Even though it's probably gonna turn out to be a waste of time."

"'Cause Conger's gonna pop him, you mean?"

Janzek nodded. "Yeah. Do it himself this time. Conger's more than capable of doing his own dirty work. D-Wayne, for starters. Then back in college, Conger, I suspect, helped beat the shit out of a rival drug dealer. Probably a few other violent acts on the guy's resume."

"Like Leah Reynolds," Rhett chimed in.

Janzek nodded.

"All right, so what are you gonna do now?" Brindle asked.

"At the moment, just wait," Janzek said. "And hope like hell that whatever Parris's next move is he tells us about it from his car or his office."

"I still don't get the golf thing," Brindle said. "Why don't they just meet somewhere, Conger pretends to give him the golf case, then takes him out. What's the point of playing golf?"

"'Cause, when you think about it, a golf course is a perfect place to whack a guy. Lots of woods. Maybe a swamp or two. Or, hell, dump him in a pond. Parris has been doing what Conger tells since they were in college. Forty years of Parris saying, 'yes, boss.' Plus, like I said, my guess is Parris trusts him completely. Never had a reason not to."

Brindle nodded slowly. "Make sense to me," he said. "Okay, boys, time to stop talking and get doing."

Janzek stood up. "But first, we're gonna pay a visit to Cotton Conger. Find out where her husband tees it up."

*****

Janzek and Rhett walked into Cotton Kelly's gallery, a newspaper under Janzek's arm. Cotton was sitting at her desk at the rear of the gallery and this time didn't get up or even bother to change her expression.

"Good morning, Ms. Kelly," Janzek said, "I'd like to introduce you to my partner, Delvin Rhett."

Nothing.

"Hello, Ms. Kelly," Rhett said, "nice to meet you."

Nothing.

"Just a few routine questions," Janzek said. "Did you get a chance to see the paper this morning?"

He held it up.

She didn't answer.

"Very interesting article about how they had a camera at D-Wayne Marion's house the night he was murdered. Did you see it?"

"I don't read that rag."

"Oh, a *Wall Street Journal* gal, huh?" Janzek said.

"What do you want?" Cotton said wearily.

"Well, the article says—very well written, by the way—that the image of the man they got on tape going into D-Wayne Marion's house is kind of grainy," Janzek said. "But the producer of the show told me he had silver hair, kind of swept back. A distinguished-looking older gentleman, was how she described him."

Cotton Kelly started typing on her Mac.

"I have a question, Ms. Kelly," Rhett said.

She looked up at Rhett, looking relieved not to be hearing another one from Janzek.

"What is it?"

"Your husband... is he a golfer, by any chance?"

She stared at Rhett. "What kind of question is that?"

She started typing again.

"I don't know," Rhett said. "Just curious. Distinguished man, looks like the type of fella who'd be the local club champ maybe."

Cotton shook her head. "Don't you two have better things to do than come around and ask stupid questions," she said. "He plays at Yeamans Hall. Now why don't you go be curious somewhere else—" she shot Janzek a look "—seems like there're women in this town who like having you around, I don't happen to be one of 'em."

"I'm sorry to hear that," Janzek said, folding up his paper. "And I can certainly take a hint. Good-bye, Ms. Kelly."

Janzek walked out, side by side with Rhett.

Janzek opened the door to the Charger and got in.

Rhett turned to Janzek. "Kind of a cheap shot she took at you, Nick."

"Yeah, I know, but sometimes you gotta take one for the team," Janzek said, "That Yeamans Hall is exactly where I would have guessed Conger played."

"Never heard of it," Rhett said.

Janzek laughed. "Which is just the way they like it."

SIXTY-SIX

Five minutes after they left Cotton Kelly's gallery, they listened in on the call they had been waiting for.

"Meet you there at two?" Parris asked.

Short pause.

"They have clubs there I can use?"

Short pause.

"And you went to the bank?"

Short pause.

"And it's all packed up?"

Short pause.

"Okay, I've got a reservation for ten tonight out of Charlotte," Parris said. "I told my wife I had a little business trip that just came up. Then I gave her a nice, big kiss—" Parris laughed "—she didn't know it was the last one."

Pause.

"That's what I hear," Parris said. "Sex slaves for a buck a day. See you in a while."

Click.

Rhett turned to Janzek. "I figured the guy for a total pig."

*****

They had Googled Yeamans Hall club, had gotten directions, and were on their way there. Rhett was driving and Janzek was dialing his cell phone. He clicked on speaker.

Sheila Lessing answered. "Hi, Nick. I had a really nice time the other night."

Janzek glanced at Rhett and blushed. "Yeah, me, too. You're on speaker. I'm in the car with Delvin."

"Oh, hello, Delvin."

228

"Hey, Ms. Lessing."

"It's Sheila," she said. "You boys need me to help you solve a crime or something."

"Yes, we do, but first, I have a big favor to ask."

"Sure, what is it?"

"Can I be a guest of yours at Yeamans Hall. Delvin and I need a little R&R."

She didn't say anything right away. "The only problem is that a member has to play with their guests. Guest can't just go play without a member. Let me think of a way around it."

"Thanks, I appreciate it."

A pause. "Okay, I might have to tell a little white lie. Tell you what... I'll call the starter in the golf shop and say that you're going to go play and be my guests and I'm going to catch up with you on the third or fourth hole. And then, well, I'll call and say I had car trouble and couldn't make it."

"This isn't gonna get you in trouble, is it?"

"Nah, no problem. I give him a big tip at Christmas, just for these little emergencies."

"Thanks, Sheila," Rhett said, "I get off at Beasley Road, right?"

"Yes, then you go straight until President, hang a right there. Then after you cross a railroad track you get to a big wall and a gate with a little guard house. Just tell the man there you're my guests."

"Thanks," Janzek said, "I don't know if we look like Yeamans material, but we'll fake it best we can. At least we left our cut-offs at home."

"Yeah," Rhett said, "But I'm guessing the only black guys there are luggin' bags."

Sheila laughed. "That's not entirely true, Delvin. Quite a few are in the kitchen."

Rhett laughed. "Us folks are really good at luggin' bags *and* cookin'," he said.

Sheila laughed. "By the way, the caddies there, someone got the bright idea to dress 'em up in those white jump suits—"

"Just like at the Masters, you mean?" Janzek said.

"Yes, as if one Augusta's not enough."

"Well, hey, thanks," Janzek said. "We'll try to conduct ourselves in such a way that won't embarrass you too much."

"I'm not worried."

"I really appreciate it," Janzek said.

"Yeah, thanks," Rhett said.

"Have fun, boys."

Janzek clicked off and Rhett turned to him. "I don't know the first thing about this game."

"You're a quick learner. You'll pick it up."

"I don't know, man," Rhett said, shaking his head. "Never hit a golf ball once in my entire short, sadly deprived life."

SIXTY-SEVEN

Janzek had an idea right before they got to Yeamans Hall. He ran it by Rhett who chuckled and said he was good with it.

So, with another call to Sheila Lessing, he was able to get Rhett outfitted in a white caddie jumpsuit. The trick was for them not to get spotted by Conger and Parris, who, the starter said, had just teed off on the first hole. From behind, Janzek saw the two driving down the fairway in a white and blue golf cart, Conger at the wheel.

Janzek looked like an actor trying hard to disguise his identity as he approached the first tee. He was wearing Wayfarer sunglasses and an oversized straw hat, pulled down low, which he had bought at the pro shop. Rhett was wearing a ski cap and white plastic wraparounds as they stood at the first tee.

"What club would you like, sir?" Rhett asked, his hand on a seven iron.

"Jesus, don't you know anything?" Janzek asked. "A driver, that thing with the big sock on it."

Rhett put his hand on the four wood.

"No, that's a little sock."

Rhett put his hand on the driver.

"Atta boy."

"Hey, just 'cause I'm a caddie, doesn't mean you can call me boy."

"Sorry," Janzek said, "I'll be needing a couple of tees, too."

Rhett pointed to the ground. "Thought this thing *was* a tee," he said. "You called it the first tee."

Janzek laughed. "Tees are also those little white things you put the ball on—" he pointed "—in that pocket there."

Rhett unzippered the pocket, reached in, and brought out a handful of them.

"Tees," he said, handing them to Janzek, then he pointed down.

"First tee—" he shook his head "—very confusing. I think I better stick to fishing."

Janzek bent down, teed up a ball and looked down the fairway. "We want to stay close to them, but not too close."

"Gotcha," Rhett said.

Janzek took a couple of practice swings. "Shit, man, I'm way out of practice."

Rhett looked around. "Are you allowed to swear at a place like this? It's so... clean."

"Oh, yeah," Janzek said, "they encourage it."

He stepped up to his ball. "They're out of range now. I can't hit them from here."

He swung hard at the ball.

He topped it and the ball dribbled off the tee and went fifty yards down the fairway.

"Hell," Rhett said, "I'd say they were safe ten minutes ago."

"Fuck off."

"Whoa!" Rhett took a paranoid look around them. "I really don't think you should be dropping the f-bomb at a nice place like this."

*****

Janzek got a quadruple bogey on the first hole, four over par.

They were on the second tee, watching Conger and Parris up ahead.

"Parris looks as bad as you," Rhett said.

"I'd like to see you play."

"How much worse than you could I be?"

Janzek chuckled and looked away. "Got lots of woods up ahead. Looks like a stream up on the left, too."

"I know what you're thinking," Rhett said.

"Out in the middle of nowhere, no houses around. Nobody to see anything."

"I saw Conger look back at us a couple of times," Rhett said. "Then it was like he picked up the pace a little. Started to go faster."

"Yeah, I noticed, like he wanted to put some distance between us," Janzek said, looking around. "Not a lot of other people out here."

"All I saw was two other... what do you call 'em?" Rhett asked.

"Foursomes?"

"Yeah, there you go."

"Sheila told me they're only about two hundred members at this place."

"Okay, man," Rhett said, as he handed Janzek a driver. "See if you can do a little better this time."

Janzek addressed his ball and swung. This time he hit it cleanly, though it had a hook to it.

"See that," Janzek said. "Gotta a nice little draw to it."

"I have no idea what that is."

"Ball kinda goes left a little."

"Yeah, whatever."

On the next hole, Conger and Parris didn't go to the third tee. Instead Conger drove their cart over to another tee about a hundred yards away.

"Okay, man, we gotta pick up the pace," Janzek said. "Conger might be making his move. Trying to get as far away from everyone as possible."

"Yeah, but if we follow them, they'll suspect something?"

"Agree," Janzek said. "So, we'll just go to the next tee, keep an eye on 'em."

"Sounds good," Rhett said, watching Conger tee up his ball off in the distance.

Conger and Parris were on a hole that had thick woods to the right and a marsh on the left.

Conger hit his drive. "It went to the right," Rhett said. "Way into the woods."

"Wonder if it was intentional."

"Exactly what I was thinking," Rhett said, watching Parris take a practice swing.

Parris waggled his driver a few times and then, hit his ball. It didn't go very far but it was straight. The two got in their cart and started down the fairway.

"My gut's tellin' me we should get close to 'em," Janzek said.

"Yeah, help Conger find his ball."

＊＊＊＊＊

While Parris helped him look for his ball in the woods, Stanton Conger slid the Beretta .22 out of the long, narrow pocket of his big, brown leather bag. Looking over to make sure Parris was far enough away from him, he screwed on the silencer, which he had taken out of the same pocket. Galen Parris was off to his left about twenty yards away. Parris stopped walking, reached down, and picked up a golf ball.

"Was it a Titleist number five?" he shouted.

"No, a Callaway," Conger shouted back.

He started walking toward Parris, the gun behind his back.

"I don't know, man," Parris said, "you might have to drop another one."

Conger didn't answer.

Parris looked over at Conger, fifteen yards away now. Conger was pointing the Beretta at him.

Conger's hands shot up. "Jesus. No—"

He turned and started running as Conger squeezed off three shots.

One of the shots caught Parris in the back of the leg and he went down, taking an overhanging branch with him.

Conger took his time getting to Parris, in no big hurry to end their long relationship.

Parris got to his feet and tried to run, dragging his wounded leg.

Conger was ten yards away. He raised the gun with both hands and took aim.

"Drop the gun and put your hands up," Janzek shouted, fifty yards away.

"Do it," Rhett said, on the other side of Conger.

Conger didn't react at first. Like he was considering his options. Finally, he dropped his gun, apparently deciding that making a run and getting shot in the back wasn't a good option.

Rhett ran up to him and pulled out his handcuffs. "You're under arrest, for attempted murder."

Janzek came up behind him. "Not to mention the four or five successful ones."

Stanton Conger had nothing to say.

Janzek read him his Miranda rights.

Rhett went over to Galen Parris. He ripped off a sleeve from his caddie's jumpsuit, wrapped it around Parris's thigh, and pulled it tight.

Parris nodded, wincing in pain.

"I owed you," Rhett said. "That Budweiser."

SIXTY-EIGHT

The rats couldn't abandon the ship fast enough.

First Parris, then Cotton Kelly.

Cotton, it seemed, had simply gotten tired of her husband's philandering, bullying ways. Not to mention, she was looking to save her own ass. In any case, she said in a written statement that it was her husband who shot D-Wayne Marion while she was in bed with him.

She gave a vivid description about being splattered with blood and thinking for a minute that she, too, had been shot by her husband. No doubt if Conger had a do-over, he would have.

*****

The day after the arrest of Conger and Parris, Janzek got a call from Holly Barrow.

"Excuse the last-minute invitation, but our wrap party's tonight," she said. "A couple of cast members suggested I invite you."

"But not you?" Janzek asked.

"I'm still mad at you," Holly said, "for making me plant that article."

"Holly, cut the crap. You know that article is gonna get you another couple thousand viewers."

"Well, actually, I'm hoping more like a couple *hundred* thousand," she said. "So, you know what, Nick? All is forgiven."

*****

Someone who worked at Yeamans Hall had taken a shot on their cell phone which ended up on the front page of the *Post & Courier*. It

235

was of Janzek, his gun out, walking through the parking lot of Yeamans Hall to his car with Stanton Conger ahead of him, handcuffed and trying to hide his face. Rhett had gone in the helicopter with Galen Parris to Roper Hospital.

*****

At the wrap party at Husk on Queen Street the next day, Saxby Wentworth-Kuhn was holding a copy of the newspaper in his hand when he went up to Janzek.

"I know it's supposed to be the other way around—you wanting my autograph," he said. "But sign this for me, will ya, hero? Let's just say it's for one of your adoring fans... my mother."

"Okay," Janzek said. "How is she anyway?" It had been three days since she stopped by his office to drop her little bomb.

Saxby got close to Janzek's ear and whispered. "She's okay," he said. "Still getting over her little affaire de coeur with that douchebag."

Saxby glanced across the room to where Rip was chatting up Samantha.

"So, the question is, Saxby," Janzek said, "gun or no gun?"

Saxby didn't understand the question at first. Then: "Oh, you mean, that horse and carriage thing? Nah." he raised his hand and pointed his index finger. "No gun."

"That's what I figured."

"But sometimes, I could kill those drivers. I mean, totally oblivious to making you go five miles an hour."

Janzek agreed, though he kept his opinion to himself.

Samantha walked across the room and came up to them. She nodded at Saxby.

"Hey, Sax," she said.

"Hey, Sam," he said.

Then she turned to Janzek. "Nice goin', Nick. Rounded up the bad guys."

"Thanks."

"I was at a cocktail party once," she said, "that guy Conger tried to hit on me, along with every other skirt in the room."

"Well, I can see, three's a crowd," Saxby said, shoving off.

"See you, Saxby," Janzek said, then turning to Samantha. "Yeah, that was Conger's MO, I guess."

"Along with killing off half of Charleston it seems." Samantha tilted her head to one side. "So, I have to ask, are you still...?"

Janzek nodded.

"She's a lucky girl. Well, I guess, I'm going to wander along."

"See you around, Samantha."

Janzek walked over to the bar and got another beer.

"So, this time you made the headlines," said the voice behind him, "instead of just writing them."

He swung around. It was Hudson Rock.

"Hey, Hudson," he said, noticing his purple bow tie. "Spiffy tie. You're lookin' like a regular Charleston blade."

"Thanks. So, ah, Holly and I were talking—" he flicked his head so Janzek would follow him.

What the hell, thought Janzek, and followed him over to a corner of the room a few feet from the bar.

"Yeah, you and Holly were talking," Janzek said. "And?"

"And we want to put you in the show."

Janzek had to laugh. "That's very flattering."

"So, what do you say?"

"Problem is, I don't think I'd score too well in those focus groups. You know, where they rate the characters."

"Don't sell yourself short, Detective," Rock said. "We're sure you'd do fine."

"Nah, but thanks," Janzek said. "There's something in the Charleston Police hand book about us not participating in anything that would draw undue attention to the department."

What Janzek was really thinking was that he would rather be on *Keeping up with the Kardashians* or slumming it with Snooki on *Jersey Shore* than on a show where someone with a hokey name like Hudson Rock bossed you around.

SIXTY-NINE

Ernie Brindle suggested that both Janzek and Rhett take a week off. They had earned it. Rhett, having had a brief taste of the game of golf, told Janzek he was thinking about going up to Myrtle Beach, where they had lots of golf courses, and whacking around the little white ball. He had gone onto the internet and found they had a bunch of cheap, not-too-challenging courses. Perfect to cut his teeth on.

Janzek was long overdue to take a trip up to Sheila Lessing's house in the mountains of North Carolina.

When he called Sheila, she was ecstatic and started talking about throwing a dinner party for him, taking him to the club with all her friends, the whole thing. She even mentioned flying him up on her chopper so he could get there faster. He nixed that quick.

It ended up taking him a little over five hours to get there, his Camry struggling mightily on the last steep hill. He was surprised to find out that the highest elevation east of the Mississippi was in North Carolina. Mountains in excess of six thousand feet.

He got to Sheila's house in Cashiers at just before six. He hit the horn a couple of times as he pulled into her driveway. She came to the door, wearing white slacks and a simple green, collared shirt. He'd never known what it meant when he'd read about a woman glowing or looking radiant, but now he did. Or maybe it was just that she had laid out in the sun for a few hours that afternoon.

He opened the car door, got out and hugged her.

"You made it... finally," she said. "How was the drive?"

"Not bad," he said. "Thanks to Jack Reacher on tape—" then looking around at the towering evergreen trees and her perfectly tended garden—"I forgot how fantastic this place is."

"Thanks," she said, grabbing his hand. "Come on in and make yourself a nice, big drink. We're going to the club for a quiet dinner— just the two of us."

'The club' ordinarily might conjure up a place outside of the Janzek comfort zone, but in this case, he had been to it once before and knew it was his kind of low-key, relaxed place. Not the kind of club where men wear red pants and fancy silk pocket squares and the women sashay around in splashy Lily P. togs. No, the Chattooga Club's dress code was casual, even though the main clubhouse was imposing... but in a good way. It was constructed of rustic timbers and massive, hand-hewn beams with several stone fireplaces that a six-foot man could walk into without stooping.

They were sitting facing each other having cocktails on a porch, which had a view of the sheer face of a mountain less than a mile away.

"So, I heard something about the Boy's Club being history," Sheila said, taking a sip of wine.

"You mean, because one of its founding father turned out to be something less than a choir boy?"

"I'd say something less than a maggot."

"His right-hand man, Galen Parris, is apparently ready to spend a few days on the stand telling the world what a swell guy his old boss was," Janzek said, cutting into lamb chop.

"Those two had a long history," Sheila said.

"Almost forty years' worth. Which is probably about what Conger is going to get."

He decided to change the subject, now officially sick of the subject of Stanton Conger and Galen Parris. As well as D-Wayne Marion and Saxby and Rip and Holly and the rest of the gang.

Instead, they talked about what they were going to do the next day. The Chattooga Club reminded Janzek of a little place he'd gone to up in New Hampshire when he was a kid. In a typical day there he might have climbed a mountain, gone sailing on the lake, played eighteen on the shaggy little nine-hole golf course, gone trout fishing, swum out to the raft, and slid down a slide half dozen times into the cool lake water.

They decided on a less ambitious schedule: a workout in the gym in the morning, golf after an early lunch, then kayaking for a while.

After Janzek ordered seconds on dessert, they went to the parking lot, got in Sheila's car, and drove home.

Janzek didn't think anything of the car that pulled out of the parking lot after them. It followed them on the five-minute drive to Sheila's house then went straight after they took a left at her house.

Sheila had an outdoor living room that was open on two sides and had comfortable all-weather furniture centered around a large stone fireplace. Fireplaces, Janzek noticed, were clearly a mandatory part of living in the mountains.

They went through the house, out to the outdoor living room, and sat down side by side in the large sofa outside.

"God, I love how it smells up here," Janzek said. "A little bit of pine, a little bit of hemlock, and a little bit of I-don't-know-what."

"My perfume maybe?"

Janzek laughed. "Yeah, that's it, Chanel Number Five."

"Joy, actually."

He put his arm around her. "Feels like it's about twenty degrees cooler than Charleston."

"Yeah, that's about right. That's my only complaint about Charleston."

"Too hot in the summer?"

"Exactly," Sheila said, resting her head on Janzek's shoulder.

"I can't believe how quiet it is."

He felt Sheila nod.

He turned to kiss her when there was a sudden loud crack. Like the sound of a branch breaking.

Sheila bolted upright. "Jesus, what was that?"

"Got bears up here?"

"We got everything up here."

Janzek pulled her closer and kissed her. "Well, don't worry, I'm packin'."

"A gun?"

Janzek nodded. "Force of habit," he said, pulling up his pant leg to reveal the Seecamp 32-cal in his leather ankle holster.

"You're going to have to take that off in a little while."

"I'm looking forward to that."

"You really think that could have been a bear?"

"I wouldn't worry," Janzek said. "They stay away unless you got a big, old ham sandwich in your hand."

"They'd better. Now, where were we?"

"I was about to give you a nice, long—"

He saw a flash of light, then heard a sharp pop and something ripped into the needlepoint pillow six inches from him, followed by several more shots.

He grabbed Sheila, pulled her down to the floor, fell on top of her and pulled out his Seecamp. He blindly fired four rounds where he'd seen saw the flash come from.

He was preparing to pop up and fire again—nine bullets left in his clip—when he heard a moan.

"Jesus Christ," a voice shouted, "I been hit."

He felt Sheila's short, fast breaths against his chest. "Come on out," Janzek called out, getting into a crouch, gun up.

"I can't, I'm dying…" Janzek thought he recognized the voice.

"Throw your gun out," he hollered.

A moment later a pistol clattered across the flagstone terrace.

Janzek peeked around the edge of the sofa and recognized the gun. It fit the description of the pistol that Penelope Kuhn had found in Rip Engel's sock drawer four days before.

SEVENTY

Rip Engel was not dying. Just being melodramatic.

He had been hit just below the left bicep. Janzek put an electric cord he found nearby around it to staunch the bleeding while Sheila called the local police.

"The hell's this all about?" Janzek snarled at him.

"Sorry, man, I needed money," Rip said. "They canceled the third season of the show. Conger told his lawyer—"

"Told him what?"

"Where you went. Conger found out somehow, and told him," Rip said. "Lawyer gave me twenty thousand to... you know. I'm sorry, Nick."

Janzek heard a siren way off.

He turned and saw Sheila sitting on the couch ten feet away, looking dazed.

He put the pistol up to Rip Engel's head. "I should put an end to your pitiful, sorry-ass, life," he growled. "You could have killed her."

"Please," Rip said, trying to cover his head. Then he started bawling.

Janzek shook his head. "You're too pathetic to waste a bullet on."

*****

It was 7 a.m. the next morning when he woke up. Sheila was not in bed. Janzek put a bathrobe on and walked down to the kitchen.

Sheila was cooking eggs and bacon and was dressed in sweatpants and Day-Glo yellow Nikes.

"Morning," he said. "You plan on sprinting up the mountain?"

She smiled, walked over to him, and gave him a kiss. "I need

242

another big hug. I didn't sleep too well last night. We don't have a lot of shoot-outs up here."

"I'm sorry, honey. I promise, it'll be okay now."

Her head snapped back, "Wait. What did you call me?"

It was a first.

"I must still be in shock," he said.

Sheila laughed. "You know, Nick, I'm well aware of the fact that you're a big, macho guy. But it's not as if a term of endearment is a sign of weakness, you know."

Janzek joined in her laugh, trying to hide a blush. "Honey, honey, honey, honey…"

Sheila laughed. "Okay, okay, okay," she said, putting her arms around him, "you don't need to overdo it."

"I just can't win with you," Janzek said.

"Yeah, you can," she said. "Now go get dressed, we got a big day ahead of us. I recommend sneakers, blue jeans... and, oh yes, you can leave that pistol of yours behind."

"What about bears?"

"Don't worry. We're not bringing ham sandwiches."

THE END

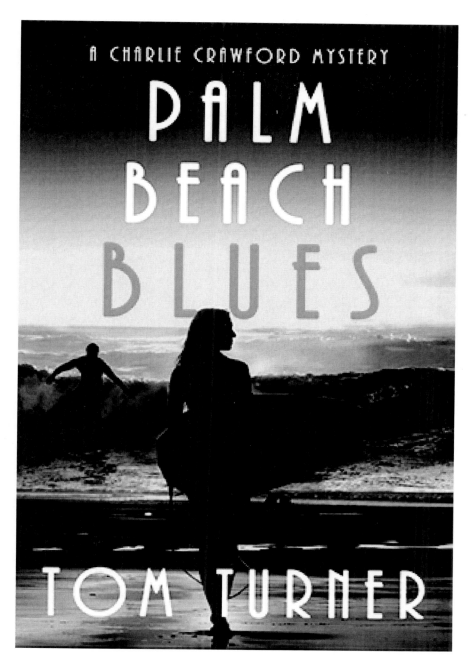

A CHARLIE CRAWFORD MYSTERY

PALM
BEACH
BLUES

TOM TURNER

Charlie, Mort, Dominica and Rose return in early 2020!
The first three chapters follow.

CHAPTER ONE

Sunny Hedstrom was on her way back from the gym.

The gym was her new favorite place—more so than any bar, restaurant, or Worth Avenue clothing or jewelry shop. That was because, as of last Thursday night, her trainer had become her lover. She hadn't seen it heading in that direction during their first workout, a month back, but as the great philosopher once said, *Shit happens.* Anthony had a gentle soul and spoke soft and patiently as he guided her through her 45-minute workout. But in bed....*watch out.* The guy was an acrobatic maniac, a Flying Wallenda of the boudoir.

Sunny's only concern was that Wayne had found out about Anthony. Or maybe not found out, but at least suspected.

"I called you for three straight hours," Wayne told her the day before. "Where the hell were you?"

Fortunately, she'd thought up an excuse in advance, knowing how possessive Wayne could be. "Didn't I tell you before? At my nephew's basketball game. I left my phone behind."

"No, you never told me," Wayne said. "How was it?"

"The basketball game?"

"Yeah."

Like he cared. "It was okay. Not that I'm a big basketball fan or anything. My sister and I just yakked a lot."

"Where was it?" Wayne asked.

"Worthington High. The gym there."

Wayne snickered. "Well, yeah, no kidding. I didn't figure they played in the library."

Her much-older landlord had a lame sense of humor.

"How'd he do? Your nephew?"

"Pretty good."

"Score many points?"

"I think so. I wasn't really keeping track."

"What's his name?"

"Danny."

"Danny who?"

"Harris."

Sunny knew Wayne was asking her about facts he could check. He couldn't have cared less about her nephew or his basketball prowess.

She was heading north on South Olive and hit her blinker for her house on Granada Road in the El Cid neighborhood of West Palm Beach. Well, not her house; it was Wayne's. Wayne, she knew, had a number of houses sprinkled around the area. She'd guessed, not inaccurately, that they were for Wayne's gal pals, and for the last ten months, which was as long as she had been living there, he hadn't charged her rent. But, of course, she did pay a price.

As she turned onto Granada, she hit her garage-door opener the way she always did. Her house was the fourth on the left. She was thinking about Anthony and the grueling abductor-muscle exercises he'd put her through as she turned into her driveway.

That was when she saw her beloved Westie puppy, Winston, with his leash around his neck, dangling from the handle of the opened garage door.

CHAPTER TWO

It took Sunny a moment to comprehend what she was seeing, that she'd accidentally hanged her own dog.

She quickly hit the button again to close the garage door, and slowly—too slowly— it descended. Like it was in slow motion. Winston was writhing on the cement as she braked, jammed the car into park, and started running.

She heard the hysteria in her voice as she screamed, "Help!" Then, "Oh my God, Winston...." She reached down and loosened the leash but she could see it was too late. Little Winston was a goner.

*****

Wayne Crabb described himself as a real-estate developer, but others called him a grave dancer. By that they meant someone on the lookout for projects that were either financially shaky or in default. Overleveraged, under-financed, or poorly managed—better yet, all three. He'd swoop in and buy the property at a discount, then nurse it back to good health. His biggest coup was buying a casino in the Bahamas for eighty-seven million dollars, then flipping it two years later for a hundred seventy-eight million while spending only a few million to renovate it. The profit from that deal had helped pay for a lot of smaller projects, one of which was located in the heart of Palm Beach.

Crabb was in his office with his assistant, Mary Beth Hudson, whom he kept very busy. Unlike most Florida real-estate offices, whose walls were decorated with photos and architectural renderings of tall buildings, apartment complexes, or luxurious resorts, Wayne Crabb's office at South County Road was dominated by blown-up posters of surfers cutting through the water, arms extended for balance, mountainous waves behind them. If a visitor looked closely, they would see that the primary surfer in the photos was Wayne himself. Tanned and, if not chiseled, at least in good shape for a sixty-one-year old. Whenever Wayne took a vacation, often with a woman less than half his age, sometimes two, he would go to places famous for towering waves and exotic beauty. Hawaii, Australia, New Zealand and Peru had become his favorite destinations.

Palm Beach, while a long way from any of the surf capitals of the world, did have a dedicated group of surfers who rode the waves up on the north end of the island. Crabb surfed there four or five times a week with a revolving cast of twenty- and thirty-somethings—mostly men, but with a few women thrown in. Wayne, known as "the geez" or just plain "geez" to the young surfers, was universally reviled as a wave-hog. That is, he'd paddle after every wave that had potential, often blocking others from having their shots at the rollers. Sometimes he'd ride his board perilously close to another surfer; other times, he'd cut them off altogether. The younger guys got silent satisfaction when Wayne would end up in a body-churning wipe-out and it annoyed them when he'd bob to the surface with a *far out, that was fun!* smile on his face.

Having read through all his emails, Wayne looked up at Mary Beth. "I want you to evict Sunny Hedstrom from the house on Granada."

Mary Beth nodded. "Okay, on what grounds?"

"Since when do I need grounds?"

"I just—"

"That she's ten months late on her rent."

"But she never had a lease."

"Well, back-date one and forge her signature," Wayne said, like that was a normal business practice. "We've got her signature somewhere."

Long ago, Mary Beth had gotten to the point where she accepted the fact that forging signatures was a normal part of her job. Wayne Crabb, after all, tended to be quite generous with Christmas bonuses. Evictions like this were typical operating procedure for Wayne who seemed to be subsidizing anywhere between four and seven women at any given time. He expected those women to be on call whenever the spirit moved him, and it moved him a lot. He also expected them to be exclusive to him. That meant no boyfriends, lovers, or even one-night stands.

Mary Beth assumed that Sunny Hedstrom had violated Wayne's code, and her boss was an unforgiving man.

"Process server?" Mary Beth asked.

"Yeah, get that weasel from Collectron on it."

"Chris Carter?"

"Yeah, tell him I want her out by the end of the week."

Mary Beth nodded. "I'm on it," she said. "You want me to do anything on the Sabal House today?"

Wayne thrummed his desk top and emitted a long, slow sigh. "You know what's bothering the hell out of me about that place?"

"What's that?" She had a pretty good guess.

"That Platt's out there tooling around in that shiny new yacht he bought with Sabal House money."

He was referring to Preston Platt, his partner in the now-notorious Sabal House on Royal Palm Way in Palm Beach. They had bought the former hotel together to convert into high-end condominiums. The deal soon went sideways, however, taking down some twenty-odd investors in the deal.

"So, what are you going to do?" Mary Beth asked.

"What I always do, sue the bastard," Wayne said with a throaty rumble of a laugh.

"You think that will do any good?"

Crabb sighed and thought for a moment. "Not if I can't track down the money."

They heard footsteps in the reception area, then a shout. "You sadistic son-of-a-bitch!" a woman's voice rang out, then Sunny Hedstrom burst into Wayne's office.

Mary Beth shot from her chair to intercept Sunny as she charged at Wayne.

"You evil, evil pig," Sunny said, jabbing a finger at the seated Wayne. "How could you do such a cruel thing?"

"What are you talking about?" Wayne asked. "I have no idea what—"

"Bullshit. It had to be you. You killed my dog. You're the only one who has the key to the house."

Wayne held up his hands. "Think what you want, but I have no idea what you're talking about." He glanced at Mary Beth standing between him and Sunny. "By the way, I'm afraid you're going to have to vacate the Granada Road house."

Sunny put her hands on her hips. "What? Why?"

"Well, for one thing, this unrestrained outburst of yours accusing me of such a barbaric thing. I can't have someone living in one of my houses calling me a son-of-a-bitch and a pig. And for another, because you haven't paid rent for the past ten months."

"Are you crazy? That was never the deal, paying rent."

"Sorry, Sunny. You're going to have to pack up and go."

Sunny took a step toward Crabb, but Mary Beth blocked her. "You'll have to leave now, Ms. Hedstrom."

Sunny shook her head. "You are the sleaziest, creepiest low-life I've ever met."

Wayne made a shooing motion with one hand. "Good bye, Sunny," he said. "Have a nice life."

CHAPTER THREE

With Mary Beth still in his office, Wayne slipped off his khaki pants, revealing long, flowery-patterned swim trunks underneath. Then he shed his white button-down shirt, under which he wore a vintage yellow T-shirt that read *Hobie Surfboards*. He hung up his khakis and the button-down in a closet and slipped into a pair of flip-flops.

"I'll be back later," he told Mary Beth, who was accustomed to her boss interrupting work with his favorite activity. Well, second-favorite actually... his favorite being to drop in on nubile tenants.

"Have fun," Mary Beth said.

She'd once said, "Hang ten!" but he'd just looked at her funny.

*****

There were four surfers up on the north end—three guys, appropriately blond-streaked and hard-bodied, and a raven-haired woman whom Wayne had never seen before.

Needless to say, he tried to hit on her. The way he looked at it, with Sunny Hedstrom having been just cut loose from the team, he had a vacancy.

The woman acted friendly enough but didn't encourage anything more than a quick conversation. The surfers always shook their heads—half in disbelief, half in grudging admiration—whenever Wayne tried to put his well-worn moves on women forty years younger than him.

A few minutes later, Wayne and one of the young surfers were sitting on their boards on the lookout for a wave.

"Who's the babe, anyway?" Wayne asked, flipping his head in the direction of the woman, board in hand, leaving the beach.

The surfer shook his head. "You're relentless, man. Don't you have a wife or something?"

253

Wayne nodded. "I do, but she's really old."

The surfer chuckled. "Got news for you, dude. So are you."

Wayne shrugged. "You're as young as you feel," he said, then pointing. "Hey, what's that?"

The surfer looked off into the distance. "I don't know, man, kinda looks like a drone."

A silver-colored drone was flying fifty feet above the ocean and coming toward them.

Wayne huffed. "I thought Palm Beach outlawed those things."

The surfer shrugged. As he watched the drone approach, it suddenly stopped in midair, steadied, and made a loud crackling sound, which was followed by a sharp groan from Wayne. The surfer turned to see the older man's chest was bloody. Another crackling sound emitted from the drone, and Wayne's forehead became a patch of red. Without a word, he fell headfirst into the ocean.

"Holy shit!" said the surfer, leaning low on his board and paddling furiously for shore.

As the other surfers watched from the beach, the silver drone exploded, sending shards of metal in all directions.

As several beachgoers grabbed their cellphones and began dialing 911, Wayne's body sank beneath the surface of the sea. His surfboard, though, was caught by a big wave and flipped high up in the air, a ribbon of blood near its tip.

The sexagenarian surfer, Wayne Crabb, had ridden his last wave.

ABOUT THE AUTHOR

A native New Englander, Tom Turner dropped out of college and ran a Vermont Bar… into the ground. After limping back to college to get his diploma, Tom became an advertising copywriter, first in Boston, then New York. After ten years of post-Mad Men life, he made a radical change and got a job in commercial real estate. Not long after that he ended up in Palm Beach, buying, renovating and selling houses along with collecting raw materials for his novels. On the side, he wrote Palm Beach Nasty, its sequel Palm Beach Poison, and a screenplay called Blood Red Sea.

While at a wedding a few years later, he fell for the charm of Charleston, South Carolina, and moved there. Recently, wandering Tom moved again. This time, just down the road to Skidaway Island, outside of Savannah, where he's writing a novel about passion and murder among his neighbors.

Learn more about Tom's books at: www.TomTurnerBooks.com

And on Facebook at Tom Turner Books.

OTHER BOOKS BY TOM TURNER

CHARLIE CRAWFORD PALM BEACH MYSTERIES
Palm Beach Nasty
Palm Beach Poison
Palm Beach Deadly
Palm Beach Bones
Palm Beach Pretenders
Palm Beach Predator
Palm Beach Broke
Palm Beach Bedlam

NICK JANZEK CHARLESTON MYSTERIES
Killing Time in Charleston
Charleston Buzz Kill

STANDALONES
Broken House

For a current list of all available titles, please visit:
www.TomTurnerBooks.com/Books